BOOKS BY TAMMARA WEBBER

CONTOURS OF THE HEART® series:

Easy

Breakable

Sweet

Brave

BETWEEN THE LINES series:

Between the Lines

Where You Are

Good For You

Here Without You

tammara webber

Brave

a Contours of the Heart novel

BRAVE

Trade paperback ISBN: 978-0-9994264-2-5

Cover Design by Damonza

To MiShaun

Who once upon a time
was brave enough to ask her unpublished,
aspiring-writer friend to put her in a book

Prologue

1980

Jeffrey McIntyre grinned as he shut the door of the cramped, ramshackle trailer serving as on-site office, boardroom, lunchroom, and occasional nap quarters for the small, would-be construction company he and his partner had pitched to the men he'd just escorted out the door. All three were prominent local businessmen, and all three were loaded. They were too sharp-witted to give immediate approval, of course. They hadn't gotten where they were with knee-jerk decisions lacking due diligence, and Jeff respected that. But his hand burned pleasantly from their firm-gripped shakes, each grasp imparting a soundless but undeniable gut-level verdict: *yes*.

The stuffy loan officers at the big banks, high-and-mighty gatekeepers of industry, hadn't wanted to take a chance on a couple of twenty-six-year-olds with vision. He and Zeke had been shown the door enough times for lesser men to give up and slink away like chastised schoolboys. Well, all those arrogant pricks could keep their damn money and fuck right off, because McIntyre & James Construction was about to have *investors*.

Jeff yanked at the unfamiliar tie and popped the top button clear, freeing his thick neck from the stranglehold of the starchy shirt his debutante fiancée had declared obligatory if he really meant business. He might resent her snooty interference, but she'd been right and he knew it, so he'd heeded her advice. Grin spreading, he turned to meet his partner's more restrained smile.

Ezekiel James had always been more naturally cautious. He was the voice of reason when Jeff wanted to barrel ahead, eternally certain of victory and dead wrong as often as he was right. Despite his characteristic composure, Zeke's eyes were wide and lit with expectant eagerness. Elbows on knees and hands knotted, he sat forward in one of two worn leather desk chairs they'd found at a used-office-furniture store in east Fort Worth. His wedding band glinted yellow against his dark skin. His pretty little wife was ready to start trying for a baby, he'd confided last week. He wanted to make her happy, but his prudent temperament told him he and Jeff had a company to establish before either of them could start a family.

"So. What do you think?" Zeke asked. His soft-spoken inquiry was almost frustrating. How could he not be crazy with excitement when Jeff was barely containing the urge to whoop with pleasure and curse all the naysayers they'd encountered right to their smug faces?

But Jeff knew his friend's grim history—his parents breaking their backs, working their hands raw at multiple menial jobs to put food on the table for Zeke and Lila, his little sister. His mother had died of lung cancer without ever picking up a cigarette; they'd buried her eight years ago. His father had lost the use of his right arm a few months later when a heavy piece of machinery fell on him at his warehouse job. He'd been slightly inebriated at the time, and before he'd even left the county hospital, the company had fired him and stripped him of disability benefits. Though he could have sued to regain them, it was hard to find a lawyer who'd take the case of a drunk-on-the-job black laborer—or so he'd told Zeke when pressed.

"It's too late anyways now, son," his father had said. "Best to just push on through."

Zeke had known who'd have to do the pushing.

Eighteen and quietly ambitious, he'd planned to go to college. But he couldn't afford to attend classes at the junior college while supporting his motherless sister, himself, and a father whose sorrow clung to his skin like days-old sweat, so he got a job working construction. It was grueling, sometimes dangerous work—especially for a young man who couldn't keep his woolgathering mind from envisioning ways to make the spaces he built more useful and visually appealing—but it paid better than anything else he was qualified to do.

A year prior, he'd been paired with Jeff on a North Dallas site. As the August temperatures soared up to and over one hundred degrees, they framed track houses—every one a cookie-cutter version of all the rest. While they worked, he'd told Jeff about the luxurious-for-the-client and practical-for-the-company concepts he'd proposed that the housing foremen always dismissed. Recessed lighting and niches, alcoves, and seating nooks, built-ins that took advantage of otherwise unserviceable spaces. Over lunch at a nearby hole-in-the-wall barbeque joint, where Jeff was often the lone white man, Zeke sketched out customizable alternatives to the floor plans.

"They keep on telling me some manner of 'We got us designers and architects for that shit, man—nobody needs your big ideas here. Just get back to work and hang the damned cabinets,' and that was that," he said.

"Idiots," Jeff mumbled, thumbing through the neatly drawn, detailed sketches. "They wouldn't know a good idea if it bit 'em in the ass and turned into a tail." He'd looked Zeke right in the eye.

"We should form our own company, man. Make some real money. We ain't cut out for this small-minded shit."

Lila, Zeke's little sister, had just graduated with honors from Texas Tech and was a newly minted teacher in Burleson. Alcohol had preserved their father's grief rather than chasing it away, but he was an unobtrusive, desolate drunk, and neither of his children could bear to rebuke him for it. They'd made a pact between them to care for him. For the first time, Ezekiel James was his own man, ready to take a Jeffrey McIntyre sort of risk.

"Well?" he pressed, bringing Jeff back to the present. "Do you think any of them will lend us the money?"

Jeff grinned like a man who meant to run the world and had just acquired the clearance to do so. "I think their rich asses want in, my brutha," he drawled, throwing his six-two frame into a creaky desk chair and sprawling his long legs wide. "This whole goddamn area is set for a population explosion in the next decade. We know it. They know it. There's fortunes to be made, and if they have a lick of sense between the three of them—and buddy, we know they do—they'll *all* want in."

chapter *One*

2014

Daddy had whistled his way past me and out the door two minutes ago, ready to drive us both to work. *Work*—as in my first postcollege job. Where I would be working for my father. Or rather, working for someone who reported to the someone who reported to my father. I felt certain that all the employees who'd *earned* their positions at Jeffrey McIntyre Custom Homes were thrilled shitless to have me coming on board.

Checking the three-way mirror nestled into the sconce-lit alcove of the mudroom, I scanned myself one more time. Sensible three-inch Ferragamo pumps (nude), sensible DVF wrap dress (chocolate), sensible Michael Kors bag that felt like luggage on my arm compared to the lip-gloss-and-ID-holding crossbodies I was used to flinging over my shoulder.

In my dark shades, I looked like my mother. I might not mind if I weren't twenty-two and in no rush to look "amazing for fifty-seven"—a commendation she received often from envious peers. Mom wasn't opposed to availing herself of the best personal trainers and cosmetic procedures money could buy, and her stylist was booked out months in advance despite fees that would choke a horse.

Her entire social circle did the same, though few got her results. Hence the envy.

Despite my lack of enthusiasm to ever be middle-aged, the mirror told me how I'd wear it when it came. *Could be worse.* For some blasted reason, that thought unnerved me rather than inspiring appreciation for my genetics. I felt hollow, as if there was nothing of *me* about me. But that was nothing new.

In my giant bag was a red leather portfolio with my initials etched into a gold-plated square right in the center, Mom-gifted to commemorate my Very First Day. Like kindergarten. I'd added a legal pad, HR-required documents, pens in three colors, a mechanical pencil, and an outdated finance calculator that I hoped to God I wouldn't need because I'd been into gluing rhinestones to everything when I took precal freshman year, and it was blinged to hell and back.

I looked like I was playing dress-up: Professional Business Chick edition.

Suck it up, McIntyre, I told myself. *Time to adult.*

• • • • • • • • • • •

As Daddy parked in his reserved spot, I stared up at the hewn limestone, raw timber, and glass structure that gave the impression of eighteenth-century Spanish architecture, but newer. Way newer. The office building housing JMCH was a testament to its own distinctive design abilities—just like my parents' Southlake home, which looked as though a European castle had plopped smack down in North Texas, turrets and all. It lacked only a moat and a drawbridge—something my father had pretend-lamented every time a new boy showed up at the door when I was in high school.

"Ready, Princess?"

I halted a groan before it began. I had exploited my youngest-child, only-daughter status my entire life, batting my lashes to get my way from age two if video footage could be believed. My father ate it up, and I kept shoveling. It wouldn't be fair to hold that against him now. But.

"Maybe it's time to drop that nickname, Daddy. Considering the fact that everyone in there has *correct* preconceived notions of how I got this position."

He chuckled. "You're beautiful, degreed, and perfectly suited for this position, Prin—Erin."

"I have a bachelor's degree in psychology. That doesn't exactly scream *I know everything about building custom homes*."

"Your name's on the building, honey." He pointed. "That does all the hollering necessary." He patted my knee before exiting the truck.

Which is exactly my point?

I slid down from the passenger side of his tank-sized F-450 King Ranch, holding my dress to my thigh to prevent giving a free show to anyone staring out one of those gleaming, stone-framed windows. "No need for a free show!" was a thing Nana, Mom's mother, began chiding me with when I was eleven, no matter how confusing that statement was then, how mortifying at thirteen, or how infuriating by seventeen. I'd never been able to get it out of my head.

Daddy's monster pickup could hold five big guys, tow a bunch of lesser pickups, or haul a small herd of elephants, but most of the time it hauled my parents and Jack, their spoiled English bulldog, around town or on occasional forays into Fort Worth or Dallas.

During the week, Mom drove a Mercedes SUV. To counter the environmental damage they generated, I'd requested a hybrid car for my graduation gift. I probably should have asked for a bicycle.

When we entered the JMCH building, heads swiveled and whispers hummed across the marble floor of the open atrium. I felt like a hayseed beauty queen on a 4-H float and fought an intense urge to wave like parade royalty just to be a smartass. But I couldn't blame them for staring. I was the boss's daughter. Privilege and entitlement wrapped in money. The expressions my new coworkers wore ranged from wide-eyed curiosity (the receptionist, who looked like a twelve-year-old wearing half a pound of mascara) to veiled animosity (some guy glaring down from the open gallery of the second level as though his sworn enemy had just breached the castle walls). *Sheesh.*

I thanked God that I'd always had a knack for facial recognition even if names escaped me, fixed a sensible, friendly smile on my face, and droned, "Nice to meet you," or "Nice to see you again," to anyone who made eye contact. I even bestowed a diplomatic smile toward the man on the second floor. He turned and disappeared.

"Great," I muttered. I already had a hater, and I'd barely set foot in the damned door.

We boarded the elevator and I whooped an internal *Thank you, Jesus* when Daddy pressed the three, relieved to skip a face-to-face encounter with Mr. Hostile for now. Polished marble gave way to plush, footfall-absorbing carpet as we turned toward the two huge, windowed offices at the back. Daddy rapped twice on the open door to the smartly decorated corner office of his CFO and walked in without waiting for a response.

Hank Greene was my uncle in all but actual kinship. His family and mine went way back; he, Daddy, and Bud Sager had launched JMCH before I or any of my three older brothers were born. From last-minute perusing of the website, I'd learned that Bud had retired a few years ago and his nephew, Ted, was the current Vice President of Operations. At least nepotism wasn't a new concept here. Yay?

"Erin—how are you, honey?" Uncle Hank asked, smiling and coming around the huge mahogany desk, which was so shiny I could see my shoes reflected in the glossy front panel as I stepped forward.

I stretched out my hand and opted for a professional greeting. "Mr. Greene—it's nice to see you again."

He and my father shared corresponding smirks. "Mr. Greene, is it? Ha. Ha." He took my hand and patted it with his other, much like Daddy had patted my knee earlier. They might as well boop me on the head and hand me a face-sized lollipop, for chrissake.

"She's worried people will think she's only here because she's my daughter." Daddy made that valid concern sound absurd.

Hank blinked and chuckled. "Now, now. Worse things to be accused of than being the beneficiary of a little harmless familial bias."

He adjusted the thin pewter frames that perfectly offset his thick graying hair and manicured brows. No doubt his wife was responsible for that flawless coordination. Miranda Greene was as much of a fashionista as my mother, if not more. The Greenes had two children—one boy, one girl—both in college now. They'd been mostly raised by a live-in au pair before au pairs were even a thing. Hank and Miranda attended championship games and recitals, but the au pair, who'd looked like a Swedish model, spoke several languages, and knew CPR, had been the one shuttling the kids to sports practices and music lessons until they could shuttle them-selves.

Miranda didn't volunteer like Mom did or have a job that I knew of. Years ago, I'd asked Mom what Miranda did all day, thinking maybe she worked at home, writing romance novels or day-trading stocks or managing a fashion blog. I was about to enter high school and was considering career options.

"Oh, she works all right," Mom said, her tone superior. "She slaves twenty-four-seven at the career she trained for—*husbandry*." She'd tapped the canvas Whole Foods bag she'd just brought in before leaving the room. "Put these things away, would you, sweetie?"

I hadn't known what she meant, but the youngest of my brothers, Pax, snorted. He was standing in front of the stainless Sub-Zero fridge, door open—per usual if he was in the kitchen.

"What," I said, confused. "I don't get it."

"Husbandry—accent on husband. *Comprende*?" He grabbed the orange juice carton labeled PAX—proof that Mom had given up all hope that he'd ever learn basic manners—and chugged it.

The mental lightbulb clicked on and I laughed and groaned, but *husbandry* sounded like a repugnant existence—looking after some man, day after day, forever. I loved Uncle Hank and Daddy, but they were not my idea of life goals.

"Dad started warning me about girls majoring in *husbandry* when I was your age. He gave me a box of Trojans and literally said, 'Wrap it before you tap it.'"

"Eww, *gross*." Fourteen-year-old me couldn't imagine any girl dumb enough to have sex with my eighteen-year-old brother at all, let alone for the purpose of having to do it with *him only* the rest of her natural-born days. Back then Pax's favorite pastime was farting all the way down the hallway like a puttering antique car that backfired once he reached my bedroom doorway. His other hobbies had included belching mangled lyrics to songs I liked, stealing food off my plate at dinner, and trying to hug me into his armpit right after lifting weights.

Hard to believe he was now a twenty-six-year-old minor league ballplayer, recently engaged to one of his groupies (she "did hair"—her words—at a Supercuts near his apartment in Albuquerque and had recognized him when he wandered in for a cut). He'd rejected all my parents' efforts to convince him to finish school or "get a real job" and seemed determined to grow up at his own pace. While Daddy hadn't officially despaired where his youngest son was concerned, he'd long since begun directing his unsolicited career advice on the older two—Leo, a construction foreman at JMCH, and Foster, a junior associate at a Dallas law firm.

Last Christmas, Daddy grilled Foster about how soon he might make partner.

"Dad, that's a decade or so away. Jesus."

"Don't cuss in front of your mother," Daddy said, as if Foster was still a kid. "If ten years is average, your fancy-schmancy degree oughta bring that down to six or seven, eh?"

Foster side-eyed Pax and mumbled, "Living six hundred miles away. You lucky bastard."

"Luck's got nothin' to do with it, bro," Pax answered, using the tongs to grab a second slab of ham off the platter and plopping it onto his already-full plate.

The management of me had been left to Mom for the most part, though my parents had joined forces in attempting to talk me out of majoring in psychology, even after I'd declared it. At first, I thought it was because they didn't consider the study of the mind and associated mental illnesses a real science. This was the philosophy of some people in their circle, no matter how many of them were high-functioning alcoholics or consumed anti-anxiety meds like candy while feeding their kids whatever amphetamines would control their nonconforming behavior and boost their GPAs, because God forbid anybody try a little *talk therapy* along with the pills.

It wasn't until winter break of my sophomore year that I figured out my parents' chief motive for urging a change in my course of study even though I had never expressed any interest in swapping majors. Events had occurred the prior semester that had solidified my desire to be a therapist. My boyfriend's best friend had assaulted and stalked my roommate and raped one of my sorority's little sisters. I was the person they'd both turned to first. I'd listened and advocated and stood by them when some of the Greek leaders just wanted it to all go away. I had never in my life felt so influential and necessary and useful.

Not that I ever discussed stuff like that with my parents, but still.

One morning over breakfast, out of the clear blue sky, they brought up other majors I might like better. *Again.* "Public relations or marketing would be fantastic for a people person like you, Princess," Daddy said, slathering a bagel with nonfat cream cheese.

"Or management—you'd be a wonderful manager." Mom grinned like she'd discovered the Holy Grail of nondescript careers.

I tried to connect the dots in the parental logic but couldn't. "*Psychology* is fantastic for a people person like me," I said, remembering Jacqueline's quiet revelation in our dorm room and the sorority meeting during which Mindi held my hand so tight that my fingers went numb. "I want to help people. I don't see how *marketing* would fulfill that desire."

"Well, yes, but—"

"I know it will take a little longer." I frowned, wondering if they were stressing over the cost. But they hadn't balked at paying Foster's exorbitant law school tuition, so that didn't add up. "I'll need at least a master's if not a doctorate—"

They exchanged a quick glance then, identical hesitant expressions, and *click*, I knew. The career paths they'd suggested didn't require demanding advanced degrees like psychology did. They didn't think I could do it. That was the only explanation. They didn't believe I had the intellectual capacity or maybe the work ethic required to go to graduate school. I put a bite of egg in my mouth and chewed robotically to cover my muteness.

Daddy had steered Leo toward summer construction internships while pushing Foster toward law school, and I'd eavesdropped on enough conversations with and about my brothers to know why. Leo was the football jock who couldn't care less about school; Foster was reading by age three, and by ten he would throw a tantrum if some hapless teacher gave him a B. He'd been his class salutatorian in high school (twelve years had passed and he was still bitter about coming in second), graduated college in less than four years, and started law school at twenty-one. Pax had been Pax—as smart as Foster and more athletically gifted than Leo, he just about drove Daddy off his rocker with his lack of drive to do any more than scrape by academically, play baseball, and hook up with as many girls as possible.

I'd been the popular cheerleader with a healthy social life and a B average. In college I'd traded cheering for sorority life and kept my adequate-but-not-exceptional GPA. They'd forever been on my brothers' asses about education and career ambitions and working smart as well as working hard. But with me, they advocated sorority alliances and my volunteering efforts and maintaining a part-time job to help pay for my shoe-buying habit and give me work experience. Every semester I brought home a B average, and that was good enough. I never got the lectures about earning an A in any class I could.

When I swallowed that bit of egg, it lurched down my constricted throat like lightly chewed rubber, determined to stick where it was. I coughed, not quite choking, and Daddy pounded my back a couple of times. I didn't retain the rest of the conversation, but I'd never forgotten the unspoken *Oh, dear* between them, my silent comprehension of it, and the difficulty swallowing—an occurrence right up there with suddenly being unable to breathe or finding your heart pounding after an unexpected scare. We don't notice reflexive motions like heartbeats or breathing or swallowing. They just happen. Until they don't.

I wallowed in self-pity for the following semester, thinking maybe they were right, maybe I wasn't capable of graduate work, but then I stepped it up and started studying harder. Despite the demanding upper-level coursework, my grades were solid and my GPA inched higher. But my parents never asked when I was planning to take the GRE. They never suggested a tutoring course as they'd done before Foster took his LSATs. So I resolved to handle all of that myself. To show them that their little girl was a perfectly capable, motivated, self-sufficient woman.

And then the past year happened, and I fell into an emotional spiral I couldn't pull out of no matter how hard I tried. Still full of faith in my chosen career, I made appointments at the campus counseling office, but it didn't seem to make any difference. I began skipping sessions and eventually stopped going at all. I saw a private therapist off campus, once, but he targeted current stress and anxiety—as though the enormous guilt weighing on my soul day after day was a by-product of being a frazzled college senior instead of the other way around. I didn't return, and the fact that therapy had failed so miserably made me question what the hell I was basing my future on and why I assumed I could help anyone when I couldn't even help myself.

The worst part? I was completely cognizant of all of it—the plunging lack of interest I had in every aspect of my life. The way I walked around like Eeyore with a small, persistent gray cloud always overhead. I was sinking lower every day, and struggling only hastened the descent. A few of my more perceptive Chi-O sisters tried to cheer me up, but ultimately they didn't get it and I had no desire to elaborate. Once, maybe twice, I almost called Jacqueline—the one and only person I could have blurted the ugly truth to. But she was hundreds of miles away and caught up in her happy life and I couldn't bear to drag her down. So I sent her carefully constructed, upbeat texts, and left superficial voicemails full of amusing stories and lies when I knew she was in class or studio and couldn't answer or call back.

Finally, I used every ounce of energy I possessed to do what I'd always done best. I slapped on my sunny Erin mask and let everyone off the hook so they'd stop asking if I was okay, stop with the apprehensive "Are you sure?" inquiries and the benevolent "I'm here for you" avowals when I said I was fine. And every one of them looked relieved as hell.

My grades kept slipping and so did my GPA. I crawled across the finish line and graduated as planned, but I neglected to sign up for the GRE in time for fall deadlines. I abandoned partially completed grad school applications without submitting them. I failed to turn in reference requests to professors who'd expressed prior interest in recommending me.

Now I had to prove myself at this job because otherwise I had nothing, and I *damned* sure hadn't trained for a job in husbandry.

chapter *Two*

Uncle Hank gestured me toward a chair at a small conference table on the opposite side of his office, spent a few minutes describing my position as client liaison, and handed me some forms to fill out for "the HR girl"—a woman in her midthirties named Connie who'd probably devised sensitivity training regarding this very issue, which clearly had not imprinted itself on upper management. While I filled in blanks on the stack of paperwork that would make me an official employee, Hank launched into a praise session about the remarkable combination of intelligence, drive, patience, and personality that comprised the supervisor I had yet to meet, Isaac Maat.

"He's a young fella, but sharp as a tack and hardworking. Respectful too. Everybody likes him. When you work finance in a construction company, that's no mean feat." He went on to explain how my new boss's degrees, a BS in architecture and an MBA, emphasis finance, made him the perfect candidate for the dual role he currently held at JMCH: financial analyst plus client liaison manager. I wasn't sure what a financial analyst *did*, exactly, and made a note to Google it when I got home instead of asking and confirming my ignorance.

"Who else does he manage?" I asked, handing over my contact information, W-4 allowances, health insurance elections, and 401(k) designations.

"Just you," Hank said, tapping the small pile of documents into a neat stack as if his answer hadn't just opened the door to making an awkward situation ten times worse.

"So the person who held the position before me was promoted? Or resigned? Or...?" An uneasy suspicion whispered his response to my brain before he answered.

"It's a new position." He clipped the paperwork and slid it into a file folder with my name on the label: MCINTYRE, ERIN R.

I looked at my clueless father, who winked at me. My stomach flipped and sank. "A new position. As in, you *made up a job* for me." I felt a surge of adrenaline signaling panic born of (totally valid) mortification. "Oh my God. *Oh my God.* Is there even a job to *do*?"

"Uh," said my father, catching on and looking to Hank to impede my escalating freak-out. *Fat. Chance.*

I imagined the formidably talented, genial but diligent Mr. Maat whipping up simple little projects to keep the owner's incompetent, otherwise jobless daughter busy, like when I was six and Mom towed me along to her book club meeting because my sitter had the flu. Daddy was leading a church men's retreat, Foster was on a field trip to Quebec with his French class, Pax was too young and untrustworthy to be charged with watching another human, and Leo, at sixteen, was incapable of keeping himself out of trouble, let alone his six-year-old sister.

"If I hadn't chosen this month's book, I would skip," Mom had murmured aloud, eyeing me with just enough annoyance that I felt defensive. Book club night was sacred, and through no fault of my own, I was throwing a wrench into it.

Scanning the kitchen counter, she'd grabbed a handheld game of Pax's, a banded set of Latin flash cards belonging to Foster, a random sketch pad and two pencils, and Leo's box of Whoppers. He would rant like a bratty toddler when he found out his baby sister had eaten it, which daunted me not at all. Ushering me toward her SUV, she said, "We'll get you McDonald's on the way."

We *never* got McDonald's, so I brightened at that sweet kickback. An hour later I was in a food-coma from chicken nuggets, fries, Dr. Pepper, and candy, bored out of my mind with Pax's tedious game, and *so done* trying to draw something identifiable with the dull graphite pencils. I crossed "artist" off my list of potential brilliant careers and glared at the Latin flash cards. *No*. I'd ended up devouring a shocking edition of *Cosmo* from a stack I discovered in the guest bathroom while a dozen wine-drinking mommies argued over whether reading *Pride and Prejudice* or watching Colin Firth spar verbally with Miss Elizabeth and dive into ponds was a better use of their time.

I could not spend my days at JMCH reading Cosmo!

"Oh sure, sure—we've been in dire need of a specified client liaison," Hank assured adult me, sputtering a little with the obvious lie and adjusting his glasses while his eyes darted between my father and me before glancing toward the door and beaming. "Ah, Isaac—perfect timing!" His gleeful appreciation of the interruption was palpable.

I turned, and my earlier relief at having bypassed the second floor and the rude man I'd hoped to escape meeting on my first day, if not forever, crashed and burned. My smile faded before reaching full wattage as I stared at the very last person in that building I wanted to encounter. *This guy* was the sociable, even-tempered, model employee I'd just spent fifteen solid minutes hearing all about?

Up close, he was beyond good-looking, which just pissed me off more. Attractive men have no right to be assholes. They were starting ahead of the curve. At frat parties, I had downgraded the pretty ones in my head before they spoke. Beautiful eyes: minus two points. Tall (unless lanky): minus three. Muscular: minus five. The cuter they were, the more I made them work for my attention. It was only fair.

Isaac Maat's medium-brown skin held a hint of red, like a warm sepia polish. His lashes were long, thick, and curved, framing large, nearly black eyes. Sharp cheekbones. Wide nose balanced over full lips. Square, stubborn jawline shaded by a dark, neat scruff of beard. Dressed like a *GQ* cover model. His physical appeal handicap was so low he could turn pro.

Lucky for me his personality left a lot to be desired. Unlucky for me that brushing him off was not a viable option as he was now my freaking *boss*.

His earlier scowl had been replaced with a placid, not ill-disposed expression, but then, he hadn't shared my surprise. He'd known *exactly* who I was when he'd glowered down at me like I was an avowed nemesis instead of his new report. Okay, sure, I was the owner's daughter, and it probably irked him to no end that he'd lost the rock-paper-scissors match and had to take on babysitting duties, but I hadn't come to wreak cosmic havoc on the place, and I wasn't remotely qualified to commandeer his job out from under him. So what the actual hell was his deal?

"Good to have you on board, Ms. McIntyre," he said, nodding across the expanse of polished teak between us, unbuttoning his perfectly cut suit jacket and sitting directly opposite me, one foot atop the opposite knee and large, well-manicured hands loosely clasped in his lap, casual as the devil. His voice was deep and soothing, like a tranquil country stream leading to a fishpond with no visible bottom. Mistake it for a harmless swimming hole and you could get tangled up in submerged weeds or bash your head on an unseen rock.

Despite his reserved demeanor and sincerely expressed words of welcome, I knew he no more welcomed me here than a cantankerous cat welcomed a yappy puppy to share the sofa. I felt the insult of his presumptions, whatever they were, but I was more miffed than nervous. If he thought I was going to let his surliness intimidate me, he could guess again. I'd grown up with three older brothers and a gruff bear of a father. I'd put up with four years of inaccurate frat-boy assumptions about what amount of unsolicited handiness would or would not earn a knee to the balls. Dude was gonna have to up his game.

"Mr. Maat. Pleased to meet you." If words were visible, mine would've had icicles dangling from them.

His eyes narrowed for a split second before he noticed my awareness of his puzzling animosity and shut it down.

Oh ho. There was a concealed jut of jagged stone under this man's surface, and I felt a dangerous, unnecessary impulse to unmask Isaac Maat. I knew better, I swear. But I've never been good at steering clear of temptation, especially when it came packaged like Satan peddling original sin.

After a five-minute discussion of client and project updates and something about the previous weekly report that sounded like finance, Hank dismissed the two of us, but not without parting decorating advice. "Fix up your office however you'd like, honey. Artwork, plants, framed photos of your favorite uncle..." He chuckled. "My secretary, Mrs. Gardner, even has a few of those beanbag bears sitting on her credenza." His mouth puckered on one side and his brows drew together as he seemed to reconsider. "Can't say I recommend that style of *décor*, as Miranda would say, since you'll be working directly with clients and you still look about fifteen."

Through obstinate, concentrated effort, I kept my mouth from falling open and steered my vocal inflection away from affronted and toward amused. "I'm well past my Beanie Baby stage, Uncle Hank. Bratz dolls too. I might have a My Little Pony lying around somewhere, but I'll leave him at home."

Isaac Maat snorted but converted his grating amusement into an extended throat-clearing as Hank said, without a trace of sarcasm, "That would be best," and Daddy sat there smiling and oblivious, as though I hadn't just been demeaned for looking like a child in the presence of my new supervisor, who'd already formed an adverse, invalid opinion of me.

The walk to my new office was silent, even while waiting for the elevator and during the unbelievably slow one-floor descent. We exited, he turned down the nearest hallway, and I followed. He gestured toward an open doorway and said, "This is my office." Sliding a key from the front pocket of his perfectly tailored slacks, he continued to the very next door. Once it was unlocked, he stepped back and motioned for me to precede him inside. I would have assumed that to be a gentlemanly action if not for the fact that there wouldn't have been enough floor space for both of us if he'd entered first.

My office was microscopic. Like used-to-be-a-supply-closet tiny. There was just enough square footage to cram a desk and a file cabinet inside without blocking the door. One narrow, east-facing window—more suited to a cell than an office and partially blocked by a tall file cabinet—was directly across from the door. Hot, blinding sunlight streamed in through the pane, unimpeded by a shade or blinds. The room was several degrees warmer than the hallway. A cloudless blue sky and the terra-cotta tops of the posh shopping strip across the street was the view. Upscale was how we did things around here, whether the structure housed a James Avery or a 7-Eleven.

I was obscenely conscious of Isaac Maat standing just behind me, silent. I imagined him staring at the back of my head and struggling with a desire to strangle me or step into the hall, shut my office door, and padlock it from the outside.

"It's small," he offered.

I clamped my lips shut to keep from retorting, *No shit.* "It will do just fine," I said instead, turning toward him. He was ridiculously close. I had to tilt my face up to make eye contact. "Although if I'm supposed to work with clients, there isn't room for chairs."

"When you're ready to meet with clients"—his tone implied that might be never—"you can reserve one of the two conference rooms off the first-floor atrium. The walls are covered in enlarged floor plans and detailed pics of finished homes—with available upgrades magnified, of course." His full lips pressed together and one brow lifted in a conspiratorial smirk.

"Of course," I said, returning the smile, thinking that maybe he was just initially hypercritical. Maybe he was actually a nice guy and I'd judged him too hastily.

The grumpy expression slipped back into place and he took a half step back, away from me, which put him into the hallway. "I believe Hank has explained your job title and duties. Basically, you're to placate disgruntled clients. The hard files are stored, alphabetically, in the filing cabinet, there." He pointed, though there was only the one cabinet in the room.

I prevented a sarcastic *DER* from escaping my mouth.

"Each client's corresponding emails, scanned contracts, blueprints, and change orders are kept in data files shared with other departments—Sales and Design, and to a lesser degree, Construction. You'll find those on your desktop computer." He indicated the large monitor. "Don't delete, move, or modify any files until and unless you know what you're doing. If you revise or erase something from your computer, the identical revision occurs to everyone's files."

Wait. It was possible for me to delete files? That the whole company used? I felt like I was being set up to crash and burn. "Isn't there a backup for those somewhere?"

He breathed an annoyed sigh. "Yes. But we'd prefer not to waste time and energy hunting for and replacing information that shouldn't have been altered. I'm mentioning it because it's been done once before." It was obvious what he thought of anyone dumb enough to do such a thing.

He glanced around as though verifying that there was nothing more to discuss. He'd already mentioned both pieces of furniture and the computer, so unless he wanted to explain how to look out the window or sit in the chair, we were probably done. "I'll let you get settled in. I suggest you browse through the printed files first—well, after you decide how to 'decorate' your space, that is. I have work to do." His eyes landed on mine as he dropped the key into my hand, the meaning behind his words ricocheting off the walls and slamming into me like hard little projectiles. "Let me know when you have questions. I'll be in my office."

I watched him go, fists balled at my sides. My lips were buttoned, but my mind shrieked, *Asshole!* I wanted to *decorate* one blank wall with a life-sized picture of him kissing my butt when I killed it at this job. Right after I figured out how I was supposed to accomplish that.

chapter *Three*

It was late afternoon when I scooped up a stack of folders, took a deep breath, squared my shoulders as though I were about to do a roundoff, and walked next door to Isaac Maat's office.

Daddy and Hank had stopped by my door just before noon and invited me to lunch to celebrate my employment. I had agreed without thinking, if only to escape the silent judgment emanating from the adjoining office. Since I had read through a few of the files, I'd also hoped to pick their brains some more about what I was meant to accomplish, but the way they hesitated and stammered—trying to align their clarifications without contradicting each other—was damning. They had no idea of me accomplishing anything.

If walking out the door had felt awkward as hell, returning was even worse. How often are company peons escorted to a two-hour lunch by the president and the CFO on their first day of employment, for chrissake? I had skittered up the staircase to my office instead of waiting for the elevator with Daddy and Hank.

Now I stood watching my supervisor for a moment, his forehead marred with a pinched crease of concern or irritation. Attention on his monitor's screen, he either didn't notice me standing there or he was pointedly ignoring me.

I cleared my throat. "Excuse me, Mr. Maat?"

His eyes shifted to me, and I swear there was a tic near his jawline that was becoming all too familiar. "Yes?"

I took one step into his office. Here, the afternoon sunlight had been filtered by a shade through which the blue sky was still visible. The interior lighting was all strategically positioned lamps—the harsh fluorescents weren't even on. Warmth and masculinity exuded from matte taupe walls and rich furniture—dark, burnished walnut and darker leather, professional with a suggestion of both comfort and power. The space suited him. But unless the interior decorating fairy had paid a visit when he wasn't here, he had a lot of nerve belittling me for taking time to personalize my own teeny, tiny space. He'd clearly done so, and the results were stunning.

Even so, I felt as though I was entering a cave inhabited by a menacing bear with a short temper. He stared at me from behind his desk—eyes never wavering from mine, mouth uncurving, expression frozen—making his annoyance at my interruption, or perhaps my mere presence in the building if not the *world*, all too plain.

I barreled ahead despite his lack of enthusiasm at my existence. "So, I have a file cabinet full of green-tabbed projects that appear to be on target and have satisfied clients. And then there are a couple dozen clients ranging from not-so-satisfied to hostile, as determined by the notes and email trails. Their folders are tabbed yellow, orange, or red."

No response. Zilch.

Under his inflexible gaze, I felt like a tiresome nitwit babbling nonsense. "Um, what do those tabs mean? I thought maybe they were divided by the budgets of the projects, but that doesn't appear to be the case."

I trailed off when I spotted that little spasm at the edge of his jaw again, like he was trying to crush glass with his teeth.

Lord love a duck, I thought, staring back. *What?*

He blinked and took a moment to pull a long, slow breath through his nose as if he was gearing up to deadlift a new world record. Or explain something simple to an unwelcome new employee who should have been able to figure it out herself. "They're client risk levels. Hazard ranks, if you will." Why, God, why did his voice have to be so velvety when he clearly wanted to see my backside running out the door, never to return?

I focused on the words. "Risk levels, as in how unhappy they are with us? How likely they are to try to terminate the project and refuse to pay?"

He nodded, brows lifting about a millimeter, which might indicate reluctant approval. "Or litigate. Or both."

"So the Beadles"—I tapped the yellow-tabbed folder on top—"are a level one? More salvageable?" I pulled a red-tabbed folder from the bottom. "And this Mr. Jansen… He thinks his ass is on fire and we're holding the lighter, the kerosene, the marshmallows, and a couple of wire hangers?"

A short chuckle snuck through his exasperated mien, but he cleared his throat and flattened his expression as though it hadn't occurred. This guy *really* didn't want to like me. "Uh, yeah."

I worried that behind his exasperation was real indignation, regardless of that brief, husky laugh. Attempting to break through that wall might be a catastrophically ill-advised move.

"Should I begin with the red-tabbed clients, then, since their projects are deemed most at risk?"

He cocked his head, the movement a trivial provocation, like a matador flicking the edge of the sword-concealing cape at the wary bull. "There's only one red folder at present, and you're holding it."

I felt the tug in my chest, a stirring of the Erin I used to be, who never backed down from a dare or surrendered to ultimatums. He was laying down a challenge. One I knew he didn't want me to take and certainly didn't expect me to succeed in conquering.

"Oh. Well. Let's make that *no* red folders then," I said, knocked sideways by a spark of confidence I hadn't felt in ages. I would wheedle into this Jansen guy's psyche to find the thorn in his paw. Everyone had one.

Isaac Maat clenched his jaw, and I saw my chance slipping away.

"I'll just go set up an appointment to see Mr. Jansen. The folder contains all the details of his complaint and what we've done to appease him thus far, right?"

He gave a reluctant nod, and I knew he was debating whether he ought to forbid me from diving right into the feasibly perilous deep end with our most irate client.

I didn't intend to give him time to interject any of his misgivings.

"Cool. I'll let you know if I have any questions."

I all but ran back to my shoebox and studied the contents of Wayne Jansen's folder with increasing apprehension and a healthy dose of *Oh fuck.* And then I took a deep breath and tried to read between the lines.

Everyone in management had weighed in on the shitstorm this guy had caused over the past year. His profession was listed as "commercial airline pilot" and he had no construction experience that anyone knew of, but that hadn't deterred his relentless torrent of criticism. There wasn't a single aspect of the project he *hadn't* nitpicked or filed complaints over, from framing to interior trim to the texture of the kitchen cabinets' wood grain. He'd chosen and approved the interior color only to insist—after over six thousand feet of wall had been painted—that it looked like puke. He'd left a scrawled note and sent seven follow-up emails citing a "defective faucet with a too-wide stream." He was prone to popping up at the job site without warning to berate the laborers.

We couldn't really tell clients they weren't allowed on their own home site, though when I asked Leo, he said we tried to discourage it. My oldest sibling had always lived by the tenet *It's easier to ask forgiveness than permission.*

"Yeah, man, that guy's a giant douche," he said, once he bothered to return my call. "Glad he's not one of mine. I'da throat-punched him by now if one of my guys didn't beat me to it."

Construction wasn't easy work, whether it was highly skilled electrical labor or a newbie nail-gunning wallboard to a frame. While I couldn't imagine that these rough-edged men were easily butthurt, nobody needed some raging fuckwit criticizing their work while they were trying to *do* it. Report notes from Kenny LaCross, the unfortunate construction foreman on the Jansen project, indicated that he'd had to dismiss teams for the day more than once to prevent them from resigning altogether.

There was no way in hell Isaac Maat believed I could appease this client.

Which made me more determined to do it.

• • • • • • • • • • •

"Hello, Mr. Jansen?"

My nails tapped out a quick staccato on the laminate wood

desktop, and I braced for his reaction, anticipation stilling my breath and revving my heart as though he could breathe fire through the corded receiver. I was sure he'd read the caller ID before he picked up. People who got their jollies berating the world at large often suffered from low self-esteem, and people who suffered from low self-esteem were frequently distrustful if not outright paranoid.

"Who is this?" Jansen—I assumed—growled the words. This dude was the epitome of hostile.

"This is Erin McIntyre from Jeffrey McIntyre Custom—"

"What do you want now? Did you replace those defective faucets? What about the substandard cabinets? I want you to rip those cheap-ass things out of my kitchen—they look like shit. Speaking of which—that paint color. It's hideous and there is no damn way I chose that. I haven't heard from anyone in well over a week. It's like you people don't know a goddamn thing about customer service."

I swear my hair blew back a little. *What a nutjob.* He wasn't passive about his complaints either. He must have known that whatever my job at JMCH was, I wouldn't be personally replacing the faucets or cabinets, but that's how his demands came across. In addition, within the past four days, the Sales VP had emailed him and the construction foreman had called and left a voicemail. He hadn't responded to either attempt to contact him.

I wouldn't be able to temper his outrage by arguing those points, and coaxing him to calm down and sign off on this project was my job. So I forced myself to smile, because even if you're in a total funk, the smile comes through your voice. Props to my middle school cheer coach for that one, which I'd used on everyone from parents irked about a curfew violation, to teachers ticked off over incomplete assignments, to Jacqueline—my initially reserved freshman-year roommate who'd quickly become my best friend.

"I've spoken to the foreman and read over your concerns, Mr. Jansen, and I'd appreciate it if you could meet me at the site this evening at say, six o'clock?" I maintained my daft grin by envisioning myself elbowing this asshat right in the windpipe, a move I'd learned in a self-defense course I'd taken sophomore year. "We'll do a walk-through and address each of those concerns so we can get you into your new home as soon as possible."

"Make it five."

"Well, the workers will still be there at fi—"

"I don't give a flying crap. That's when I'm available, Miss— What was your name?"

The imaginary throat punch in my head became a knee to the nutsack. "Erin. McIntyre."

I waited, but instead of any further comment from Mr. Jansen, the annoying *onk-onk-onk-onk* reorder tone sounded in my ear. For one harebrained moment, I assumed the call had been dropped and started to dial him back. And then I faced the startling realization that he'd disconnected, on purpose, without so much as a *Later*, let alone a more polite *I'll see you then* or *Goodbye.*

I stared at my phone. "That cretinistic *dickhead.*"

"Bad time?" I heard from the door. I turned to see one of the three sales agents—the only guy—leaning against the frame, arms crossed over his chest. He smiled conspiratorially and one dimple appeared. "Or do I need to kick somebody's ass for sassing the new girl?"

I sighed and gave a little chuckle as though I appreciated his useless, unsolicited rescue offer while I struggled to recall his name among the two dozen people I had met this morning. My brain had experienced near power failure by the time we got to Sales. I'd filed Cynthia Pike in my memory bank because she was the VP but blanked on the rest of them. This day was sucking ass hard enough to leave a mark.

"Oh, ha ha—nothing I can't handle…" *Jacob, Justin, Jasper—*

"Joshua Swearingen at your service, ma'am." He was all frat-boy cuteness in a late-twenties package—a bit less hardbody, no less cocky swagger. He touched his finger to his forehead in a flirtatious little salute.

Maybe it was the channeling of my mother this morning, or maybe it was the fact that I had brothers and had long been subjected to an excessive amount of their bodily emissions and thought processes—such as they were—but Joshua Swearingen seemed like a mischievous kid, and I was in no mood.

Fabulous. I'd started my first full-time job and swerved hardcore toward middle age. If I'd had a lawn handy, I'd have ordered him off it.

"*Joshua*—yes, sorry, I almost had it." Not.

"No big. You met lots of folks today. Can't be expected to remember everyone. I'll just have to make sure to impress you enough to be memorable." He winked. *Seriously.* "Sure I can't defend your honor to whoever you were just talking to?" He glanced over his shoulder and his voice lowered. "It wasn't Maat, was it? Most everyone thinks he's kind of a dick."

Despite the fact that I'd had similar contemplations, Hank had said the opposite, plus it kind of pissed me off that one of our sales agents would refer to my boss like that so casually.

"Uppity, you know?" he all but whispered.

No, I don't know. What do you mean, exactly? was on the tip of my tongue, but I never got a word out because the subject of this unsettling comment appeared over his shoulder. Joshua should have looked sheepish at what he'd just said, but instead he straightened in the doorway and threw his shoulders back, his eyes hard.

"Excuse me, Swearingen," Isaac Maat said, his voice a smooth, deep well of sound, far from juvenile. He stood equally straight and tall, but on him it was his natural posture, not the issuing of a silly macho challenge. "I need to speak with Ms. McIntyre if you don't mind." His tone said he didn't give a goddamn whether Joshua Swearingen minded or not.

"Yeah, sure." Joshua shrugged and stepped back into the hallway. "Later, Erin," he said, his eyes flicking over my boss as though his appearance at my door was an unreasonable intrusion.

Isaac didn't appear to have overheard Joshua's derogatory comment or noticed his peacocking, and I was relieved because I didn't want him to think I'd welcomed or initiated a conversation that was definitely gossipy and possibly bigoted. I might dislike my new boss at the moment, but that was my business, and I'd learned not to place blind trust in first impressions because (a) I'd been wrong before, and (b) I didn't like it when people judged me on superficial traits like my looks or my parents' money.

Like Isaac Maat had done the moment I walked in the door, if not before.

But it was day one, and I still had hopes that the indignant, preemptory scan he'd given me when I entered the building this morning and his derisive tone since the moment we met would become irrelevant to our working relationship going forward.

I forced a pleasant expression and waited patiently as he looked down at the papers in his hand, rolling them into a tube. His silent examination of what he held—or his pause until Joshua was out of earshot—allowed me both time and excuse to stare.

My new boss was as easy on the eyes as he could be. His was a face of contradictions—soft and hard, curved and honed, at odds with itself. I wondered what that told me about the man inside, if anything. Because his outside was as hot as bare pavement in the middle of summer, and that was pretty damned inconvenient in a hundred and ten ways.

That was when I realized a pop-sexy soundtrack of my perusal was issuing from my computer speaker. I fought the urge to mute it out of fear of what he thought of the spoiled white girl listening to Taylor Swift. I could feel the word *predictable* circling the room even though he had given no indication of his thoughts about my music choices. *This is your office*, my inner voice groused. *You can listen to whatever you want.*

And then the end of that track blended into the beginning of the next and it didn't take long before I realized that yes, it could actually get worse. The beat pounded as Usher promised to make the object of his affections scream.

"I'm heading upstairs for a meeting and wanted to make sure you have everything you need before I'm inaccessible," Isaac said, eyes back on mine.

I searched frantically for the Mute key. It wasn't where I thought it should be, and though I knew it was somewhere on the keyboard, I couldn't find it. We were a captive audience as Usher progressed to picturing his would-be lover naked in the club. I felt my face catch fire. Some people ugly cry; I ugly blush. I prayed my Urban Decay foundation would conceal the inevitable blotches.

"I think I have what I need for now!" I bellowed in my thunderous cheerleader voice.

What the fucking hell with this damned keyboard? my mortified mind wailed. The layout was nothing like my MacBook. Did assholian designers make different models backassward out of spite, just to screw with tech-challenged people like me?

Meanwhile, Isaac's expression went from impassive to that face people make when they believe someone is experiencing a psychotic episode right in front of them: eyes widened, brows high, no sudden movements.

"I'm actually about to head out to meet Mr. Jansen at his home site," I all but roared as Usher promised an entire night of his highly proficient company.

"Tonight?" Isaac deadpanned, with such impeccable timing I almost thought he did it on purpose.

Finally I located the button and slammed my index finger on it, putting a blessed end to Usher's litany of fuck skills.

I nodded. "At five." My voice emerged breathy with relief that had nothing to do with my impending appointment. "I know construction teams are likely to still be there. I was just about to message Kenny LaCross to give him a heads-up."

He scowled, a line darting between his brows, as if I'd just said something so outrageous and wrong that he didn't know where to start in telling me so. But he pinned his lips like he was physically holding in the words and gave one curt nod. And then he turned and left.

chapter *Four*

Wayne Jansen pulled up in a sleek silver Jaguar. Not a fleck of oil or a smudge of dirt dared mar its polished surface. Its shiny hood ornament gleamed mid-pounce.

I'd arrived an hour early and had been over every detail, with and without the foreman, who gave me the grand tour and then vanished, overjoyed that someone else was taking this guy on.

For all its absurd grandiosity, the house was superbly and solidly built—glazed lava countertops from France, artisanal Amish-built cabinets, Waterworks faucets, Brazilian hardwoods, and single-pane floor-to-ceiling glass walls in the master bedroom, overlooking a walled, landscaped garden with a fifteen-foot waterfall fountain in the corner. The craftsmanship and materials were top of the line.

There was no reason whatsoever for this client to be disappointed with a single detail, so there were only two possible explanations for his groundless rants.

Less likely: he could no longer afford the house and was trying to weasel out of the contract and take his big fat pile of earnest money with him. After perusing the file, I'd called Cynthia, and she'd shared that during the recent economic recession, especially at the onset of it, they'd had a few clients press for that escape and leave JMCH holding the bag on a half-completed custom home—customized for *them*. But I'd checked Wayne Jansen's financing, and he was good to go. If reneging on his contract without paying out the nose was his motive, he was going to fail.

The reason for the incessant confrontations, then, probably had nothing to do with JMCH or price and everything to do with Wayne Jansen's personality: his self-worth, his self-image, his colossal but fragile ego.

I had less than five minutes to figure out which version fit the bill with this jerk—the overreaching, in-debt-to-his-eyeballs asshole or the dude with a tiny penis and a big, swinging dose of arrogance to make up for it.

My money was on tiny penis.

Pulling the heavy front door closed behind me, I raised my chin, displayed my premium, competition-winning smile—wide eyes, just the right amount of teeth—and strode down the hand-placed-slate path to greet him. Time to unravel this guy's issues—sufficient to get him to sign off on the ostentatious monstrosity my father had built for him, anyway.

He exited the car and sauntered forward while I dissected the superficial clues. Expensive haircut and color. Likely Rogaine addict. Mirrored aviator Ray-Bans. Neon-green Hugo Boss golf shirt. Pressed khaki slacks. Two-tone loafers—handcrafted by the look of them—that hopefully had the fairway spikes taken out. If he meant to score that imported wood floor on purpose, I would shove those fancy shoes—spikes attached—where the sun had never shone.

"Mr. Jansen—thanks so much for coming." Smile intact, I stuck my hand out as he stepped up onto the curb and stared down at me from behind those reflective lenses, his lips a thin, flat line. He enclosed my hand in a grasp meant to fracture digits, but I had forearms of steel and a grip to match from years of cheer drills and strength training. *Nice try, mister.* I fake-winced to salvage his ego—no sense antagonizing it further—and glanced down at the left hand balled at his side. No wedding band, so no Mrs. Asshole to pity.

"Lovely to meet you," I lied, gushing as if he were the legendary golf pro his outfit implied instead of the all-too-common rich bully he was.

He grunted in response. *Grunted.*

Daddy loathed guys like Wayne Jansen, and I was pretty sure Hank was shielding him from this shitshow while hoping Isaac could get the project back on track without my father ever knowing the details. "Defective" and "substandard"—them was fightin' words. My father had anger-management issues and was liable to meet the guy rage for rage like a couple of Rock 'Em Sock 'Em Robots. At home, he was all bluster, though he did tend to yell and bang on things and send poor Jack struggling to wedge himself behind the nearest sofa, where he had a doggie panic attack, whining and shaking, until Mom pulled him out by his butt and fed him treats. In public though, Daddy had been known to throw a punch or two back in the day.

I wasn't supposed to know about those, so I pretended I didn't.

"I'm Erin McIntyre, and your satisfaction is my number *one* priority at the moment! I know you're more than ready to get into this gorgeous house and start entertaining. Your friends are all going to be *green* with envy." I touched a finger to the sleeve of his bright lime-green shirt and smiled, turning to lead the way up the path before my inner *blech* took control of my face.

When we reached the front door, I pushed it open and stood back so he could enter ahead of me and get an unencumbered view of the two-story-high ceiling of the huge foyer, which boasted tons of natural light somewhat spoiled by a spectacularly garish chandelier —five feet wide, gold-plated, dripping in crystals, with more bulbs than I could estimate from twenty-five feet below. He'd selected it, of course. I was surprised he hadn't papered the halls in C-notes.

He removed the sunglasses and walked through the door, his fists on his hips, sneering as if he were a conquering warrior-king who was none too pleased with all he surveyed. For all the vicious emails and voicemails, let alone our phone conversation not two hours ago, I was kind of shocked that he wasn't already off on a vocal enumeration of JMCH's offenses. He hadn't said a word.

"I've made a mental note of each of your worries," I began, "but why don't you show me the things you're unable to sign off on, and we'll see what we can do to make you happy?" And then I waited for him to launch into his exhaustive list of grievances and accusations. It wasn't a long wait.

"The kitchen cabinets." His tone was drenched in predictable disdain. "There are protruding knots in the wood. The whole mess is unfinished and dark. They look like the side of a decrepit, termite-ridden barn, not cabinets that belong in a luxury home." He spit *luxury* as if it was the farthest thing from this structure.

As I turned toward the hallway leading to the kitchen, I took a breath, imagining how my father would respond to this. *Not. Well.* "Okay. Let's go have a look." I heard the scrape of toolboxes and scuff of work boots in the distance, laborers scurrying out one end of the giant room as we entered the other. This guy had the whole team freaked out.

The cabinets were indeed rustic, but they weren't crawling with termites by any stretch. They were durable and distinctive. My mother would kill for them. She'd had her kitchen redone right after I left for college four years ago. She'd gone all ornate cherry woodwork and quartz countertops, right before high-end turned to varnished concrete and butcher-block counters and one-of-a-kind, custom made, artisanal cabinets—like the ones in Wayne Jansen's kitchen.

He crossed his arms over his chest, sullen. Apparently his knowledge of what constituted sophisticated luxury ended with golf clothes.

I took out my iPad and pulled up several saved interior design sites, each of which proved that this kitchen was all that and a bag of money. Swiping through Pinterest posts I'd earmarked ahead of time, I pointed out the current stampede for cabinets like his. Consumers couldn't get enough of them.

"Now, I agree that they're a bit dark." I didn't, but that was a subjective point and it was his house, not mine. I stroked my fingers over one of the detested knots. I loved them. "What about a bit of sanding and a *low*-level varnish for polish and light reflection? That should give you what you want without sacrificing this fabulous pastoral look that everyone is dying to have." I made these suggestions sound spontaneous.

"What about the hideous paint?" he asked.

I wasn't sure if that meant we had just reached an agreement on the kitchen cabinets, but I wasn't about to ask. "Again, Mr. Jansen—you chose the absolute *perfect* shade of cream—"

"It looks *green*."

The walls did look a bit minty, but it wasn't revolting. "As the light moves through the house during the day, the color will actually change," I said. "The kitchen is on the east side, so this is its darker tone. Let me show you the difference between this and a room in full sun, as the kitchen will be in the mornings." *Please, God, let me not be full of shit*, I prayed, hoping God wouldn't respond with *And you are?*

We crossed through the entry toward the other side of the house and entered one of the guest bedrooms, which was flooded with light. And hot damn if the green cast wasn't completely undetectable. *Yessss*. "See? Bright and creamy. No green." I high-fived myself in my head. "Your guests will never want to leave. I guess it's up to you whether that's good or bad, eh?"

"Humph," he said.

All righty then.

I started to leave the room, his bathroom faucets and their *wide streams* the next item on the list, but he cleared his throat. Linking my fingers in front of me, the picture of benign fortitude, I tried to prepare for a brand-new complaint. Cynthia Pike would choke the life out of me with her bare hands if this venture resulted in yet another objection.

"Did you say your name was Erin *McIntyre*?" he asked. "As in—"

"Yes, sir. Jeffrey McIntyre is my father." *Where the hell is this going*?

"You get along with him then? You work for him, so I assume you don't have a contentious relationship."

What the? "Um, no—not at all. Our relationship is excellent."

He turned slightly and glanced around the room. "My daughter is going to be visiting for a month. At the end of the summer. I was thinking this room would be hers."

"That's awesome!" *Tone it down, Erin. Get him talking*. "How old is she?"

"She's eighteen. About to head off to college. She lives with her mother." He was staring out the window, which was still a bit construction-grimy. "We haven't spoken in almost four years," he added.

Whoa. I'd been mad-searching for the thorn in the lion's paw, but I didn't think I'd find it this easily. My brain whirred and I chewed my lip, glancing around the fifteen-by-fifteen-foot room, the vaulted ceiling, a closet the literal size of my office, and its own bathroom. Plush for a secondary bedroom, but it was located at the mouth of the main hallway.

"Let's take a look at the other bedrooms." I led the way out the door. "Just to make sure we've got her in the best one for a young, adult woman. The room's placement and furnishings should convey the fact that she's not merely a guest. That this is her home, the room belongs to her, and she's welcome to return, anytime."

• • • • • • • • • • •

I drafted an email around midnight, feeling so self-congratulatory I could have spread my smugness on a piece of toast. First thing the next morning, I did a quick reread, added Uncle Hank to the CC, and pushed Send before I could chicken out.

From: McIntyre, Erin
To: Maat, Isaac
Cc: Pike, Cynthia; Sager, Ted; Greene, Hank; LaCross, Kenny
Subject: Wayne Jansen

Mr. Maat,
Mr. Jansen is willing to sign off on the house and close as soon as it's completed so long as the following changes are agreed to and implemented:
1) Gently sand and lightly varnish kitchen cabinets
2) Move custom guest closet to bedroom four (at end of the hall)
3) Add built-in window seat to bedroom four
4) Make bathroom three privately accessible only through bedroom four (remove hallway door; add door into bedroom)
He is withdrawing all other change requests/complaints and is willing to pay the reasonable cost of these changes. Preliminary addendum attached. Please let me know if this is acceptable, and also the date he may plan to take possession of the house. I have also referred him to an interior designer who will need access for measurements ASAP, especially to bedroom four.
E. McIntyre

Less than two minutes passed before I received a reply, but it wasn't from Isaac Maat.

From: Pike, Cynthia
To: McIntyre, Erin
Cc: Maat, Isaac; Sager, Ted; Greene, Hank; LaCross, Kenny
Subject: Re: Wayne Jansen

Erin—How the hell did you do this?!?! Never mind. I don't care how you did it. I might not want to know, HAHA. I'll get this addendum to the contract executed as soon as I have financial approval. (Hank?) Ted and Kenny—if I were you I'd

get busy on a cost list pronto and let's get this fucker out the door. Pardon my French.
CPike

And then another. Also not from Isaac Maat.

From: Sager, Ted
To: McIntyre, Erin
Cc: Pike, Cynthia; Maat, Isaac; Greene, Hank; LaCross, Kenny
Subject: Re: Wayne Jansen

Agreed! On it!
TS

Finally my supervisor replied.

From: Maat, Isaac
To: McIntyre, Erin
Cc: Pike, Cynthia; Sager, Ted; Greene, Hank; LaCross, Kenny
Subject: Re: Wayne Jansen

Good work.
IJM

chapter *Five*

I'd no sooner read those two pithy, barely congratulatory words when my desk phone—a corded piece of antiquity left over from some previous decade, which I was sure I'd seldom use and had relegated to a far corner of my desk—emitted a shrill peal like a horcrux being stabbed dead.

"Je-SUS!" I gasped, flinching so hard my chair nearly rolled out from under me. As I stared, heart racing, it shrilled again. I snatched up the receiver and ended the obnoxious ringing. "Hello?" I wheezed as though I'd been doing calisthenics.

"Ms. McIntyre. It's… Isaac Maat. I'd like to speak with you in my office when you have a minute."

I wondered whether he would ever give me permission to use his first name or if we were going to *Ms. McIntyre* and *Mr. Maat* each other forever. He *was* my boss, but what was the proper way to address one's boss when one was on a first-name basis with the CFO and the owner was *Daddy*? I filed this riddle away for later consideration.

"Okay. Sure. Right after I figure out how to turn the volume down on this thing. I swear that ring took a year off my life."

"On the bottom."

"What?"

"The volume control. It's on the underside of the phone base."

"Oh, ha, gotcha. I've never used a phone like this. You know, with a cord and everything. I thought these had all been relegated to government offices and maybe phone museums. I guess they still make them though. Who knew?"

Everyone but you? He hadn't spoken the words, but I heard them just the same. I was torn between irrational anger and feeling like an idiot.

"Be there in a sec." I turned the heavy contraption upside down, looking for a volume switch and trying not to become further riled by Mr. Insufferable right before today's first face-to-face.

A couple of minutes later, I strode next door with my game face securely in place, dropped into the leather-upholstered chair facing his desk, and crossed one leg over the other. Very professional and astute and ready to tackle the challenges I wanted him to lob my way so I could slam them back, accomplished without a glitch, to his side of the court.

He glanced up. And then down.

My clingy yellow knit dress inched up my thigh just a hair, which I might not have noticed had he not sneered directly at my leg, after which he scanned up to the skin peeking from the cutout cold-shouldered design and then up to the loose, somewhat chaotic twist at my crown, which I'd spent half an hour arranging. Tendrils escaped to tease the tops of my bare shoulders. It wasn't Cynthia Pike's taut, no hair unconstrained, facelift-replicating bun, but *Vogue* assured me it was perfectly acceptable workday chic. I fidgeted, almost raising my hands to shove loose hair behind my ears.

And then I heard Coach Oxby's *Get a freaking grip, McIntyre*, because whenever I barked self-directed orders in my head, they emerged in the voice of my high school cheer coach, who'd been rumored to strike fear into administration, teachers, the school board, and all the other coaches.

I straightened my spine and fortified my expression into a blend of pleasant and intrepid—neither of which I felt. "Is something wrong?"

His eyes flashed to mine as if he'd been caught staring at something he shouldn't. Bracing for some unreasonable reproach of my appearance, I wasn't expecting him to switch gears. "I'm curious about your meeting with Mr. Jansen. It was very productive. No one's been able to get him to sign off on anything for weeks, but suddenly he's got a few semi-reasonable demands and he's ready to move in. What's up with that?"

I brushed a few of Jack's bristly gray hairs from the hem of my dress, hoping to bring Isaac back to my dress code grievances, whatever those were. I didn't want to divulge Mr. Jansen's anxiety about his child's looming arrival. He had purchased a home from JMCH, but he'd opened up to me on a deeper level, trusting me with distress beyond the mere construction of a house. My psychological training prohibited sharing a client's confidences except in cases of harm to self or others. I had no intention of disclosing things unrelated to the house itself to anyone.

Isaac Maat waited, silent. He knew I had information he didn't have, and he wanted it.

"I guess he just wanted someone to hear him," I said.

The scowl returned. "We *all* heard him, most often during some groundless tirade. We haven't been sitting around with our thumbs up our—uh, rears, expecting him to arbitrarily accept the status quo. We've offered compromises and made concessions and multiple modifications. Nothing made any difference—until a couple of hours spent with you."

I barely kept my mouth from dropping open. "What exactly are you implying? That I put him under a spell? Or gave him a lap dance?" He recoiled with a choked gurgle and I briefly hoped he might asphyxiate with revulsion, but I wasn't finished. "I was hired to pay attention to dissatisfied clients in hopes that they would feel more valued, and surprise! It worked!"

His livid gaze swung away and back, and I knew I'd been right. He'd expected me to fail.

"But you didn't expect it to work, did you?" I pressed.

His lips flattened. "In *one day*? No, Ms. McIntyre, I confess I didn't. I'm merely asking what was said or promised—"

"That's between Mr. Jansen and myself," I replied.

Silence stretched and I barely breathed under his narrow stare, but I didn't squirm or shift my eyes from his. I was grateful for the large desk standing between us. He looked like he wanted to murder me and was simply racking his brain over how to do it and where to hide the body. I had become this man's primary tribulation an hour into my second day of employment, and I clearly had a lot of competition for that position.

"You aren't Wayne Jansen's doctor or his attorney." He feigned composure, but a razor-sharp edge was all too audible under whatever self-restraint he was utilizing. He didn't want to reason with me. He wanted to throttle me. "There is no client confidentiality clause within this company. If you offered him something we can't supply or condone—"

"I didn't promise anything more than what's laid out in that addendum. As for what he and I discussed, that's off-limits." I lifted my chin a fraction higher. "Clients should view me as a sort of in-house advocate. I won't be able to help them if I know I'll have to spill things shared in confidence to everyone in the office. I was asked to get him to sign off on the project and I did."

Through his teeth, he said, "With additional design alterations." He was reaching and he knew it. Nothing I'd requested for Wayne Jansen would require major design revision.

"The alterations are necessary."

"Why?"

I crossed my arms. "I'm sorry, Mr. Maat. I can't reveal that."

He twisted to grab a file folder from his credenza and slid it to me across the polished surface of his desk. "Fine. Here's your next chance to perform miracles."

I recognized this particular folder, because I'd left it right next to my keyboard when I'd gone to meet Wayne Jansen yesterday afternoon. Not that client files belonged to me, but seeing the Hooper file on Isaac Maat's desk when I'd left it on my own made me feel like I was being spied on.

"We've barely begun framing, and these clients are already causing headaches for the folks in design and the foreman," he said, neglecting to inform me that the foreman on this job was my brother Leo. "The details are all there. Have at it."

The folder was currently orange-tabbed, but the clients were borderline red. Mr. Hooper traveled globally for business and wanted nothing to do with the house-design particulars, so Mrs. Hooper made every decision and seemed to think it was her sworn duty to argue the rate of every single line item charge as if haggling prices in the Grand Bazaar. She'd also changed her mind again and again and again.

"No problem," I said, standing.

His gaze returned to his monitor, fingers flying over the keyboard's numerical section, dismissing me without a word, civil or otherwise.

Miracle number two, coming right up.

• • • • • • • • • • •

As I flipped through the paperwork, one odd fact stuck out: Richard and Iris Hooper hadn't once signed the same document, not even the original contract. It was as if they were never in the same room. That had resulted in duplicates of the contract itself and every single change or addendum—one initialed and signed by him, and one by her. All of his signatures were faxed or electronic. All of hers were signed in ballpoint pen. Their current residence was about twenty minutes away in Keller, which made me wonder why she'd want to spend forty minutes driving to and fro when she could digitally sign from her computer, at home.

If I could manage to trick Leo into a levelheaded conversation, I would grill him about them. I sent him a text and knew it might be all day before he answered. My oldest brother was a belligerent ass, and even if they all tolerated each other now, there was no way our middle brothers had forgotten how much of a bully he'd been when they were younger. I'd escaped most of his jackassery thanks to being a girl, but he was on Foster's permanent shit list, and Pax only abided him because when he was seventeen and Leo was twenty-three, Pax had gotten so riled that he broke Leo's nose and knocked him unconscious with one punch.

Leo had been slapping him in the head for grins at the time.

That tender show of fraternal affection had taken place on

Christmas morning, right before we were supposed to open gifts. Mom lost her shit, but Leo roused after a minute or so. Daddy handed him an ice pack for his bulging nose, checked his pupils, and told him he should probably lay off his no-longer-little brother from then on. After the two of them left for the ER to get Leo's nose set and make sure he didn't have a concussion, Foster fetched an ice pack for Pax's knuckles and told him that punch was the best damn Christmas gift he'd received, ever.

Mom opened a chilled bottle of chardonnay, poured herself a glass, and gave us all the stink-eye in case we planned to comment on the fact that it was nine a.m.

Leo didn't have the good sense to recognize that he would have never landed a job remotely like the one he had if it wasn't for him being a McIntyre, not that I could talk. But all he did was bitch—about the clients, the other foremen, the sales team, the construction crews, the weather. Everyone and everything was always out to get him and nothing was ever his fault. The only thing that shut him up was when Daddy told him he was welcome to try his luck elsewhere. He only said that because he knew Leo would never do it.

Meeting Mr. Jansen at the site had made perfect sense because his house was almost done, but the Hooper house was months from completion. I wasn't sure whether either of them was capable of viewing the framed structure—like a skeleton of some animal they'd only seen sketches of—and imagining what it would look like when it was built. For some people, it was better not to walk the slab until the roof, walls and windows were in place and the home could be more easily visualized.

"Hello?" Iris Hooper sounded exhausted. I checked the time: eight thirty. I hoped I hadn't called too early and woken her.

"Mrs. Hooper? This is Erin with Jeffrey McIntyre Custom Homes, following up on some requested alterations to your new home. Is this a bad time? I can call back later."

As if in answer, a piercing scream from either a very small person or a demon from hell echoed from the receiver. I yanked it away from my head. *Holy shit.* My ear was in actual pain, and I wasn't even in the same room. I put the phone on speaker and lowered the volume.

"Morgan, please don't scream at Mommy. I thought you liked Cheerios?"

"Nooooooooo!" the screamer declared, drawing that one syllable out as far and high-pitched as it would go.

"I'm sorry—what did you say your name was?" Mrs. Hooper asked.

"Erin."

As the demon's mother attempted to cajole it into eating breakfast, I contemplated getting my tubes tied, because my answer to that scream probably would have been something wildly inappropriate along the lines of *Eat it or starve.* If my biological clock ever started ticking, I planned to chuck it against a wall or smash it with a hammer. I'd seen enough snot-nosed tantrum-throwers and preadolescent nightmares during my tenure as a restaurant hostess in college.

"Erin..." She returned to me. "Your name isn't familiar. I've been working with Joshua? And Leo?"

"Yes. They are your salesman and your project foreman, but I'm the client liaison at JMCH. It's my job to make certain that your needs are communicated to the project team, any and all issues are resolved to your satisfaction, and your home construction advances on schedule. I can provide reputable interior design and landscaping references as well."

She was silent for a moment. In the background, I could hear the kid whining about what it wanted to eat for breakfast. Apparently the answer was mashed potatoes.

"We don't have that, Morgan. How about some French fries?"

That offering was rejected with more ferocity than a Northerner declining grits.

Mrs. Hooper sighed heavily. "No offense, *Erin*, but I don't know you. I've never been contacted by a *client liaison* before. Where have you been for the past five months?"

The reason for Isaac Maat's *Go do miracles with this one, I dare you* smirk was becoming clearer by the minute. "I'm new to the company. The client liaison position was recently created to enhance customer service to our most important—"

"Hold on." Her voice took on a stiffer edge. "Is this some bid to block me and my 'inane complaints' from the sales guy who made promises that aren't being kept and that boorish Bob the Builder who dodges my calls until I have to show up at the site to get anything done?"

I fought a guffaw, envisioning Leo's most probable reaction to being called *Bob the Builder*. He'd shit a brick.

"Ashatatoes!" the kid sobbed.

"I'm sorry you've had a difficult time—"

She wasn't having it. "And now I'm expected to sit back and play guinea pig for some inexperienced underling hired to calm the hysterical client?"

Well, that was partly accurate. I did not comment. Wisely, I thought.

"No offense, but your company assuming I want to deal with *you* instead of the men responsible for building my house makes me feel pretty low on the totem pole of *importance*."

No offense but was the sort of passive-aggressive crap most liable to raise my hackles, but I couldn't be unpleasant back to a client no matter how warranted, and from the pint-sized waterworks gearing up in the background regarding inferior potato offerings, I knew this lady was at the end of her emotional rope. So I gritted my teeth and forced that smile on my face.

"Mrs. Hooper—I want to be your advocate. Give me the chance to do my job and take some of the hassle and stress of this project off you. That's what I'm here for."

I waited for her answer as the kid wailed and blubbered something unintelligible to anyone but its mother. I all but held my breath. And then she sighed. "Fine. Okay. When do I have to come out?"

"You don't. Just take care of little... Morgan, and I'll come to you. What's the best time?"

She sighed again, this time with weary resignation. "There's a fifty-fifty chance she'll go down for a nap around two. Please, for the love of God, don't ring the doorbell. I'll be watching for you."

"Love a dog! Don't! Doorbell!" the kid squealed.

"I'll be there at two o'clock. See you then, Mrs. Hooper."

chapter *Six*

On my third day, my office phone rang for the second time, but it didn't scare me out of my wits as it had the first time because I'd successfully turned the volume to a normal level. I answered, "JMCH, Erin McIntyre speaking," with as much courteous professionalism as I could muster. Playing hostess at a posh restaurant for three years had come in handy for more than bankrolling my shoe addiction.

There was a pause, and I almost said *Hello*? But then an equally formal but far less courteous voice (he was definitely not smiling) said, "Isaac Maat here. Please come speak with me when you have a moment. Before you leave for lunch." There was another short, weighty pause. "Or the day."

I pondered what the hell that meant and how to respond, but it didn't matter because the *click* and dead air told me he'd already hung up.

"Yes sir, your assholiness," I mumbled. I hung up more forcefully than intended and forced myself to do two minutes of *ujjayi pranayama* to take the edge off. Day three and I was resorting to yoga breathing. Not good.

When I walked into his office, his eyes didn't budge from his monitor. I took a seat in front of his desk and waited as I had yesterday, making an all-out effort to channel positive energy.

Finally he turned to me. "You were out all afternoon yesterday—"

My hackles rose like I'd been plugged into some sort of auto-defensiveness device. "You were gone when I got back."

He stared.

"I mean, it was nearly six, so I didn't expect you'd still be here or anything."

"Six," he said, head cocking to the side, skeptical. He didn't believe me.

My hand flew to my mouth and then dropped into my lap. "Oh my God—did you think I just ditched?" I'd left yesterday afternoon and—as far as he knew—had never returned. "I should have emailed an update. I just ran in to grab a few folders to take home and I was *starving* since I missed lunch, so I forgot."

"Update?" he repeated like a disconcerted parrot.

"I could give it to you now? Or would you rather I go to my desk and email it?" I started to rise.

"No." He leaned back, resting his elbows on the arms of his chair, and laced his fingers. His thin smile was more derisive than pleasant. "Now is fine." He was, I thought, attempting to seem laid-back, but his entire posture was a dare.

Perching on the edge of the chair, I said, "Okay. Well. I met Iris Hooper at her current home instead of the site because she's got a little kid and also their house isn't that far along, so I didn't think it would do any good to meet there. Plus hello—June in Texas. Excess heat and humidity don't exactly inspire equanimity, right? When I met Wayne Jansen to walk through his place, my antiperspirant was working like a moth— Um, anyway—I told Mrs. Hooper I'd be happy to drive over with the proposed blueprint copies and discuss her issues there."

He didn't respond, so I continued. "Basically, I think Mrs. Hooper has been indecisive when it comes to the house because she's felt unsure about making those judgment calls."

Once I had diverted her by spreading the blueprints onto her kitchen table—people are eager to examine the plans at that stage of a project—I'd surreptitiously analyzed her current home. The architectural style and the décor she favored, the toys stacked everywhere, the books, magazines and art displayed, the family photos revealing that Mr. Hooper was considerably older than his wife. I began probing for what sorts of changes she wanted to see in her new home and wasn't surprised to find that she knew exactly what she wanted, but her husband's sporadic, lackadaisical input confused her. He would insist she make decisions only to circle back and question her choices. Her authority felt more theoretical than real to her, so she second-guessed *everything* before he had the chance to.

Isaac Maat's forehead was creased. He was either perplexed or agitated.

"I'm going to work with her on that," I said, which didn't seem to help.

Without meeting Mr. Hooper, I wasn't certain whether he was purposefully undermining her or attempting to placate her anxieties with input. Either way, the result was a feeling of powerlessness leading to perpetual vacillation—and that had to stop or little Morgan would be getting her driving permit before their house was completed.

"I'm confident we can get the Hooper project on track."

"It sounds as if you're *psychoanalyzing* our clients," Isaac Maat said.

I gave a cursory, faintly guilty shrug. "Figuring out who people really are and assessing their inner workings is my strength. I might as well use it to do my job."

He looked dumbfounded. And more distrustful than ever. His left hand was a tight fist, as though his state of mind was held constrained within its grip, and he drummed a pen on a blank notepad with his right. *Tap tap tap.* He noticed me looking, dropped the pen, and loosened his fist, but his chin was still tucked low like a grouchy turtle. As if I'd verbalized that thought, his chin popped up and out. His whole body was poised for conflict.

Maybe because I was staring at every move he made. I began to inspect his office instead, giving him time to unwind and hoping for clues to why he didn't want me here—aside from the obvious.

"So, Wharton MBA, huh?" I commented.

"Hank tell you that?" The words rang subtly, like a curbed accusation.

I pointed over his shoulder where his diploma—in all its triple-matted, professionally framed glory—hung. His magna cum laude architectural undergraduate degree hung just below it in a matching gilded frame, the archival mats Pantone-matched to the schools represented.

"Ah," he said, caught off guard. "I forgot that was there."

"That's pretty impressive."

"Does that surprise you?" he asked, his words low but snapping like hot oil.

Holy banana nuts—what had I said now? "Why should it?"

"Why remark on it, then?"

"I was trying to make conversation. Futile endeavor, I guess." I rose and stomped toward the door, muttering, "I withdraw the commendation." As I reached his doorway, the implicit meaning behind his comments became appallingly clear. "Wait." I turned. "Was that some sort of assumption of micro—what's it—microaggression? Like, a racial thing? Because I'm not like that. I don't think like that. You don't even know me!"

My anger dissipated before I stepped foot into my office, to be replaced by unanticipated insights into my supervisor, and right on the heels of those, nagging questions. *Had I meant it like that? Even if I didn't see it?*

I'd never known anyone who went to Wharton, though Christina—my studious chore of a roommate for the past two years—had mentioned it once, when we were still on limited speaking terms. Our rare conversations had been ninety-five percent me asking questions that she answered with barely veiled annoyance and five percent stuff like "Excuse me," necessitated by the cramped shared quarters. She had never inquired about my life, goals, or relationships. I'd been evaluated as deficient the moment we met—chirpy, airheaded sorority girl—and her initial estimation never changed. Senior year, I hung out at the Chi-O house to study and socialize, and our dorm room became little more than the place I slept and kept my stuff.

In a singular show of insecurity during junior year, she'd confessed her first choice for grad school, Wharton, and her concern about being accepted. "I'll have to work for two or three years after graduation before even applying—something innovative and distinctive that will stand out to the graduate committee—or I'll never get in."

I knew her grades were stellar; I'd once overheard her tell someone that she'd had "another" 4.0 semester, and her tone was more blasé than thrilled. The fact that *she* had fretted about getting into

Wharton left me with the impression that it was a top-tier school, but that was all I knew about it.

I considered my father's company a last-ditch springboard for me to ever go on to be anything, yet here was this guy with an MBA from a big-deal university, working at a Podunk construction company. Okay, so it wasn't exactly *Podunk*. We did build multimillion-dollar mansions. But still—why would anyone be *here*, with a degree that could open doors *anywhere*? Not to mention his with-honors degree in architecture.

He'd identified my amazed response correctly, but not the reason behind it. I'd told him he didn't know me, but the truth was I knew as little or less about him. Those degrees and our combative exchange told me two things though. He was brilliant, even if his social skills needed some serious work. And he was defensive about being a highly educated black man.

Defensiveness is often rooted in fact, and I got the feeling that Isaac Maat relied heavily on facts. Either he'd experienced racism personally or knew he was susceptible to racial prejudice because he'd observed it firsthand. I considered the possibility that he'd encountered it here, in my father's company. From Joshua Swearingen, maybe, with his "uppity" comment and his unjustified grandstanding posture.

From me, when I appeared to be surprised that he'd earned a degree from Wharton. That wasn't what had surprised me, but he couldn't know that.

He was defensive because he had to be. Anything could resemble an affront because anything could *be* an affront.

After my sorority sister, Mindi, was sexually assaulted at a frat party, a restraining order and even her rapist's eventual incarceration wasn't enough to quell her disquiet, because the threat wasn't confined to him. Once she was aware that evil could exist in plain sight—in a place she'd felt safe, in the guise of someone she'd trusted—she knew it could lie in wait anywhere. Every shadow on the wall was a potential menace, and if the danger turned out to be real, survival depended on an immediate, suitable response. Her personality around guys went from convivial to cagey in the space of that one night. Now, after almost three years, she'd made transformative progress, but she would never be that trusting, bubbly girl she had been.

My mindless reaction to Isaac's response—my own defensiveness—had done nothing to alleviate the perceived offense. I'd only made it worse. With my training, I should have recognized his reaction for what it was. I should have known better, but where Isaac Maat was concerned, I couldn't think straight.

Sounds like a personal problem, as my brother Pax would say.

When I'd agreed to work for Daddy and Hank, the last thing I'd expected was a supervisor so blazing hot I just wanted to stare at him. He was what—twenty-eight, thirty? He could have at least had a little gut going on, for chrissake. Hair loss? Dry skin?

Freshman year, I had compared life-with-brothers notes with my lab partner. She'd had to teach her skin-care-clueless sibling how to exfoliate. "Him and his cheap soap and 'moisturizer is for girls' foolishness, taking twenty-minute, use-all-the-hot-water showers. He looked like the black undead, I swear to God."

I'd snorted. "Brothers and their long showers. Like—*we know what you're doing in there*. Ugh."

"Right?" She'd laughed. "Boys are so nasty. It's a miracle any girl with brothers ever wants a man at all."

Isaac Maat's chestnut-toned skin had no trace of undeadness, and his stomach looked flat in his fitted dress shirts, which strained across his wide, rounded-with-lean-muscle shoulders just enough to flaunt the chiseled definition underneath. Even his hands were a perfect balance of rugged and refined—as he was tapping his pen with irritation. At me.

He'd seemed appalled that I was *psychoanalyzing* our clients, which made no sense considering the fact that it appeared to be working. I wasn't doing anything I hadn't done my whole life—encouraging people to talk to me, to like me, making them happy so I got what I wanted, whether that was a better grade, a social invitation, or the loan of a pair of killer boots. I simply observed people's fears and insecurities and quirks, drew conclusions about what they wanted, and then I gave it to them—or didn't, depending on my objective. Admittedly, some—like Christina—were so resistant to forming attachments that there was no altering their initial reserve. I wondered if Isaac was like that.

Maybe he thought I was analyzing *him*? He was my boss, but my father owned the company that employed him. That had to be awkward but didn't account for his unease over my opinion of him, unless he thought I would go crying to my daddy if I got sulky. Which I would *not* do, but he didn't know that.

"I owe you an apology." I stood in his doorway, hands loosely laced in front of me. "I made that about me, and it wasn't about me. Or it *was*, but I shouldn't have made assumptions or taken offense like that. I'm sorry." He watched me, deconstructing my words to extract the truth or deceit in them, perhaps. I moved into his office and lowered my voice. "The thing is, I've grown up with *Jeffrey McIntyre Custom Homes*. I know it's a successful company and it makes total sense for you to work here. But I know just enough about Wharton to wonder why you do."

"I don't follow," he said, but then he seemed to understand. "Are you saying you think I'm *too educated* to work for your father's company?"

"That's not what I—" I stopped. Only honesty would work here. "Okay, yeah, I guess that's what I meant. But—"

"I took the job I could find at the tail end of an economic recession—a downturn based on a rupture in the housing market. Just because you and your brother landed well-paying jobs through no personal effort of your own doesn't mean the rest of us get that opportunity, Ms. McIntyre."

Ouch. "You're right, of course." I nodded and backed toward the door, volcanic insecurities erupting from the accuracy of his words. "I'm just gonna go contact the next client."

"Wait," he said, and I froze two steps from the door. "You didn't finish giving me the details about the Hooper project."

"Oh." I straightened my posture and cleared my throat like a kid giving a book report, trying not to fidget under the teacher's gaze. "Where was I?"

"You were psychoanalyzing the client."

Iris Hooper had been unreceptive at first, but I'd pretended I didn't notice. "Many clients who travel full-time are less confident in their spouse's judgment so they check up on every detail, micromanaging from afar. We turn into amateur marriage counselors just to get their house built. Ha, ha."

"My husband hasn't called you—?" she began.

"No." I suspected the primary conflict might not be confined to the home build. I was prepared to hold her hand until the project was done if I had to, but I hoped to actually help her. I inched out on a limb. "Perhaps he just worries that you'll think he's not contributing if he doesn't give feedback?"

She sighed. "Maybe?"

We went over the items at issue. That activity, coupled with a little positive feedback, proved that as long as she ignored how or why her spouse might object she had no problem identifying what she wanted.

"Well?" Isaac asked now.

"I'm going to work with her on trusting her gut and sticking to her decisions."

One eyebrow rose. "You're going to 'work with her.' How, exactly?"

I shrugged one shoulder and he rolled his eyes and tapped his pen.

"I can do this. Just... trust me." I was floored by how much I needed his trust. "I know I'm not what you imagined for this position." My chin rose a fraction of an inch. Acknowledging that I knew he hadn't wanted me here was mortifying, but I persisted. "But this company is my father's baby. He built it from the ground up. I wouldn't do something stupid and cause problems for him. I want to do a good job, I swear. So I'm just going to believe you're willing to reconsider your incorrect preconceptions about me. And... I'm sorry for any I had about you. Maybe we can start over from here?"

His assessment was guarded, searching my face for clues while giving nothing away, but he was diplomatic, if reluctant. "All right."

I left before he could rethink it.

chapter *Seven*

Since I was working with Iris Hooper every other day while trying to keep her project foreman—my lughead of a brother—from crossing paths with her at all, I decided to dispatch a few of the low-priority, yellow-tabbed clients.

Some of those were nitpicking, trifling specifics like an outlet placed a foot farther left than they thought it should go or cabinet hardware that looked a shade darker than they recalled. With clients like that, I indicated on their contract where they'd signed off on said outlet or knob finish and then explained the cost they would incur and the amount of damage it might cause to alter the original, agreed-upon plan. I exaggerated a bit for effect when required.

When those efforts failed or a client had an understandable complaint about work done shoddily or incorrectly or not at all, I worked with them to order the changes. That often meant shielding them from construction division wrath and reminding foremen in particular that if we (he) had screwed up or the client was paying to have something changed, it was part of his job to make the change without going into a man-baby sulk. (The man-baby was Leo four times out of five. *Shocking*.) Alarmed that my brother had his big, dumbass hand in so many of our miffed to hopping-mad client files, it was all I could do not to tattle on him. Nose to nose over a mistake one of his subcontractors had made in the Hooper's kitchen, I made that very threat, which worked as well now as it had when we were five and fifteen.

By the end of my first month, I felt like I was doing work that mattered to my father's company. Work that no one had been able to do before I arrived. I grew more confident with every mollified or downright delighted homebuyer. The green-tabbed client list grew, and with it my cockiness. My parents hadn't believed in my ability to use my powers of negotiation and persuasion for anything but getting my own way, but I was kicking ass and carrying my own weight. Joshua had confided that Cynthia Pike wanted to steal me for the sales team.

I'd declined. I had come to relish the way Isaac Maat's jaw hardened when he knew my psychoanalytical mumbo-jumbo had resulted in another satisfied client. Not that he wanted disgruntled clients, he just didn't want me to be right, especially when it made him wrong. He never stated any of that explicitly—his body language and facial tics spoke for him.

Being right became my new favorite thing.

No surprise then that when my comeuppance came, it didn't blow in gently—a storm moving in from the horizon that gives you time to batten the hatches and soften the damage. Oh no. It was the thin funnel of a tornado at the moment it descends from the sky like an accusatory finger—dooming one unfortunate structure to wreckage and leaving another intact. There was no moderating the devastation, though I couldn't say there was no foreseeing it had I not been drunk with my own success.

I just wish it had been an actual tornado so it could have been an act of God and not an act of Erin.

The Andersons had never been cause for concern. Recently

retired, with West Texas oil money out the ass, they were "downsizing" to a six-thousand-square-foot, five-bedroom home with a meticulously landscaped garden for her to putter in and an air-conditioned, eight-car garage to house his vintage sports car collection. They could have been a perpetual pain in the ass. But all through the design phase, they were model clients, deferring to their architect's expertise with a balanced amount of trust and involvement. Likewise, their build had moved along beautifully until they wanted permission to make an artistic modification just before the house was complete.

A world-renowned artist was in the area for an exhibit of his early work at The Modern, and somehow they'd managed to get him to agree to paint a *mural* on their towering great room wall, which they technically wouldn't own until August. When their request was summarily denied—clients were never allowed to make non-JMCH customizations to the property until they owned it—they dug in their heels. As days passed, they began calling or emailing every day and were beginning to rumble to Cynthia about making their complaint public.

During the weekly planning meeting, Uncle Hank didn't seem worried. "We're just following the rules in their contract. There's no valid grievance to make public."

"Sheila Anderson is a piranha in a sweet-little-old-lady pantsuit from Neiman's," Cynthia said. "She was an executive editor for the *Star Telegram* in her former life. Those warning shots aren't blanks." She passed me the file. "Work your magic, Erin!"

I caught Isaac's furtive eye-roll though he pretended to concentrate on flicking a crumb from his cuff-linked shirtsleeve in an effort to hide it. When he glanced up, I stared straight into his insufficiently stunned face and said, "Done!"

As though I would reach into my oversized bag, pluck out a wand wrapped in enchanted unicorn mane and glitter, wave it around a bit, and *poof*, obstacle dissolved. I think my dumb ass half believed my own mythical hype as the Cranky Client Wrangler.

When I contacted them, Harold Anderson harrumphed and handed the call off to his wife.

She was all charm, sensing the probability that someone with the title Client Liaison could be persuaded to her side of the dispute. "His work is *ahh-mazing* and highly distinguished! This is a once-in-a-lifetime opportunity for us and for McIntyre Homes! He's legendary, and a *friend of a friend*, you know."

I didn't know, nor did I have a clue who this legendary guy was, but I googled him and was duly impressed. My brother and everyone else at JMCH, not so much.

"He's never even had an exhibition in Texas before and may never again! He's returning to Stockholm in three weeks, and we aren't set to close until mid-August!" Sheila Anderson had contagious enthusiasm. "Surely these are the sort of extenuating circumstances calling for laxity in the usual policy?"

I tried to resist, I swear.

"Well," I said, not indifferent to her cause and aware what a coup it would be to include images of that room's incredible focal point on the JMCH website and in future promotional brochures. She seized my *Well* and made it as close to a *yes* as a word that is not *yes* could be.

"Hurrah! I just knew if I could find a fellow devotee of art and culture that he or she would champion our cause with management!"

Uh-oh bounced around inside my skull like an internal warning of an impending malfunction. I could already picture my boss's tightly contained smile and shaking head. He was going to say no and keep saying no, and he would enjoy doing it; the rules were on his side. "I'll have to run it by my supervisor before I can confirm—" I began, my brain speeding toward and discarding tactics that might change Isaac's mind.

"Of course, of course! These *men* build opulent, impressive homes, but they clearly lack the refinement essential to appreciate the magnitude of this fortuitous chance." *Did she—did she just play the fellow-woman card?* "I can tell that you know just what to say to persuade whomever needs persuading." Okay, so her woman card was a bit outdated and veering toward sexist.

Leo had grown up in Southlake but had no concept of artistic refinement, and he only broke rules when they applied to him. Of *course* he'd said no. But why had Isaac Maat refused to listen to reason? He struck me as a thousand times more cultured than my brother—not that it would have been a difficult feat. Surely my supervisor could be made to see the advantage in approving the Andersons' request? Even if it meant making me look right. Again. *Ugh*. He was going to say no so hard I would feel it.

I gave myself a stern talking to. I could do this. I *would* do this.

It was too early for celebration, no matter my burgeoning confidence in the outcome. "I'll do my best," I said, smiling into the receiver.

• • • • • • • • • • •

Isaac Maat wouldn't budge. "We have rules about things like this for a reason," he said, wearing a satisfied, pig-in-shit smirk while issuing his *we have rules* decree. "He could damage the property."

I stood in front of his desk, my head tipping to the side in honest-to-God disbelief. "You think a brilliant, distinguished artist is going to damage a *wall*."

He shrugged one shoulder, up-down, as if he couldn't be bothered to shrug both. "Our workers and city inspectors will be in and out of there every day toward the end of this project, finishing up, checking code compliance. Someone could damage his... *art*." He made air quotes.

He had a point, but I loathed disparaging air quotes, particularly where the derision was invalid. "So we'll block it off. Screen it from the workers with plastic sheeting or something."

He shook his head, unmoved. "Nope. Sorry." He was the most *unsorry* man on the face of the earth. "You'll have to find some other way around this one. Maybe you can hypnotize one of the Andersons and instill an aversion to murals. Or pretentious artists."

Oh he did *not*. My mouth dropped open and I snapped it shut. I left his office without replying, convinced, now, that he was just dying for me to be wrong. I couldn't prove myself right without the mural's ultimate completion and he knew it, the jerk.

• • • • • • • • • • •

That thing I said I would never do? I did it. I went over his head. I wasn't proud of one-upping him like that, but *desperate times*, et cetera. I would wheedle into his brain later—if his head didn't explode first—to figure out why he stubbornly continued to despise me no matter how well I did my job. I didn't have time for that bullshit now. I was too busy impressing everyone else.

I didn't run directly to my father, who would undoubtedly hold the same unqualified, overly conservative opinion that Isaac, Hank, and Leo did, if not worse. Instead, I confided in Mom, who (hallelujah) knew the artist and immediately flipped out over the notion of him custom painting a one-of-a-kind mural in a JMCH home. Feeling a slight bite of self-reproach—even though it was for a good cause—I left her to it. I was Pontius Pilate washing his hands.

"I don't make a habit of butting in on these sorta decisions," I heard my father say, while eavesdropping on my parents like a manipulative child who just set off a parental squabble to further her own conniving scheme. *A scheme that will benefit everyone*, I assured myself in an attempt to mollify my conscience. I could imagine Isaac Maat's dark, narrowed eyes and clamped jaw of fortified steel. I swung between surging dread and the desire to laugh out loud, but the latter was less genuine glee and more hysterical surplus from the former.

"Jeff, this is the definition of an extenuating circumstance! This isn't a client who wants some would-be trompe l'oeil yahoo to sponge on a tacky faux texture. This is a client who's chummy with a gifted contemporary artist. Do you want Jeffrey McIntyre to be known as the clueless hick who wouldn't allow a highly acclaimed artist to contribute to the magnificence of one of his homes?"

Wow, Mom, below the belt. On target, but damn.

"Jesus, Cheryl—"

"I'm sorry. But is it your company or not?"

She was as *not* sorry as Isaac Maat, but Daddy must have just glared at her over his coffee before giving some sort of affirmative gesture because she continued.

"Then simply tell this Isaac person that you've approved the exception. Done and done. You don't have to explain yourself to an employee, especially one who isn't even a direct report. Perhaps he needs to be reminded who the real boss is." *Shit.* Mom was veering off course. "He's the—you know—" Her voice lowered. "*African American*, right? Are you sure Erin should be working under him? Hasn't Leo had trouble with him?"

Oh. Hell. Leo was a boneheaded dipshit who had trouble with *everyone*. Isaac Maat and I just had a difference of opinion, and I had access to a higher authority, which I'd used.

"Hank hasn't had any problems with Isaac, and his opinion is the one I give a crap about. From what I hear, Erin is doing a bang-up job, but she's still new. Her boss is a stickler for following rules. I like that in an employee."

"But you'll veto his verdict on this." Her tone made that a declaration, not a question.

This exchange was the audible version of a rapid-fire game of Ping-Pong. Not the game we all played badly as children or drunken undergrads—more like unsmiling competitors in the Olympics and a match of furiously slammed white missiles that could put an eye out.

He sighed. "Yes. If you feel this strongly about that artist doing that mural. If this isn't about your little girl getting her way, or because he's her supervisor and he's— Some other reason."

"Of course it's about the artist. What do you mean, *some other reason*?"

"You know what I mean and how I feel about it. We're not going there again. I always respected your father as a businessman, but we're not going there again."

"Good Lord, Jeff, will you ever just move past that? It was more than thirty years ago and wasn't even your decision—not really. You have *nothing* to feel guilty for."

"Drop it."

"The world is a different place now—"

"*Drop it.*"

A chair squealed across the kitchen tile, and I slinked back up the stairs, my brain churning. I should be ecstatic. I'd fought for my client's perfectly reasonable request and won.

But the rest of my parents' conversation didn't pertain to the client, or the artist, or the mural. What had happened more than thirty years ago and involved Grandpa Welch? What could it have to do with Isaac, who hadn't been born yet?

My grandfather was one of those old guys who said some racist shit sometimes, and you just hoped it was over Thanksgiving dinner and not out in public. But he had retired and become a silent partner long before Isaac came along, so he couldn't have had anything to say about the one black man who worked at JMCH in a professional capacity. Right?

chapter *Eight*

Joshua Swearingen invited me to lunch. We were leaving the building at the same time, so he made it seem like no big deal—but his flirtatious half smile showed definite interest. Likelihood of persuading him to reveal any noteworthy workplace gossip: high. Also, he was sorta cute, and not my boss.

"Why not?" I said, slipping on the mirrored shades I'd had to wear in my office some mornings before having a motorized shade installed in that damned east-facing window. I'd felt like chicken under a broiler that first week, slathering sunscreen on my left arm and shoulder to prevent disproportionately dark freckles on one side.

"Cool. I'll drive."

Joshua turned to walk toward his SUV after that statement, a small but telltale indication that he might be one of those guys who preferred to dictate everything from the car to decisions about vacation destinations to how big his girlfriend's ass would be allowed to grow before she was teased or scolded for it. If he thought I would tolerate that bullshittery, he was prowling up the wrong family tree. I was my mother's daughter, and we didn't take orders unless we wanted to. But I was curious enough to follow, plus my fuel gauge was behaving as if my little hybrid was running on fumes. Might as well waste his gas on in-town traffic instead of mine.

"Sure. Where to?"

He opened the passenger door of his shiny, metallic-blue Range Rover and leaned in to clear a Malouf's shopping bag and plastic panini container from the passenger seat and a gym bag from the floor. Tossing everything into the back, he asked, "Sushi?"

Dry cleaning hung on a hook behind the driver's seat—starched pastel dress shirts and slacks with perfect creases. There were Starbucks cups of various sizes in every available cupholder and magazines—*GQ* and *Men's Health*—crammed into the door pockets. It looked like he lived in his car.

"Sounds good. I could use some Zen."

I was relieved that Zushi was close to the office given Joshua's antagonistic driving performance on the short trip down the boulevard. Muttering rude asides about anyone going slower than he was, i.e. pretty much every driver on the same stretch of road, he cut people off right and left but got instantly riled if someone dared to move into his lane. I was reminded—and not in a good way—of ninety percent of the testosterone-fueled boys I'd dated in high school and college. *So much for Zen.*

When I was fifteen and dating older boys, I didn't want to be accused of being a grandma in the passenger seat. So I'd clenched my teeth, closed my eyes, and held on to the door grip to brace for the eventual impact. But eventually I'd stopped worrying about wrecking my adventuresome persona and asked my dates to slow the hell down. Some grumbled or tried to sass their way out of yielding, but they shut it quick when I threatened to call my father to come get me—something I would have likely walked home before doing—but they didn't know that and they'd all met Daddy or knew who he was.

By college, that warning had become null and I switched gears accordingly.

"Do you always drive like you're in a live-action video game?" I'd asked a guy on our first date, after he'd NASCARed around everyone on 21st between DKR Stadium and my favorite pizza dive on Guadalupe. The 'Horns had trounced Nebraska 20-13, our first win after a couple of humiliating losses. It was time to celebrate with our collective group of boisterous friends. Chaz was tall, blond, and smoking hot, but his driving was scaring the bejeezus out of me.

He'd smiled as though I'd paid him a compliment.

Um. No.

"Maybe you should get in the back seat and let an adult drive," I'd snapped as he cut off some dude in a pickup who blared his horn and hollered obscenities.

Instead of being offended, he'd laughed. "Don't worry baby, I'm in complete control of this car." He'd flashed a sexy smile that almost maybe might've worked. Then he ruined it. "I turn this wheel or hit the gas and she obeys."

"Ah, so your car's an obedient, controllable female? Then maybe you can get freaky with *her* later tonight, because I won't be getting back into this car unless you quit driving like a dick *right now*."

He'd slowed right down and snapped a chivalrous, "Yes, ma'am," without a trace of sarcasm, and I'd never had to say another word about his driving.

"Erin?" We were parked in front of Zushi, and Joshua was looking at me; I'd zoned out thinking about my college ex. Awesome.

"You in there? Man, you *do* need some Zen."

I wasn't going to find any *Zen* riding with this clown, but I hoped to ply him for intel on my boss so I could prepare for surefire backlash when he found out I'd outflanked him to get my way. *For the Andersons*, of course.

"Sorry. Just debating how to handle an issue with one of my clients."

"The Andersons? The whole place is buzzing about the sorcery you're working with our VIP PIAs."

He twirled his keyring as we walked toward the door, waited while I pulled it open, and entered in front of me. I couldn't help comparing him to Isaac, who automatically opened doors, whether for me or Cynthia Pike or the UPS guy. My mother, who took being "ladylike" way too seriously, would have wondered aloud about Joshua Swearingen's upbringing. I huffed a small sigh and reclaimed my feminism. I opened doors for myself all the time, for chrissake. Ordinarily men didn't enter in front of me afterward, but whatever.

"PIAs?"

"Two," he said to the hostess and then turned to me to clarify. "PIA—pain in the ass."

What a super classy way to describe our clientele. I thought of Wayne Jansen and Iris Hooper, "PIAs" to people like Joshua. To me, they were clients who needed a sympathetic ear.

"I think most of them just want the beautiful home they were promised."

"Yeah. Sure." He winked like I'd just run a marketing line while simultaneously knowing it was categorical bullshit.

Once we were settled at a table near the window, having ordered and run through small talk mostly focused on him, he returned to my earlier bait like a predictable guppy. "So this issue with a client. Wanna bounce it off me? Voicing it out loud might help you work toward a solution. Who knows? I might even be able to help." He might have wanted to help—his complacent smile said he was certain he could—but he was practically salivating over the chance to exchange gossip about our wealthy, often eccentric clients.

I leaned up, staring down at my colorful Oaklawn roll as though I was planning my chopsticked attack rather than hiding my eagerness to know why Isaac seemed to hate the sight of me. "They want to have some contracted work done in the house before it's complete. It will all work out, I'm sure." I shrugged and popped a spicy, caviar-topped piece into my mouth.

"So Maat decided to be all hard-ass about it? That guy has such an giant ego."

I looked back down at my plate. I was exasperated with Isaac Maat. He *had* been tyrannical about the Anderson's request. But Joshua made it plain, whether he meant to or not, that his dislike of my supervisor went beyond work.

"He's just a stickler for following procedure," I said, echoing what I'd heard Daddy say. "I'm more of a think-outside-the-box sort of girl. I'm sure he'll come around eventually."

"When? You should reconsider a transfer to Sales. Cynthia would probably let Ashley or Megan go to make room for you, but I'm number one in sales, so I'm safe. No worries on that account."

Joshua's loyalty to his coworkers: zero. He took my lack of response as deliberation.

"I could, you know, show you the ropes, teach you whatever you need to know. I'm sure Maat would be glad to let us have you. He's probably all wound up that you're making the clients happy when he couldn't." He laughed. "You're showing him up."

I thought of all the green-tabbed folders in my file cabinet—the dozens already there when I'd arrived—and felt unreasonably defensive of Isaac Maat, who wasn't here to defend himself. "Most of the clients were perfectly happy before I came along," I said, moderating my tone in hope of giving an impression of benevolent diplomacy rather than protectiveness I could not justify to myself, let alone anyone else. "Does he usually get his way?"

"Maat?"

I nodded.

"Seems like it. I mean, he pisses off enough people."

Again, Hank had said the direct opposite. Had he played Isaac up to sell me on working for him, or was his difference of opinion the result of upper management bias toward educated, white-collar workers like themselves? I dismissed the former. Hank and Daddy wouldn't lie to me about someone and then put me under his supervision. So either Hank was ignoring complaints about his chosen one, or Joshua was a jealous liar.

"Can I try one of these?" he asked, lifting the largest piece of my sushi roll off my plate before I'd said yes.

It was all I could do to keep from stabbing him in the hand. In my family, there was no compulsory sharing unless someone wanted to end up wounded. He popped the bite in his mouth and then swirled his chopsticks over his bento box.

"Feel free to take anything you want from mine," he added, as if that would absolve him of straight-up stealing part of my lunch.

I don't want yours or I would have ordered it, I thought, scooting my iced tea glass between him and my food. "No thanks. What do you mean by 'He pisses off people'? I haven't heard that from anyone else."

I was starting to think the only people who didn't like Isaac were Joshua... and me. As much as I found Isaac judgmental and condescending, no one else—Joshua aside—remarked on it. Which just meant that Isaac didn't like *me*. But why? *Oh my God.* Was that my only real problem with him? That he didn't like me? How pathetic and juvenile that would be.

"Well, yeah, management doesn't really see it, you know? He's just smart enough to stay under their radar," Joshua said, as if he meant to school me on what management at the company my father owned was thinking. And what the what with that *just smart enough* baloney?

"He got his MBA at Wharton," I countered. "That's kind of a big deal. And I've seen the weekly financial reports he puts together for the CFO. They're insanely complex and detailed."

Joshua's dismissive gesture was a rapid, all-body sneer, as though a wave of derision had coursed through him. "Like I said—he's smart."

I'd gotten no closer to preparing for Isaac's reaction to being overruled, which would come any minute now. Maybe even when I returned from lunch.

"What do Harold and Sheila want to have done at the house? They're rich as fuck, man, and old. *Isaac* shouldn't be telling them no. They might not appreciate it coming from him, if you know what I mean."

While he was correct that rich people don't care for being told no (who does?), I didn't like his implication that the Andersons were racist but absolved of it because they were elderly and had money. That was all kinds of gross and probably defamatory.

"It makes sense that a denial would come from Finance and Legal because of the liability aspect," I said. "But that doesn't matter now because they aren't getting denied."

"I thought Maat said no." His eyes widened and I realized my mistake, too late. "Wait. You pulled rank and got him vetoed?"

I flushed, not with shy satisfaction over my victory, but with shame. *What had I done?*

He hooted, grinning. "That is the best thing I've ever heard. Ha ha!"

I considered stuffing my napkin in his open mouth.

"Man, you just went full boss on your *boss*. He's going to lose his *shit*. And he can't do a damn thing about it because it's coming from the owner of JMCH!"

Which went right to the heart of my dread. Just because I liked getting my way and believed in the end result didn't mean I enjoyed confrontation. I was not a hostile person. In a disagreement, my plan of attack centered on persuasion, not bullying. "I know you find this *really* humorous and all, but seriously—is he going to flip out?" So much for my plan to make a subtle inquiry. But if Joshua had a clue to what might happen next, I needed to know.

"That's the beauty—he *can't* flip out. He can't risk being rude to you. You're the owner's daughter."

"Hasn't stopped him before," I mumbled.

"What'd he say to you? If he's being disrespectful, you should report him."

Right. Report my supervisor for being disrespectful—a subjecttive accusation if ever there was one. I wasn't about to run into my father's company demanding respect for my ideas— *Oh, hell.* I just had.

"It was just normal supervisory criticism, not character assassination. I'm fine."

I was so not fine. I still had no idea how Isaac might respond. And while I didn't relish the thought of being justifiably reprimanded for subverting his authority, I didn't want to push him over the edge and cause him to lose his *job*. If a confrontation over the Andersons' great room wall happened—*when* it happened—I would have to pacify him and keep whatever angry shit he said to myself. *After the house is complete, our clients are ecstatic, and this nonissue is resolved, he'll get over it*, I thought.

That wasn't how it worked out. But I wouldn't know that for a while.

• • • • • • • • • • •

There was no immediate showdown. Isaac didn't even bring it up. In fact, he didn't speak to me about anything the rest of the day. Or the next day. On Thursday, in the weekly meeting that I was only invited to because of my surname, he introduced talking points, held conversations, and put forth a good case for continuing to use subcontractors instead of assuming that economic recovery in the housing sector would be steady and the current summer boom at JMCH was permanent. But none of those exchanges included me.

Hank sided with Isaac, reminding my father that JMCH had, in part, weathered the recession because we weren't beholden to contractors like we were to employees, who required steady salaries and benefits and would put us at risk of layoffs if the growth fizzled.

My father sighed, agreeing with a reluctant "Point taken," though it was obvious he was partial to his viewpoint of nothing but blue skies.

"Unless Erin has an objection?" Isaac said then, and everyone's heads swiveled toward me.

I glanced up from my notepad where I'd taken a few client notes but was mostly doodling a pair of perforated wedges with a perfect little ankle strap that I wished someone would design and produce. "What?" Why would I object to something I knew nothing about? My puzzled midafternoon I-need-caffeine brain tried and failed to process that question until I realized Isaac's dark-as-bitter-coffee eyes were boring into mine for the first time that week.

Unless Erin has an objection.

Oh.

I stomped my guilt and righteous indignation down—an uncomfortable mishmash of emotions that made me want to hide my face behind my hands while screaming—and cleared my throat. "No objection. Sounds reasonable to me."

"Relieved to hear it."

I wished he would look elsewhere so he wouldn't see the remorse I didn't want to feel or the fact that it didn't keep me from wanting to strangle that smartass glare right off his face.

"Great."

"Good."

chapter *Nine*

Three weeks later, days before the Andersons' closing date, Erin's Horrible Downfall kicked off with an alarming text from my eldest brother. I'd just left a promising on-site meeting with a new client and had run by QuikTrip for gas and caffeine before returning to work. Perspiring from less than five minutes in ninety-seven-degree heat, I'd just taken a sip of my iced coffee and fired up the AC.

Leo: It wasn't my fault. The plumbing subcontractor can't speak English. He didn't do what I said. He's just trying to cover his ass.

I reread the text three times, hoping the words would rearrange themselves into some semblance of rationality instead of jumbled justifications for an unspecified horror. During the next exchange, my heart began a slow-motion *thump, thump, thump*—the kind that occurs when a homicidal clown has just grabbed the heroine's ankle in the horror flick, or something unspeakable has happened in real life and you are to blame.

Me: What?

Leo: The wall. I never said to go through it.

Me: What wall?? Please don't mean what I think you mean.

His next text was a pic of the Andersons' custom great room mural, no longer a triumph of art and perseverance over dogmatic rules and shortsighted management. Since yesterday, when I'd last been on-site, the wall had become a hideous disaster of Leo proportions. A tire-sized portion of wallboard at the center of the painting had been damaged and patched over.

Patched. Over. As in mudded and sanded, as though it were a nondescript section of a regular wall, no big deal.

One justifiable fratricide, coming right up.

Me: JESUS FUCKING CHRIST LEO WTF???

Leo: Hey shut it I'm not the one that bends over and takes it up the ass for some whiny fancy ass bitch.

Me: First, Sheila Anderson is one of our most important clients and you don't like her because she's a WOMAN with more money and sense than you will EVER HAVE.

Me: Second, listening to our customers is my JOB.

Me: And third, MAKING SURE SUBCONTRACTORS DON'T MUTILATE THE PROPERTY BEYOND REPAIR IS YOUR JOB.

Leo: Face it "princess" you fucked up.

Leo: Also my guys damage and fix shit all the time. It's part of the building process and as you can see the WALL is just fine. Not our fault that you and your stick up his ass boss got something stupid approved by running to Daddy.

Me: What is the deal with you and asses you homophobic dickwad, aside from the fact that you are in fact a GIANT ASSHOLE?! Do you want me to fail at this job? Is that your endgame? Congratulations and FYVM.

I tossed my phone into the center console, so livid I was shaking and unable to get my seatbelt clipped. While I struggled and cursed the locking mechanism as though the tremors in my hands had zero to do with it, my phone trilled an alert. For once, I was grateful it sometimes decided to send calls straight to voice mail instead of giving me the option of answering, because the missed call was from Sheila Anderson's cell.

Before I could find the nerve to even listen to her message, my email refreshed and blew up from a conversation in which I'd been copied. The thread began with Mr. Anderson, whom I'd never actually corresponded with directly since he was fond of handing all decisions off to his wife. It was addressed to my father. Cynthia Pike, Leo, and I were copied. A photo, similar to the one Leo had texted to me, was included, along with close-ups of the damage that looked—how was this even fucking possible?—*worse*.

From: Anderson, Harold
To: McIntyre, Jeffrey
Cc: Pike, Cynthia; McIntyre, Leo; McIntyre, Erin
Subject: Wall

I've attached images for how the great room wall looked before and after your construction crew of idiots managed to wreck it. The artist's remuneration was $50K; I'll expect that credited back on my house at closing. As far as the wall itself, arranging a satisfactory repair (if such a thing exists, which I doubt) and coercing Sheila to accept that proposed resolution is on you.
May God have mercy on your souls.
Harold Anderson

From: Pike, Cynthia
To: McIntyre, Jeffrey
Cc: McIntyre, Leo; McIntyre, Erin
Subject: Re: Wall

OMFG WTF

Forward From: McIntyre, Jeffrey
To: Sager, Ted; Greene, Hank; Maat, Isaac; Pike, Cynthia; McIntyre, Leo; McIntyre, Erin
Subject: Re: Wall

WHAT IN HOLY HELL??? WHO IS RESPONSIBLE FOR THIS??? CONFERENCE ROOM 2 IN 20 MINUTES. EVERYONE. NO EXCUSES.

From: Sager, Ted
To: McIntyre, Jeffrey
Cc: Greene, Hank; Maat, Isaac; Pike, Cynthia; McIntyre, Leo; McIntyre, Erin
Subject: Re: Wall

We have an interview scheduled in that conference room at 11.

From: McIntyre, Jeffrey
To: Sager, Ted
Cc: Greene, Hank; Maat, Isaac; Pike, Cynthia; McIntyre, Leo; McIntyre, Erin
Subject: Re: Wall

I DON'T GIVE A GODDAMN. CANCEL IT.

From: Sager, Ted
To: McIntyre, Jeffrey
Cc: Greene, Hank; Maat, Isaac; Pike, Cynthia; McIntyre, Leo; McIntyre, Erin
Subject: Re: Wall

Yes sir, I'll postpone it until this afternoon.

From: McIntyre, Jeffrey
To: Sager, Ted
Cc: Greene, Hank; Maat, Isaac; Pike, Cynthia; McIntyre, Leo; McIntyre, Erin
Subject: Re: Wall

POSTPONE IT UNTIL TOMORROW. MAYBE I'LL NEED TO HIRE A WHOLE NEW STAFF BY THEN.

The gas station was five minutes from the office, or roughly seven hours from the Mexican border if I drove straight there instead. As I pulled into the road, I gave the idea serious consideration.

Pros: I had a savings account into which my trust fund had dispensed quarterly cash since I turned twenty-one, and two months' worth of paychecks in my debit account. I had a credit card in my name. My car had a full tank of gas.

Cons: I'd have to go home to get my passport. I would be quitting something in the most spectacular fashion in the history of Erin Quitting Something—no living it down, ever. And I would have to take my high school Spanish and make a go of it. *Hola, mi nombre es Erin.*

I jumped like a spooked rabbit when the driver behind me honked; I'd spaced out and missed the light turning green. I did not want to face my father and his key employees (plus my idiot brother). Every one of them knew—or would soon know—whose fault this fiasco was. But above all, I did not want to face Isaac Maat. Would he be furious or smug? Furiously smug? Smugly furious? These were the only options I could conceive aside from a 450-mile-long drive straight down I-35 and a freckled as fuck future.

I pulled into the JMCH parking lot like a robot on autopilot and asked myself, *What's the worst that can happen?*

Answers spilled into my head, none of them implausible. Leo would escape unscathed, because he was right—his guys scratched surfaces, bumped frames loose, and knocked holes in the wallboard frequently in the process of doing something else. Blunders were patched up or replaced quickly, and as a rule the client remained none of the wiser. But those damages were perpetrated on standard construction drywall, upmarket countertops, and satin paint finishes in Lemon Custard or Newport Sand or Perfect Cream. Not *irreplaceable works of art.*

This was my fault, when it came down to it. All. My. Fault. I was going to have to deal with the ruined wall in a way that satisfied the Andersons or die trying. But as much as I wanted to trust in my remarkable capacity to come up with innovative solutions to predicaments like this one, nothing came to mind.

Good-bye, cruel world.

• • • • • • • • • • •

Our butts had barely hit the chairs before my father thundered into the room and slammed the door shut behind him. He paced at the head of the table instead of sitting, staring down at the phone in his hand.

"How?" The word was a long, angry growl. When no one answered immediately, it was barked. "*How?*"

Leo leaned forward, one meaty palm up. "The guys have to make wallboard repairs all the time, Dad. It wouldn't have been a big deal if that *painting* hadn't been on it."

"*You think*?" my father shot back and Leo shrank back a bit. "Who did this?"

"The damage or the rep—"

"Both. Both! Who did it? Who authorized it?"

Leo shrugged, but his shoulders remained taut. "One of Phil's crew—some guy, Pedro or Juan, I dunno—installed cabinets where the dishwasher was supposed to go—"

"What the fuck does a dishwasher have to do with the *great room wall*?"

"The kitchen is on the other side of that wall. The plumbing and gas lines enter the house there. They accidentally bumped through it when they were ripping the cabinets out. It happens." He tried another shrug.

My father pressed both palms against the table and Ted, seated nearest him, angled away, his face a blotchy mask of dread. If a door straight to hell opened up in the floor, I was pretty sure Ted would jump right in. He was not cut out for reporting directly to Jeff McIntyre.

"That mistake should have been caught before that painting was done—"

"And it would have been if procedure had been followed. Aftermarket customizations aren't supposed to be added until the house is transferred." My brother had never uttered the words *procedure* or *aftermarket* in his life. He must have consulted a JMCH handbook and a dictionary and then spent several hours memorizing those two sentences. He leaned back in his chair, elbows resting on the arms, and glanced across the table at me as if musing how this flagrant oversight could have happened. "But someone got approval to do things out of order this time."

No he didn't. That rat bastard!

"I want that laborer fired, whoever he is," Daddy snapped. "Fire the whole lot of them, including Phil."

Leo gasped, mouth agape, and pointed at me. Pointed. Like a five-year-old. "But Dad, this is Erin's fault—" Phil was a buddy of his from high school.

"Jeff, if the crew was just following orders—" Hank interrupted.

Panic clawed at my throat. I had no idea how complicit Phil was or if he was at all. No idea if the damage had resulted from a legitimate accident or was straight-up Leo sabotage for my invasion of JMCH and the subsequent loss of our father's full attention. Could he be that petty?

"Were they?" Daddy glared at Leo, who glared at me. *Question answered.*

"This is on me." Isaac's voice rose just above the others, silencing everyone.

Ted's mouth hung open and Cynthia angled one brow like a stunned cartoon villain. Leo didn't even try to hide his exultant half grin, the fatheaded asshat.

"I approved the request, and I'll have to work out how to repair the damage to the wall and salvage our image, if you will allow me that option." Isaac's gaze was locked on my father, who knew damned well he'd allowed me to circumvent the rules and my supervisor's efforts to uphold them.

Daddy nodded once, addressing Isaac without a single telltale glance at me. "Fix it, or I will make sure it never happens again."

"Yes, sir. I'll do my best."

Both behaved as though I had nothing to do with this calamity, when I had everything to do with it.

"Hank." My father inclined his head toward the door before he turned and left the room. Hank followed. "Leo," he barked from just outside the door, and my clueless brother stood and sauntered after them, happy to see someone else take the fall for his mistake, even if the intended target—me—hadn't been hit.

Without a glance in my direction, Isaac Maat rose and left the room.

"Goddamn," Cynthia muttered.

Yeah.

chapter *Ten*

That night my subconscious startled me awake with the recurrent nightmare that had plagued my nights since last fall. Christina had fluctuated between mumbled annoyance and cursed condemnation whenever her sleep had been trashed by my pitiful whimpers or shrill yells. Since graduation, it hadn't occurred once, and I'd begun clinging to a naïve hope that moving home and working full time—a signal to my brain that I was finished with school, with that campus—had made it stop.

Nope.

As I bumbled through my morning routine of yoga poses, I tried to focus on the lone bright sides: the interval between last night's nightmare and the last time it had occurred, and the fact that my bedroom was on the opposite side of the house from my parents, who slept with a white-noise machine humming to drown out Jack's bulldoggy snores (and Daddy's). My brothers had long since moved out, so since I'd boomeranged back home, I had the east wing to myself. Maybe I should have been bothered that I could be chain-sawed in my bed and no one would hear me shrieking, but I was too grateful for the privacy.

Pax and Foster had witnessed an episode on Christmas Eve. They'd each come home for a few days bracketing Christmas—Pax from New Mexico and Foster from Dallas. When I'd screamed, both of them had torn into my room half-awake, Pax wielding a bat (of course), and Foster brandishing a museum-quality sculpture not intended for home defense that he'd grabbed from a hallway niche between our rooms.

Pax had gestured once it was clear I'd only suffered a nightmare, not a murdering fiend. "*Dude*."

"Fuck!" Foster stared at the marble figure in his hand. "Mom would have murdered me!"

We'd all had a good laugh, and I'd managed to convince them the disturbance was an isolated incident. Nothing to worry about. Nothing that transpired so often I sometimes thought I was losing my mind.

The awful images that had roused me to consciousness at three a.m. this morning had refused to be banished, so I'd lain there for three miserable hours, exhausted but wide fucking awake, unable to escape a hell that had been generated by a real-life nightmare instead of a morbid, regrettably wired imagination. When my alarm chirped at six, I'd just begun to drift off and had almost thrown my phone and its jaunty time-to-wake-up tone across the room.

I'm pretty sure I fell asleep for a couple of minutes during child's pose. Also, quite possibly, during my shower.

Once the dream began, it was always inescapable, because I never knew I was dreaming. Though the sequence of events never varied, I was unable to predict what was coming next or how it would end. I lived the whole thing anew every time, start to finish—shock, hope, agony—and then I woke to debilitating, irreparable remorse. Over and over, as if my brain was determined to make me pay for the rest of my life.

"Chaz?" My throat didn't release more than a whisper, and the

only answer I got was the whine of wind, hissing in fragmented bursts through the cracked windshield. The car was entirely off the road, sitting at a sharp angle on its side. The impact had come out of nowhere. No bracing for it, no split second of awareness beforehand. Nothing but an unanticipated force slamming into us, severing our conversation midsentence—his or mine, I couldn't recall. Nothing but the shrill protest of tires and metal and glass giving way before either of us realized what was happening. Our bodies were tossed like flimsy, inanimate things, restrained in our seats as we spun and rolled into our current position.

Crumpled against the concaved driver's side door, his shoulder and face against the window, he was motionless and silent. Choking back a sob, I reached out to touch him, my fingers trembling, but he was a few inches out of reach. "Chaz?" I repeated, my voice more substantial, if disembodied—like it wasn't coming from me. Still, he didn't respond, didn't move, and I went numb with fear.

The sickly-sweet smell of burned rubber, crushed metal, and leaking engine fluids assailed my nostrils in confirmation of what had just occurred, but the speakers still emitted an upbeat, twang-filled country narrative from his brother's band's newest album, as if we were still sitting at the stoplight, waiting for green. I stretched one shaky finger to switch the sound off but couldn't reach the dash, so I balanced my hand on the center console to keep from falling onto Chaz and pressed my seatbelt's release. The rowdy music went silent with one click, and I leaned closer to hear his shaky inhalations and see his breath making faint, steamy clouds against the cracked glass of his window. I gasped in relief, silent tears tracking down my face. I heard sirens in the distance before a low drone began inside my head, like a hive full of livid bees had lodged there, buzzing.

"They're coming." I swallowed hard, trying to tamp the panic down from the space in the middle of my chest where it pressed and swelled. The moon was a sliver, and the nearest streetlamp was across the street. It was too dim inside the car to assess how extensively either of us was injured, but as my eyes adjusted, I made out the thin, dark trickle of blood seeping from his right ear. It dribbled down the valley behind his angled jaw and across his throat like a slash.

The sirens grew louder. They were coming for us—I was sure now. "Hold on, Chaz. Please hold on."

He opened his eyes and shifted them toward me, though no other part of him moved. I edged closer, hovering over him from my elevated position. "I'm here," I said, and then stupidly, "Are you okay?" His contorted limbs and the fact that he'd not moved anything but his eyelids were all the answer any rational person would need to that question.

He blinked and squinted as if he couldn't quite focus on my face. "I don't think so." He closed his eyes while I bit down on my lip and wished we could back up ten minutes and never get into this car.

"Baby?" His voice was familiar but rasped, as though it had been scraped with coarse sandpaper. He hadn't called me baby in months.

I strained to pull myself closer but my legs wouldn't move. They were dead weight. Numb. "Yes," I gasped, trying not to freak out at the realization that my legs could be paralyzed. "I'm here."

Opening his eyes again, he stared up at me. "Lie to me. Please."

"What?"

He was speaking nonsense. His head must have slammed into

the window during the crash. His throat worked to swallow, and even that ended in a grimace. "Lie... to me," he repeated.

"Don't try to talk—they're almost here," I said, unable to see the road in our twisted, angled position—but I heard the siren roar around the corner at the end of the street. Half a block. Ten seconds. Five.

"If I'd asked you again. Would you—" He gasped. "Would you have said yes, eventually?"

Lie to me.

I couldn't hold out pretending I hadn't heard. "Yes. Of course I would have. I love you." I realized that even if the first part was a lie, the second wasn't. Not completely.

The right side of his mouth turned up in the barest hint of his customary cocky smile. "Thanks, baby."

I laid a careful hand on his chest, just above his heart. It was warm. Warm and wet. My fingertips came away dark, and a trembling terror detonated in my lungs and ripped through my limbs as if I'd touched a live wire. I clamped my teeth together and tensed my shoulders and arms but couldn't prevent the shudders from multiplying or the tears that sharpened my sight of everything I no longer fought to see.

A fire engine pulled up behind the car and emergency personnel swarmed around us, their determined voices coming through the broken glass. I pressed against the console, trying to free myself from the wreckage, and the edges of my vision blurred. The next thing I knew, they were dragging me away from him.

"It's not a lie," I'd shouted, opening my eyes to the total darkness of my room. Silence, but for the whoosh of breath from my mouth and the heartbeat hammering away in my ears. No wrecked car, no paramedics, no flashing lights.

The truth rushed out from the shadows, bright and excruciating, as it had dozens of previous times. Reality returned to separate nightmare from memory. Pain came in waves, bursts of fiery currents surging through my heart and scattering to reach my skin and set it aflame. I couldn't move, and everything hurt—but it was a phantom pain more debilitating than any physical agony I'd ever experienced. Tears trickled from the corners of my eyes and streamed into my hair.

Chaz and I had broken up spring of junior year, over a year ago now. And even if it had hurt like hell to do it, I hadn't regretted my decision. In front of our friends, their smiling faces gradually fading into expressions of incredulity and dismay, I had placed my hand over his, closed that hinged box in his palm, and broken his heart as softly as I could manage.

"Oh, Chaz. I can't. I'm so sorry, but I can't." I wasn't in love with him, not like he loved me, and it would have been wrong to pretend.

After a summer of no contact, we'd begun our last undergrad fall semesters. We managed a few semi-awkward social interactions, and the story of his failed proposal gradually faded from campus gossip. Within a couple of weeks, we were both hanging out and hooking up with other people. Everything felt settled between us. So what if I caught him looking at me from across the room during his frat's first big party of our senior year? He'd smiled that familiar, affable grin and returned his attention to the girl he was chatting up, easing any lingering guilt I might have felt for not anticipating that months-ago proposal and heading it off before he'd arranged it.

Days after that party, a driver sending a text failed to notice that the stoplight ahead had turned red. She'd flown through the intersection and hurtled into Chaz's car without ever hitting the brakes.

His mother caught me alone after the funeral and told me—her red-rimmed eyes full of stark grief and her words raw with bitter reproof—that her stubborn, loyal son had never stopped plotting to win me back. That he'd never returned that ring he'd proposed with the previous spring—the one I couldn't accept because I didn't want to be anyone's wife and I'd known with utter certainty, when that diamond solitaire had winked up at me, that if I ever did it would not be him.

"You broke his heart, but he loved you until the day he died," she said before her husband slid an arm around her shoulders and led her away, sobbing.

His absolution was a trick that disappeared when I was awake, because I wasn't in his car that night. I hadn't been there with him no matter my mind's desperate attempt to invent a closure I could bear. I'd never told him that lie he wanted to hear. And he had died alone.

chapter *Eleven*

Isaac hadn't spoken to me or so much as acknowledged my existence for the remainder of the day yesterday. And after the unexpected predawn return of my guilt-induced nightmare piled atop my personal responsibility for the Anderson debacle, I was a stressed-out ball of anxiety when I slunk by his open door, wishing myself invisible, and entered my cubbyhole office. I hoped my boss would continue to ignore me for one more day so I could make it to the weekend when I would maybe, finally, call Jacqueline and dump everything on her, so I was apprehensive when he rang my antique desk phone Friday morning and asked me to clear my schedule for the morning.

"Oh?" My heart squeezed painfully. I was being fired. *I deserve to be fired!* I thought, realizing with simultaneous shock that I didn't want to leave this job. Not this way, as a failure. Not now, when it was all I had that was mine.

But no—Daddy wouldn't let that happen, bestowing both the best and worst kind of job security.

"I want you to join me on an errand related to the issue with the Anderson home," he said. He paused on either side of the word *issue*, as though separating out both the word and what it referenced, in case I needed a reminder of it.

"Errand?"

"I'll meet you downstairs in fifteen minutes," he answered. His authoritative tone told me in no uncertain terms that this request was more order than invitation.

A rather strident *click* rattled my eardrum, and I reached an immediate comprehension of those "In *my day* hanging up on people was more satisfying" memes older people passed around on social media. I glared at the receiver—opposite hand over the offended ear—before banging it down in its cradle, but with no one on the other end, my satisfaction was short-lived.

I rearranged my a.m. calendar, postponing two on-site client visits, grabbed my bag, and was gratified to see his office door was already shut when I strode into the silent hallway. I'd never been the sort of girl who arrived first, even when I was eager to meet up with someone. Especially then.

I was not eager. *I was not.*

I sauntered to the elevator, pressed the button, and waited for the ponderous response of the single car, which always took a good fifteen seconds to register the command and begin to move, another fifteen to arrive, and five to open. I knew because I'd counted once out of impatient curiosity. On most occasions, I took the stairs because standing and waiting made me want to scream. But I still had three minutes to be downstairs; there was no need to hurry to obey Isaac Maat's summons. I checked my lip gloss in the reflection of the shiny gold-toned door and fluffed my hair around my face, hoping he was pacing irritably, checking his phone or a watch. My brassy likeness gave me a conspiratorial smirk at the thought.

I regretted my decision not to take the stairs when Isaac appeared from the opposite end of the hall, where the bathrooms were, rolling the sleeves of his crisply pressed, sky-blue shirt to just under the elbow. As he came closer, his attention on fashioning a perfectly squared cuff, tiny white pinstripes became visible in the smooth poplin. No tie today, and his collar was unbuttoned. I yanked my eyes from that visible, contrasting triangle of skin before he caught me ogling it.

His steps faltered slightly—when he looked up to see me standing there, I assumed—but he reached my side and the elevator was *still* struggling to ascend one measly freaking floor.

I detected a trace of spicy aftershave behind the blended lavender and rosemary from the bathroom soap dispensers as he took his place next to me. The piquant blend made him smell like a gingery dessert, or the mulled wine and chipotle pepper garnish my mother sent around on trays at our annual holiday party. Swallowing, I tried not to breathe through my nose and concentrated on the double doors, behind which a motorized drone promised the arrival of the elevator. Any day now.

"I feel like I left my office half an hour ago," I said, attempting levity in the guise of shared frustration. "Guess I should have taken the stairs."

"I usually do." His tone was neutral, but I caught his reflection's eye-roll before he spoke.

"Why stop now?" I snapped at his gilded image.

His brows arched as he met my indignant, mirrored stare, realizing that I'd probably seen his not-so-stealthy eye-roll. "I thought it more courteous to wait with you since you were already standing here, than separate and beat you downstairs."

I didn't want his courtesy if it came with a side of disdain. "Courteous? Hmm."

"What?" He frowned, turning just enough to look down at me.

"You think I lack courtesy?"

Yes, but just to me, so please discontinue smelling so good if you're dead set on treating me like I'm a joke. I couldn't say any of *that*. The elevator emitted a sound between a ding and a honk. As the doors slid open, I stepped forward, but Isaac's hand shot out, cupped my left elbow, and pulled me to a stop, preventing me from slamming into Joshua, who was darting through the slowly widening gap, eyes on his phone's screen.

"Erin! Shit!" Joshua took hold of my right arm to stop from running me over, or to keep himself upright. "Man, I didn't even see you. I'm in a hurry to grab some numbers from my desk for this cheap-ass, time-sucking prospective I've got waiting downstairs."

And then he noticed Isaac, whose big, warm palm was still supporting my elbow. I could feel the connection to the soles of my feet and everything in between.

"I would've run up the stairs, like always, but the elevator was just sitting there open, so I took advantage."

Isaac made a low *humph* that I pretended not to hear, and for one brief, uncomfortable moment, I was a bone between two adversarial dogs. I did not appreciate the sensation and shook both of their hands loose.

"I'm fine," I said. "No harm, no foul."

I knew better than to wait for an actual apology from Joshua, who'd neglected to stuff a single, clear-cut *I'm sorry* into his litany of excuses for almost knocking me down. Like my eldest brother, he was all justifications, all the time, and I suspected he'd express the same sort of belligerence when backed into a corner. That similarity to Leo had rubbed me the wrong way the day I met him, and no amount of hallway chats or coffee runs had changed my mind. He was adept at sniffing out company gossip and enjoyed disclosing it to me—along with his unsolicited running commentary on what each tidbit signified—but that was the extent of his usefulness. I was interested in gossip concerning my boss, but most of his supposedly privileged intel on Isaac seemed like a bunch of resentful, unwarranted BS.

I preceded Isaac into the elevator and pressed the button for the first floor and then jabbed the Close Doors button several times while the two men stared at each other. The elevator sat there like all we'd wanted to do was board a cramped, stationary box for no reason. Finally, the doors jerked as if rudely awoken and then shut as slowly as possible, leaving Joshua on the second floor. I poked the first-floor button again for good measure. Twice. *Go, dammit.*

Standing a foot apart, Isaac and I faced the burnished doors instead of each other. I expected a tense, silent ride to the first floor, but he cleared his throat and I readied myself for a comment about Joshua or some sort of personal rebuke.

"I, uh, apologize for the eye-roll," he said. "That was discourteous and juvenile."

Whoa. I risked a glance at his reflection.

Staring at his shoes, he slid his hands into his pockets. "I made an assumption that you'd rather have walked down—or had me do so—than share the elevator for five seconds."

His candor was a solid gut-punch. Every time I tried to peg what he was thinking or feeling, I was mistaken. My quirky insight into other people's motivations wasn't functioning with Isaac, and I couldn't figure out why.

"Apology accepted." I watched mirror-Isaac as I spoke. "But c'mon now. Five seconds? It's more like five minutes."

He laughed softly. "True. True." His relaxed gaze rose to connect with mirror-Erin's.

I tried not to tip over, staring at the pleasant shape of his mouth, upturned at the corners, a little higher on one side than the other, while the warmth of his masculine laughter flowed over me. I wasn't sure whether it was the habitual sluggishness of the elevator or my visceral reaction to his atypical smile that made time slow. The sound of his laugh—maybe, I thought frantically, it was the close quarters that unleashed such whimsy—made my heart twist and fumble toward him as though he was everything familiar, everything safe, when he was nothing of the kind.

DONK. The spell was broken when the elevator sounded its dejected, obligatory warning and the doors slid apart, separating our images. His laughter faded, and the smile with it, his mouth returning to its characteristic taut line. He extended a hand toward the lobby, inviting me to exit first. "After you, Ms. McIntyre," he said, but that unanticipated laugh had overlaid my perception of him, and instead of the stark, professional tone he meant to project, I heard something else—the real Isaac Maat. He pushed through the lobby door and held it open for me, and we stepped out of the building's cool mid-seventies temperature into the soggy warmth of July in North Texas.

His BMW sedan was immaculate. There wasn't so much as a balled-up napkin in a cupholder or a leaf on a floor mat. This surprised me not at all.

"Nice car," I said. "Nice, really clean car. Remind me not to ever let you see the interior of mine." Mine wasn't that bad—I could still turn up my nose at Joshua's big SUV that looked like a staged version of his life: *I shop here. I eat here. I have nice clothes. I work out.*

Isaac's car gave no such clues.

"Now I wanna see it," Isaac said, pressing the ignition.

The AC blew gently, and a talk show came through the speakers. I recognized the NPR host, who was discussing a film built on the fictional premise that humans only use ten percent of their brains at any given time, leaving ninety percent untapped. They played an audio clip of the film, but the guest—a psychologist from Princeton—was not swayed by Morgan Freeman's authoritative performance. He called bullshit on the ten percent myth, stating the fact that we use one hundred percent of our brains. The host, laughing, said he didn't feel like that was true. Even though my psychology classes had debunked the fairy tale of that unexploited ninety percent, I could relate. Boy howdy, could I ever relate.

Isaac turned the sound down. "Your office is amazingly tidy, considering it's got about the same usable space as my car. Tidy and welcoming even. Can't help but believe your car's interior is comparably well-ordered."

I sensed a trap even as I tried not to gloat at his praise. My office *was* tidy and tastefully decorated—something I had accomplished on the weekends, outside of working hours: smoky gray walls, graphite-toned furniture softened by fabrics in deep amethyst and plum. I'd traded the original too-big desk and bookcase for smaller pieces that complemented the space—what there was of it—instead of over-powering it.

"And not a Beanie Baby in sight."

That smartassery earned a soft laugh, and I was grateful he was too busy merging onto 114 to watch my response. I felt like I was melting into his buttery leather seat. I'd never had that sort of reaction to a *sound* before. It was disconcerting and uncomfortable, because all I wanted was to do whatever I had to do to hear it again.

"So, um, where are we going?"

"Art studio."

"Oh?"

He didn't rise to the conspicuous desire for further information in my *Oh?*

"Whose studio? Where?" I left off the *And why?* because I was beginning to sound like a four-year-old.

"A friend. In Fort Worth."

Hence the *clear your schedule* request, I guessed. This was not an enjoyable drive in and of itself. The scenery was ass and the roads were perpetually congested and full of road-ragey people who might or might not have a concealed handgun under the front seat. We were going to be in this car half an hour in either direction, barring traffic on the multiple freeway interchanges—and there was *always* construction-triggered traffic somewhere if not numerous somewheres.

My burning curiosity over why in hell's name we were driving into Fort Worth to see some mystery artist was bubbling up like a chemistry experiment gone awry. If he didn't start talking soon, I was going to rupture something vital trying to hold it in. He'd told me this impromptu excursion had something to do with the Anderson home's *issue*, which was just a polite way of alluding to the catastrophe I had caused with the help of my judgment-deficient big brother.

All of that was before I could rationally address the fact of spending an hour trapped in a car, alone, with Isaac Maat, the most intimidating, attractive man I'd ever met. I'd always been partial to gregarious, approachable guys. I had never found an intimidating man attractive, or an attractive man intimidating—until now. I didn't know what to make of it. He made me uncomfortable, but I couldn't tell if that discomfort was because he seemed to think so poorly of me as an employee or because he was immune to any reciprocal attraction. *Ouch* and *ouch*.

I gave myself a mental shake. I didn't have time for this nonsense. We had a bigger obstacle to leap than my wounded feelings. A priceless (to Sheila Anderson—but worth fifty thousand to her husband) piece of art had been disfigured, and I couldn't imagine how adding another artist to the mix would solve that.

"So we're meeting with an artist friend of yours? You said this little field trip concerned the Andersons', um, issue." I started to ask why we needed an artist but answered my own question and went momentarily speechless as my heartbeat became heavy and slow. "Are we hiring an artist to *recreate* the damaged section?" My voice sounded like it came from outside my body.

Sheila Anderson would never allow such a thing. I'd known women like her all my life, and I would be hollered right out of North Texas for the suggestion. Her sweet-tea-sipping, hobby-gardening, arts-supporting, gracious-society-lady façade would fly right out the window. My ears began buzzing in anticipation of the ass-chewing I was going to get.

"Not exactly," Isaac said.

"What?" I wasn't sure I heard him over the panicked hum of blood swishing through my head as if it was trying to convince me to run.

"Recreate—no, I don't think so. Most artists aren't about aping someone else's creation, certainly not right on top of the original. They might draw inspiration or pay homage, but she'll have her own vision—or not. Let's see what remedy she suggests, if anything, before we freak out or give up."

"Too late," I muttered, staring out the window.

"Hmm?"

"Nothing." I was dead. I was so dead, and Isaac with me—of his own misguided volition.

Why had he done it? Why had he taken responsibility for a disastrous comedy of errors that he'd tried his best to prevent and that should have rested squarely on my idiot brother and me? He could have remained silent and let us deal with the consequences. But he hadn't.

chapter *Twelve*

We merged onto 121 and came to a halt before we'd gone half a mile. An orange sign on the shoulder read RIGHT LANE CLOSED AHEAD. In the distance, a huge flashing arrow obstructed our lane. Isaac heaved a dispassionate sigh and put on his turn signal. We scooted forward a foot or so at a time until someone waved him into the center lane. He lifted a hand in appreciation, inched over, and stopped again.

People were calling into the talk show coming through his speakers, but he'd reduced the sound, and with construction equipment tearing up asphalt just ahead, the voices were nothing but a low, unintelligible drone.

I picked at a nub on my skirt. "In case it hasn't been obvious, I'm really sorry about this whole situation, which wouldn't have happened if we'd followed procedure. You were right."

He was silent so long I almost thought he was going to leave my apology lying there between us, but after two months of working for him, I'd learned he was seldom in a hurry to respond. Isaac Maat did not react. He did not sound off. He did not shoot from the hip—not without plenty of reflection. He'd only lost his temper once, over something that made total sense, and even then he'd been low-key. He thought things out, considered every point from various angles, before revealing his opinion. I wasn't used to that kind of constraint.

It drove me a little nuts.

"You're used to getting your way, aren't you?" He stared straight ahead, and his calm tone and composed profile gave no clue as to the level of disapproval he meant to convey. The question itself accomplished that, unaided by scowls or indignant discourse.

Of course the owner's daughter is spoiled. Haven't I been battling that perception from day one?

But I'd obliterated any gained ground when I discounted Isaac's foresight about that wall and had his mandate dismissed. Because I had been so determined to play the hero to every client, and as the owner's daughter, I could.

I could, so I had.

My defensiveness melted to expose the insecurity at the core of it. "I suppose I am. Why did you agree to hire me? Or were you even given a say?" *Or did you say no but were overruled?*

"The determination to hire you wasn't my decision to make," he said, hedging. We got past the roadwork, one lane opening to three and releasing frustrated drivers from the bottleneck like a provoked swarm. He moved to the center lane. "I was asked to supervise the position once it was created, and I consented."

Consent was a funny word, with shades from coerced to enthusiastic. I couldn't envision the latter as Isaac's reaction to the thought of supervising the owner's daughter.

"I remember you, my first day. Before we met. You were watching from the second floor when my father and I came in." I thought about the tentative smile I'd given him—the one he'd snubbed. I hadn't known why then; I'd had no idea who he was. "You looked dead opposite of someone who'd happily consented to my being there."

He glanced at me and back at the road. "I said I agreed to oversee the position. I didn't say anything about *happily*." Before I could reply, he added, "You didn't even have an informal interview, let alone the sort of thorough assessment and scrupulous vetting expected for such a direct, client-impacting position." His jaw was tight, but his tone had a guilty ring to it.

"So interview me now."

His mouth twisted in a smirk half-visible to me since his eyes were on the road. "Bit late now, don't you think? Horse already out of the barn and all?"

I decided not to object to being inserted into a horse analogy. "Interviews go both ways, you know. I had no idea what I was getting into. Not really."

"Poor you, forced to accept a professional job and competitive salary right out of school." He shook his head. "All right then, tell me about your prior work experience."

I sat straighter in my seat, as if it were perfectly normal to be interviewed in a car for a job I'd been doing for two months. "In college, I was a hostess for an Austin steakhouse. By the time I left, I'd been there three years and was the hospitality lead. I coordinated weekly scheduling for all the hosts and even sat in on interviews for new hires. When I turned in my notice, I recommended the best person to replace me. They took my suggestion, and I trained her myself the last month I was there.

"Before that, I worked at a funky little clothing shop downtown. I loved shopping there and thought it would be a cool place to work. I didn't know the owner was an inept micromanager who thought every employee was out to steal merchandise or just loaf around. I hung on for four months, until I got written up for chatting with a friend who'd come in to shop. Her mom was neighbors with the head chef at Perry's; that's how I got the hostess interview. And in high school, I worked for Delia's, a retail clothing chain."

"I'm familiar, actually. My cousin worked for the one in Arlington during high school and college. You were in Southlake?"

"Yeah. It was a fun job. Grueling some days and boring others, but I liked my coworkers, and I loved the discount. Major perk, except I spent most of my paychecks there. We *all* did. Your cousin too, I guess."

"Jasmine was paying her own car payment and saving for college as soon as she turned sixteen. Helping her mama out with bills here and there. She didn't have much left over for shopping sprees."

"Oh." I kept making assumptions that turned out to be off base. I'd never imagined that people who were as educated as Isaac, as well dressed, well spoken, and driving a nearly new BMW had ever been less fortunate. "Were y'all close?"

Our eyes connected briefly. "Sure. We're family."

"Leo is family, and we are *not* close."

I wasn't sure that any of us were close. I felt a deep-rooted allegiance to them, which seemed to be the gist of what Isaac meant. But maybe it wasn't. A teenager who contributed to household bills and expected to pay her own college tuition? Those were foreign concepts to me—responsibilities I couldn't imagine within my own life, even though I knew people did it.

"Leo..." Isaac glanced at me, and we both laughed.

"Is an entitled tool and always has been. Please don't judge me by him. I'm unimpressing you enough on my own."

"I try to judge people on their own merits."

Too bad for me that my actions had caused a very recent dumpster fire.

"So how did you reach a managerial position at an upscale restaurant? And you must have been part-time?"

"It was more of an honorary title. I think I made fifty cents more per hour." Working at Perry's felt like a million years ago, but it had only been three months since my last shift. "I was good at keeping reservations straight while handling walk-ins. Seating tables—grouping them for large parties and breaking them back into four-tops for parties of two to four—is like a puzzle. I prided myself on low wait times even on busy nights. When they asked if I'd be in charge of the hosting calendar, I agreed because it gave me the power to take whatever nights off I wanted." I laughed. "I didn't consider the fact that everyone else would come at me with their own schedule requests and would be pissed off if I said no."

"I have to admit, I'm surprised."

"That I was good at something or that I was so gullible?"

"That you worked in high school and college—something many of your peers don't do."

Ah. "Because rich kids don't work?"

He shrugged. "That's the sort of thing interviewers are discouraged from prying into."

"True, but that doesn't keep an interviewee from spilling her guts, especially when the interviewer is biased about her work history, or the fact that she *has* any work history, in this case."

"Touché."

He didn't ask another question, so I elaborated.

"Growing up, Daddy told all of us—Leo and I have two middle brothers—that we might have a cushy life because of his money, but it was his money, and if we wanted to live high on the hog as adults, we would have to figure out how to earn it for ourselves."

I didn't share the fact that I only knew these instructions by heart because they'd been drilled into my brothers. *My* way of earning it had been geared toward socializing in the "right" circles and marrying well someday, even if that objective hadn't been explicitly stated. My brothers' attractiveness was never remarked on; my academics were never exclaimed or fretted over. Their jobs were encouraged to foster work experience; mine were for shopping money. One plus one equals two.

"So what's your 'high on the hog' aspiration? Where do you see yourself in five years?"

I forced a small laugh. "I can't believe you asked me such a clichéd interview question." I hadn't shared my goals or wishes with anyone in a long time. I wasn't sure what he would think of them, and for some reason what he thought mattered. A lot.

"Are you avoiding answering me?" He arched a brow, making light of the turn the conversation had taken. But when his dark eyes found mine, they were wide and curious.

"Maybe."

"Why?"

"Well. My future probably isn't in construction."

"I'm glad to hear it."

I scowled.

"Not because I want rid of you—"

"Really? Even after *the Anderson issue*?" I deepened my voice ominously, as though narrating an apocalyptic doomsday chronicle.

He rolled his eyes. "You made a mistake—albeit a monumental one—and you apologized."

"*Albeit*? Who even says that? How old *are* you?"

"Age is definitely not an appropriate interview question, Ms. McIntyre."

"I'm not the one conducting the interview, Mr. Maat. *You* can't ask *me* how old I am. I don't think the reverse is true." I wasn't sure why I needed to know. Just that I did. "I'm twenty-two."

He was silent for half a minute, and for the dozenth time in this conversation, I was sure I'd pushed too far. And then: "Twenty-six."

"Whoa. Really?"

"Yes, really." His profiled brow lowered, but he didn't turn to look at me. "Why does that surprise you?"

"I thought you were older. Mature. Set in your ways. Like, at least thirty."

"I'm not thirty, and I'm not set in my ways."

"So you say."

He frowned and stared straight ahead, and I repressed a laugh. Isaac Maat didn't like being called a stuffed shirt even though he *so was one.*

"Back to your non-construction five-year plan…"

For some reason, not telling him wasn't an option, but I took a deep breath and prepared for a response somewhere between mild ridicule and derision. Isaac Maat wouldn't dissemble. He would tell me what he really thought.

"I had hoped to be out of graduate school in five years."

"Psychology?"

"How did you know that?"

"When you were hired, I was curious about your field of study—how your skills or training might fit the job description and the corporate culture at JMCH. I asked Hank, but he wasn't certain of your degree. He said, 'Something-ology, I think. Sociology? Anthropology? Psychology? Maybe Philosophy?'" Isaac's vocal imitation was spot on.

I hid my face behind my hands and mumbled, "Oh, Uncle Hank."

"I asked if you'd minored in business at least. He said he didn't think so, which I confess I found alarming. But after you admitted to psychoanalyzing our clients and operating as if what you discussed with them was protected by doctor-patient privilege? I deduced that your degree was most likely in psychology."

His Wharton degree, his vocabulary, and the meticulous reports he generated for Hank made his intelligence clear, but that was deductive reasoning on another level.

At the same time, I'd been ten feet away and one door down from him for forty hours per week. "Why didn't you just ask *me* about my degree?"

He said nothing, and I waited, fighting the urge to fill the silence with follow-up questions or contentions like *I mean, I was right there every day. And it wouldn't have been weird for my supervisor to inquire about the degree I'd just earned. We even speak the same language. No need for interpreters or anything.*

"I don't know," he said. "I should have done that. So graduate school—private practice, not research, I assume, based on your inability to stay out of people's business?" He teased me about my innate nosiness, but he hadn't said *graduate school* as though it were a pipe dream.

"Not private practice exactly. I wanted to do therapy work in a high school or a college counseling office."

This earned me another look. "You said you *had hoped* to have completed grad school in five years. When do you plan to get started? Have you chosen a program path? Prospective schools?"

I all but squirmed in my seat. This was less like a job interview and more like *How Much Fail at Life is Erin?* "Not exactly." Once upon a time, I'd had a list of prospective schools. Dream schools. Backup schools. Program comparisons. "I'm trying to be realistic about my future. Not that I ever spelled out detailed ambitions to my parents, but they freaked enough when I brought up *graduate school*."

"Why?"

"They don't think I'm capable of it. Mentally, or whatever." I waved a hand as though I wasn't affected by the knowledge that the sum total of their hopes and fears for me had nothing to do with my intellect, work ethic, or heart, and everything to do with the genetic gifts they'd bestowed. The ones that made me the perfect ornament for the family tree. The perfect decoration for someone's arm and not much more. I wondered for the first time if that was my mother's valuation of herself.

Isaac took the Montgomery exit and moved to the right lane behind a block of cars waiting for the light to change. This was one area of Fort Worth I was acquainted with—Mindi would be back in town in two weeks to begin her senior year at TCU, and we would meet for artisanal pizza at Fireside Pies or beer and greasy nachos at the Pour House. What had happened to her three years ago, and the fact that she'd turned to me for help and support, had been the impetus behind my career choice. She'd transferred schools twice and slowly rebuilt her life, and she'd sworn I had everything to do with that.

The light turned and he took a right, glanced at the map on his phone's screen, and then turned into a small neighborhood of old, well-maintained houses. My father's company built gated communities of lavish stone and brick mansions that would swallow any one of these cozy, eighty-year-old cottages with their pier-and-beam foundations, wood siding, shutters, and porch swings. Pecan, red oak, and magnolia trees curved over streets and towered above the quiet community of pretty dollhouses they shaded. Rosebushes and crepe myrtles bloomed everywhere, and vines of honeysuckle trailed along arched gates. Sidewalks invited strolls geared more toward wool-gathering than exercise.

We parked in front of a tiny, one-story home, white with pink—*pink!*—shutters framing the two front windows. The vintage porch light was antique copper, as were the house numbers just beneath it. A letter box, painted like a bumblebee, was affixed below, as if it were buzzing around the large, flourishing pots of geraniums on either side of the front door.

The entire structure would have fit inside my parents' garage, but I'd never been so enchanted by a house.

Isaac leaned forward to look out the passenger window. "The house is both home and studio. Tuli works in several different mediums, but her first love was outdoor murals, experimenting with plaster and concrete to add texture or create separate supporting pieces. She's developed into an inventive genius when it comes to mixed media."

"You've worked with Tuli before, then?" A tiny pinprick of jealousy took me by surprise.

He nodded without looking at me, as if considering whether to say more. I waited.

"When I was in high school, I started an anti-gentrification project that turned into a community outreach. A few local commercial backers began working with neighborhood associations and volunteers to repair and weatherize homes for owners who were elderly, disabled, or so impoverished that they were unable to afford to make repairs themselves."

"Like Habitat for Humanity?"

He angled his head. "Sort of, but small, local, and all restoration and noncosmetic refurbishment to combat what investor-backed developers call *blight*, not the sort of 'beautification' that attracts too much outside interest. We focused on stabilizing neighborhoods by stabilizing homes and public areas, making them livable rather than doing trendy renos and adding landscaping, dog parks, bike lanes…"

"Things that attract chain stores and hipsters." *White, upwardly mobile hipsters who end up destroying the local culture they ostensibly seek.* "And then higher property values and taxes force original residents out. Displacing them."

"Yeah."

If those comically arched brows were any indication, I'd surprised him again.

"My, uh, minor was sociology. You started an impressive project like that by yourself? As a teenager?"

"With a couple of friends—one of whom was Tuli. It was a senior project." He grabbed his iPad from a seat pocket as we exited the car. "We graduated, I started at UTA, the other guy went off to OSU, and Tuli moved to Fort Worth to care for a terminally ill aunt, so we turned the project over to the community leaders and helped them manage it until they got the hang of rejecting the offers of assistance that come with strings attached—like developer money."

"That's so cool."

"I've loaded the images of the wall, before and after, to my iPad," he said, bringing us back to the purpose of our field trip. "If she says she can do something with it, then we'll see what the Andersons think. If not, well, we'll cross that bridge before we light it on fire, eh?"

We stepped onto the porch, where a colorful welcome mat instructed: WIPE YOUR PAWS.

"You trust her evaluation and artistic skill quite a bit."

He nodded and pressed the doorbell, which produced a muffled tinkling of wind chimes inside the house. Even the doorbell was adorable. "I do."

"Then I trust her too." I wasn't lying; I was completely disposed to trust his stupendously talented, artistic friend, who lived in the most precious house I'd ever seen.

But I'd never realized how like heartburn jealousy was. My throat burned with it. I swallowed and stuffed my heart back down where it belonged. But I couldn't seem to help the malicious wish that formed in my head: *Please don't be cute. Please, please don't be cute.*

chapter *Thirteen*

Tuli was small and dark-haired with smooth, tawny skin and friendly eyes. She was the very definition of *cute*. "Isaac, my God, look at you!" she said, grinning up at him. "You look like some sexy, bougie banker. Such a difference from your trademark worn jeans and V-neck tees."

Trademark what now?

Dear image of Isaac dressed down: get out of my head, please and thank you.

Tuli's features were Indian, from the almond shape of her eyes to her patrician nose, but her lips were full, and she wore her hair in intricately braided dreads that were fastened at her nape. A bright fuchsia tank peeked out from white, paint-splattered overalls cuffed midcalf.

"C'mon, girl, you seen me looking professional before. And at church back in the day. Quit playin'." His lips pressed tight, he crossed his arms and rocked back on his heels. He was embarrassed at her frank declaration that he was hot, while his dialect and posture were more relaxed than I'd ever witnessed. The Isaac Maat I knew was clearly not the Isaac Maat Tuli knew.

"You never filled out a dress shirt and slacks like this in high school or I'da taken notice, church or no church. Mmm. *Mmm*."

Isaac shook his head and sighed, charmingly self-conscious.

Who was this man?

"Tuli Bell, this is my coworker, Erin McIntyre. Erin, Tuli."

She turned her smile to me, not the slightest bit repentant for disconcerting him in front of a stranger. "It's great to meet you, Erin." She pushed the door shut behind us with her foot. "I'd shake your hand, but you might come away with a bit of clay. I'll just go wash up real quick. BRB." Her ballet flats moved silently across the wood floors and canvas drop cloths.

"Thank you for taking the time to meet with us," I said, my heels clacking with each step into the room.

Artwork of assorted types and stages perched, leaned, and hung everywhere. A newly begun painting waited on an easel by one window and a hand-thrown bowl sat on a pottery wheel. Sharp smells of drying paint and solvents mixed with wet clay and fresh-cut flowers.

The main room was one long space encompassing the entire depth of the house, front to back. At the opposite end of the room, a half-light door flanked by two large windows showcased flowers and fruit trees in the backyard. Tuli disappeared through a doorway on the left, likely the kitchen. A short hall leading to a bedroom was visible through a doorway on the right. I was used to soaring ceilings, so hers felt low, but the effect was snug, not oppressive. This was the atmosphere JMCH couldn't replicate. Cozy. Comfortable. Homey.

She came back, drying her hands on a tea towel.

"Your home is lovely," I said, wishing I were here alone so I could explore every nook and cranny.

She laughed. "I've seen what y'all do—on the internet, anyway. This little house is my favorite place in the world, but it can't compete with the luxury materials and square footage you're used to working with."

"Oh, you're so wrong. I just matched up a client with a specific decorator a couple of weeks ago because *this* is the sort of vibe she wanted. A home that feels like a welcoming, peaceful space apart from the world instead of a hotel lobby. To get that kind of ambiance in the gigantic house she bought from us, they'll have to fake it. This is the real thing."

She beamed. "Well, thank you."

I glanced at Isaac, who stood silently observing me with his dark, enigmatic eyes.

"Let me show you our predicament," he said to her, his eyes still on mine for two heartbeats before he pulled up the photos of the Andersons' ruined great wall, then handed over the iPad. "We're hoping you can dream up a miracle."

• • • • • • • • • •

An hour later, we left Tuli's studio with numerous sketches of her ideas and images of completed projects scanned into Isaac's iPad. Initially, she'd needed several minutes to recover from her immediate recognition of the artist's work and the fact that my donkeyhead of a brother hadn't taken basic precautions to safeguard a piece of irreplaceable artwork instead of *battering right through it.*

"I think it would be best if I never met whoever did this," she'd said, glowering at the wall's "after" pic in horror. "I am not a violent person, but I might end up in jail. Seriously. This is *sickening*."

She had also needed time to adjust to the idea of collaborating—after the fact—with this same world-renowned artist, but once her brain began firing off potential solutions, she started sketching design concepts. Marching past her initial reverence and trepidation, she began to draft bold ideas I never would have conceived.

"Da Vinci's *Last Supper* required restoration to preserve it, and if someone can man up to do *that*, I can do *this*," she'd mumbled to herself.

In the face of her confidence, my not-unreasonable fears about the Anderson project receded from the edge of certain loss, and I began to feel optimistic for the first time.

"What now?" I asked Isaac, attempting to outrun the voice in my head telling me how together Tuli's life was. How unfettered and creative and beautiful. I found myself in a peculiar mental space. Still jealous, but optimistic and grateful.

"Now we convince Sheila Anderson," he answered.

"Okay." I released a pent up breath and clicked my seatbelt into place. "How?"

The motor hummed to life and the AC blasted warm air that turned blessedly cool in seconds.

Facing me, Isaac quirked a brow. "That is *your* job, Ms. McIntyre."

Well, damn.

As we reached the end of the picturesque street, he asked, "Would you like to grab lunch before we go back? It's a little early, but we could beat the crowd here."

"Sure. There's actually a new taco place on 7th I haven't tried yet—"

"Velvet Taco."

"Yeah—that's it. The one in Austin was good. You've been?"

"I live across the street from it." He laughed. "I probably go too often."

"Oh, well, we can go somewhere else. So wait—you do this commute every day?"

"I could eat tacos on the daily. And yeah, the commute is why I got this overpriced car. Figured if I was going to be on the road that long every day, I should be comfortable. I should have better considered the gas mileage though."

"Be jealous—my Prius gets like fifty miles to the gallon. It always surprises me when I need gas because I never need gas. I wanted something more earth-friendly."

"Admirable." He smiled at me and thankfully looked back out to the road, because Christ on a porch swing, my face was warming up—literally—for a full-on blush. *From a compliment about my environmentalism.*

When was the last time Erin McIntyre had a real live crush on a boy? Middle school? Kindergarten? I did not crush; I was *crushed on.* I pointed the AC vent right at my face like I'd seen Mom do when she was going through The Change, as she called it.

Over spicy tikka chicken tacos and creamy cups of *elote*, Isaac restarted the faux interview, asking me to cite skills I possessed that would recommend me for the job.

"Wow, you were for hella real about conducting an after-the-fact interview." I wiped my lips and considered the best way to answer. "Well, I'm a likable people person, evidenced by my election to sorority leadership—I was recruitment chair. I have ample customer service skills as shown in my success as a host. I've also been professionally trained to analyze, diagnose, and treat behavioral deviations and abnormalities, which will help me locate the root problems of our clients and resolve them."

He took his time replying, as usual. "You aren't worried about overstepping? Getting too personal? JMCH is a business, not a therapy office."

A week ago I would have taken offense, but today I was basking in the glow of thwarting Leo. Also, I already had the job. "There's a reason for that old adage *Home is where the heart is*. Our product is a home. Where a person sleeps, eats, spends time with family, friends, and pets—it's inherently personal. How they feel about that place is crucial to their happiness."

After another lengthy pause for reflection (fifteen seconds, like the wait for the crotchety elevator; yes, I counted) he said, "Our marketing department could use your help, I think."

"You trying to get rid of me Maat? Sales wants me, too, you know."

His eyes flashed. *Oops*.

"I said no."

I counted to fifteen, but this time he made no reply.

As we were sorting our lunch containers into the trash and recycling bins, he asked, "So what do you believe your time at JMCH will do for you? My theory is that good workers make better employees when they gain as much—in the form of new skills, stronger confidence, clarity about where their career is ultimately going—as they contribute in labor."

He unlocked the car, which had already returned to cookie-baking temperature. With no shade like the trees on Tuli's street provided, the seats were too hot for bare skin. I slid my sunglasses on and closed my eyes. I had no idea what I would get from working at JMCH except a deferral from making a decision about my future, which stretched out before me like a barren landscape, devoid of solutions or even indistinct clues.

"We can stop if you want," he said.

"Can we find a Starbucks while I formulate my unbelievably clever answer? I need caffeine. *Bad.*"

"Sure."

My tormented night of insufficient sleep was taking its toll. Between the excitement of the first half of the day, a full tummy, and the warmth of the car, I was struggling to stay awake. I wanted to volley another astute answer back to him even if it was half-fudged. I wanted him to think he might have hired me himself if given the chance. I wanted him to *like* me.

A whole-body jolt made me realize I'd *fallen asleep* for a few seconds.

"You sure you're feeling okay?" He looked concerned. "You've been asleep the past several miles."

Oh. My. God. Several *miles?* What if Isaac had said something and I didn't hear him? What if I snored like Daddy? Or drooled? I touched a finger to my chin, which was thank-you-Jesus dry. "Yeah, fine—I had a rough night. Didn't get much sleep."

Swoop. There went that quizzical eyebrow of his, and my belated realization of what I'd just said.

"Um, I mean, I had some bizarre dreams. Probably just surplus stress from this whole wrecked-wall situation—failing at life, Daddy in an uproar, the desire to commit a wee bit of fratricide, the usual." My heart clenched at the lie, but there was no way I could tell him the truth—that I couldn't come to terms with my ex-boyfriend's death. Not when I'd caused him so much pain in the last months of his life, even if it was unintentional.

"Your father just wants the problem resolved. And your brother?

I can't be an accessory, but I'd testify for the defense. You have a sound case for justifiable homicide."

I laughed. "Don't start planning for your deposition just yet. If Tuli comes through, Leo will survive to ruin other people's lives. Hopefully I will be far, far away from his next disaster."

We got drive-through coffee, and just when I'd assumed he'd forgotten all about the interview, he reminded me of his last question: What would working for my father's company do for me and for my career?

I wanted to release a dramatic, angst-filled groan, but I pulled myself together and went for broke. "If I was going to be honest, I guess I'd have to admit that landing this job would give me the opportunity to regroup and decide what I want to do next."

"The 'I need to find myself' rationale? That sounds more like a gap year than career ambition."

"Yeah, well, I said, 'If I was going to be honest,' didn't I?" I sighed and dropped my empty cup into the cupholder between us. "Yes, I took the job because I didn't know what else to do with my life right now. I can't be the first person in the history of employment to do that, whether or not I bypassed having to tell pretty lies during a real interview to land the position."

He sipped his coffee, stared out the windshield with an indecipherable expression, and said nothing.

"What about you? You said once that you took the job you could get because of the recession." I'd circled back around to his weeks-ago reproach that my father had handed me a position created just for me and his indirect admission that working for JMCH wasn't exactly his dream job either.

"And?"

I pressed on despite the vein pulsing at his temple. "And that doesn't sound like someone who's doing exactly what he wants to do with *his* life either. But neither of us is lolling around on a beach drinking mai tais or hiking up the Pacific Crest Trail. We both have our reasons for being there. So what if we didn't disclose every motive for needing or accepting a job? That doesn't mean the work we're doing now is worthless."

This time there was no lengthy pause and then another question, just uncomfortable silence but for the murmur of talk radio, the volume too low to catch more than a word here or there. Whether due to the caffeine or the abruptly ended conversation, I was fully awake for the remainder of the trip back.

As we entered the lobby, he said, "I'll upload the scanned images to our folder and let you use your analytical expertise and congeniality to convince Mrs. Anderson of our proposed repair of her wall. Keep me informed. If she doesn't go for it, I'll have to come up with another angle."

"She'll go for it," I said. I had no idea if she would go for it.

He nodded once with the most fleeting eye contact ever, turned, and jogged up the staircase to the second floor. I could have booked it up those stairs after him, stilettos be damned. By the time I was eighteen, I was accomplished at moving through the world in heels. But he couldn't have made his desire to get away from me clearer. I followed more slowly, and his office door was closed by the time I passed it. The images were in our cloud file, as promised, minutes later, and I wasted no time in calling Sheila Anderson and asking her when she could meet me on-site.

"This will work," I told myself, staring at the images on my giant desktop screen. I wanted to fix this for the Andersons. I wanted to fix it for Daddy. I wanted to rub Leo's face in his failure to spoil everything for everyone. But most of all, I wanted to fix this for Isaac, because only his approval would fix it for me.

chapter *Fourteen*

A couple of weeks later, Daddy and I crossed paths as he huffed inside from a run when I was leaving for yoga. "Well, Princess, I guess you really are the miracle worker Cynthia calls you," he said, mopping his face with a small towel.

"Oh?"

"Harold Anderson withdrew his demand for blood money—says Sheila's happier than a tornado in a trailer park about that young local artist you helped her discover. Apparently she loves being the first in her artsy-fartsy circle to unearth new talent. The girl has agreed to start work on that damned wall the day they close. I think she's doing some other work for them too after that."

"That's great."

I knew all that, of course, because I'd kept in close contact with both Sheila and Tuli as they exchanged ideas for the wall. Tuli would be creating a set of three arched columns, floor-to-ceiling, from stone, cement, and brick: two framing the mural on the wall's outer edges, and one strategically set to screen the damage in the middle. It would cover a bit more of the painting than the ruined portion, but it would enhance the unique feature by providing dimension and a bit of protection as well.

I also knew that Isaac had planned to pay Tuli's fee and material costs out of his own pocket, which made zero sense. None of this mess was his fault, even if he'd made it his responsibility. Before I could insist on paying it myself, Tuli waived the whole cost when Sheila Anderson hired her to transform a nondescript shed in the middle of her planned garden into a she-shed, a thing I'd never heard of until that moment. I googled and found loads of Pinterest and blog pages dedicated to the adult version of backyard playhouses.

"She wants it to be a space where she can enjoy her garden, a book, and a glass of wine, instead of just a structure to house tools," Tuli told me. "She said, 'I want it to look like a storybook cottage,' so I sent her some proposal sketches that were basically miniatures of my house, and she *loved* them." Her laugh was contagious. "I gave her my quote for the work, and she not only accepted it, she added a bonus for me to start as soon as the wall is complete. I'm good. Not taking Isaac's money or yours either."

"But—"

"Nope, girl. Look, I wouldn't have this career if Isaac hadn't picked me to be on his team back in high school, and I'm elated to be able to help him now. Besides, work begets work. This gal is a big talker with a wide-ranging social circle. I make her happy? It will come back to me."

"Speaking of tornadoes," Daddy said just as I reached the door. "Cynthia wants you to go to the convention. It's a big once-a-year event. She's taking one of her people too."

"Convention? What?" I shifted the rolled mat under my arm.

The only convention I'd ever attended was my sorority's national biyearly shindig two years ago. Meeting active members from all over the country and alumnae ranging from sophisticated recent grads to refined, white-haired retirees was amazing. Three days of meetings and workshops with wall-to-wall ladies in business attire, three evenings of the same people but in semiformal dress. Collegiates weren't allowed to drink publicly, though private after-parties in our rooms happened—*duh*. But chapter advisors and GHs expected us to arrive fresh and professional the next morning and have our butts in chairs for the day's events, and woe to anyone who skipped out.

I got the feeling a mixed-gender construction convention would not be the same. *At all*. I tried to keep the incredulity out of my voice. "You want me to go to a builders' convention? With Cynthia?" If the salesperson she was bringing was Joshua, I was determined to be violently ill with some unspecified stomach virus. "Is it meant for people outside Sales?"

"Oh, yeah. It's not just for salespeople, but it's client-facing info, so we always send her and whoever her favorite of the moment is. Hank usually goes too but may send Isaac this year—some kind of conflict with Miranda and surgery."

"Miranda is having surgery?"

And Isaac might go?

Daddy's unconcern about a lifelong friend's upcoming surgery was baffling until he said, "Nothing *health related*. She doesn't have your mother's good fortune and genes." He winked and chuckled, and I wondered if he knew about Mom's trips to the spa for injectables, fillers, and peels. She always told him she was getting a facial or a mani-pedi.

"When is it? Won't it interfere with my work? I mean, especially if Isaac is going—"

"We'll manage, no problem."

Not the most solid commendation, being regarded as unessential. I'd helped a few clients, but I'd spent a huge portion of my recent time resolving the harm caused by one of those attempts to help, and I couldn't have done that without Isaac. My first two months had been like a game of Chutes and Ladders.

"Have you ever gone to one?"

"Used to go every year back when the boys lived at home." He looked over his shoulder and lowered his voice. "It was a nice little escape. Meet some vendors, learn a couple things, speak to some business-friendly political hopefuls, drink beer, smoke cigars, play some golf…" He smiled at his nostalgic memories and sighed. "What happens in Vegas…"

"Daddy, *eww*, I hope you don't mean that how it sounds because Mom would have you neutered."

He waved a hand. "Your mother knows I'm all talk. And considering the existence of you four kids, it's a bit late for neutering, ha ha!"

I sighed and covered my face with my hand. I did not appreciate the tumble of thoughts I would have to spend the next week trying to eject from my brain. "And you want *me* to go to this thing?"

"I have every confidence that you'll represent J. McIntyre more discerningly than your old man ever could." He grimaced. "And a damn sight better than your older brother. He went last year, and Hank said he was like a crazed wildcat—too much drinking and too much tail." He laughed at his own joke like he was prouder of Leo's undisciplined behavior than he should be, especially in front of his daughter.

I scowled. "You should have warned me I'd need brain bleach for this conversation."

"Sorry, Princess." He chuckled.

In truth, my brothers had casually annihilated my opinion of the archetypal male long ago. I was too close to the action. I knew too much. From the swapped boasting I overheard, to sounds and smells emanating from their rooms, to porn left on browsers of shared computers when I was still in elementary school—I was all too aware of what boys were about before my earliest notion that boys who were *not* my brothers were sometimes cute. I'd been horrified.

Clearly, I'd gotten past the horror.

But if boys and men were routinely crude and tactless and too often deceitful about what they expected, I made sure I had the power to forgive what was tolerable and reject what wasn't. If there was too much *boys will be boys* in my home and the world at large, I would be the one who could walk away from anyone—and I had, almost every time. Sure, I'd been down after a few of those necessary breakups, but guys used to doing the discarding were prone to resentment when the shoe was on the other foot. Any sadness I might have felt evaporated the minute they threw a public tantrum or wrote a vulgar Facebook post.

One night in high school, I was at Campania Pizza with several girls from my cheer squad, inhaling slices of double cheese and pepperoni after we'd come home from an all-day tournament in Waco. My most recent ex—who'd turned into a total ass in a record two weeks of going out—walked up to the table with a couple of his bros. He stared down at me, eyes narrowed, and I wondered how in the hell I'd ever liked him.

"How can you have red hair and be such a cold bitch?"

"How can you be tall and be such a whiny little shit, *Todd*," one of the girls said. Everyone laughed, including his friends.

That was the last I heard from Todd.

Sometimes breakups were mutual. Other times the guy was hurt, and I felt like I'd kicked a kitten every time I saw him. That was the case for Brian, who'd given me a handwritten note swearing he was sorry for whatever he'd done and promising he would do anything to get me back. I couldn't tell him I was just sixteen and bored. He moped for a couple of months but was never spiteful. When I saw him holding hands with another girl, I was happy for him.

I'd been so sure that would be my story with Chaz. That he would get over my refusal and move on. I was so wrong.

Yoga class was a total waste. I couldn't seem to clear my mind. The harder I tried, the more errant thoughts pushed their way through. The teacher had to correct my horrid form a dozen times though I seldom needed any adjustment at all. When thoughts of Chaz began to play as if on a loop, I knew I could expect the dream that night. I wasn't used to advance notice; it preferred to take me by surprise. Sometimes, though, I could feel it coming, and nothing I did or didn't do would stop it.

My hands went cold and I got even clumsier and more distracted, finally excusing myself after whispering to my teacher that I wasn't feeling well.

"Feel better," she said.

If only. At least it was Saturday, and I could sleep in or nap the next day.

As I drove home, I tried to force my mind to something pleasant. Something simple. Like the sound of ocean waves against the sand, or a perfect slice of cheesecake, or the heady buzz of a first kiss. For some tragi-comic reason, the thought of kissing brought Isaac Maat to mind. I laughed at the absurdity. But standing under a cool shower minutes later, eyes closed and hands sliding over my own wet skin, all I could think of was Isaac, who didn't like me. Who didn't want me working with him, for him. Who would celebrate if I turned in my notice and departed JMCH forever.

But his smile, the few times I'd seen it. His soft laugh. The sharp, masculine planes of his handsome face. The heat I felt from his eyes when he trained them on me, which he seemed to struggle against ever doing. The likelihood that he felt the same insistent pull I did was remote. A slim chance, at best. A humiliating thumbs-down, at worst. But he'd taken my one hulking failure in hand and turned it around instead of letting it ruin me. He'd risked his professional standing to do it.

And I had no idea why.

• • • • • • • • • •

I entered the break room with my empty coffee mug just as Joshua shoved the near-empty carafe back onto the drip tray, which was still on. When he saw me, he leaned against the counter and began bad-mouthing his boss in low, angry tones, ignorant of my silent aggravation. I rinsed the carafe, pulled out the coffee canister and a filter, and began making a fresh pot of coffee, after which I was obliged to wait for it to brew while he yammered on about his grievances.

Cynthia had emailed her team to announce that she was taking Megan to the convention.

"When I confronted her, she had the nerve to imply that Megan's sales record was equal to mine, which is utter bullshit, and then bring up the fact that I went last year! Like that should prevent me from going *this* year!"

Cynthia Pike, for all that I didn't relish the thought of reporting to her directly because she was always *on*, was the Sales VP of one of the largest, most successful builders in DFW. She was capable of calculating, to the penny, the sales of each of her three salespeople. I almost said *Wow—she has a lot of 'nerve' choosing which employee accompanies her to the convention* but I didn't bother because Joshua wouldn't have caught my sarcastic tone. He was one of those people who never perceived sarcasm about themselves.

Since arriving at JMCH, I'd humored him because he *did* disclose a shit-ton of info about fellow employees and clients, even if half of it was so speculative that there was no way I'd have relied on anything he said unless I heard it from a more reputable source or witnessed it myself. Erratically credible or not, however, the rumors he passed on gave me a beneficial heads-up often enough to keep me from putting an end to his gossip.

"Maybe Cynthia trusts you so much that she wants you here to handle things while she's away." I continued the placating, diplomatic cover I'd maintained for weeks.

His terse *pshaw* showed how unappeased he was determined to be. "I know why she's taking Megan, and it has everything to do with Maat and nothing to do with what I'm entitled to."

"What?"

"Hank is sending Maat in his place this year. And Megan has a *thing* for Maat. Clearly, Cynthia is playing matchmaker."

The thought of *Cynthia Pike* playing matchmaker for *anyone* was the single most ridiculous thing I'd heard out of him. The idea that Megan would find Isaac attractive was less ridiculous. The machine beeped, and I turned to pour myself coffee and take a deep breath through my nose. I had no reason or right to feel possessive of my boss or be piqued over some improbable office romance he might decide to carry on. Even if Megan seemed not at all his type.

And what is his type? my brain said, complete with mocking tone. *You?*

I added sugar and creamer and took my time stirring. "I *really* doubt Cynthia would choose who will accompany her on a corporate trip based on an interoffice crush."

He stared at the open doorway and lowered his voice to a whisper. "It's probably some sort of vicarious thing for her because she's such a hard-ass and at her age, I doubt she even has a man. She's never brought anyone to the spring picnic or the Christmas party." Just when I thought he'd said something off-the-charts offensive, he one-upped himself. "That's the sort of shit you can expect when a woman is in charge—some of them, anyway, no offense to you. You're not like her."

My feminist hackles rose like tiny livid spikes. "And by 'not like her,' you mean?"

He shrugged one shoulder. "You're logical, not so fly-off-the-handle and prone to freaking out over every little thing."

Cynthia was both logical and shrewd, and if her interactions with employees were comparable to anyone I knew, it would be my father. They were both aggressive, classic type-A extroverts. Even so, she surpassed him in the ability to be more gracious with clients even if she wanted to grab them by the throat and squeeze (this from an email about one of our orange-tabbed clients when she was at wit's end with their incessant grievances). I was forming a retort that didn't throw Daddy under the bus when Joshua changed the subject, glancing at the open doorway and still whispering.

"Speaking of Maat—what d'you think of that Ferguson shit?"

I froze. "*Excuse me?*"

"Those cop haters rioting and looting over that criminal getting himself shot. A buddy of mine lives near there. He thinks they wanna burn the whole city down. Crazy shit. Man, I'm glad I live *here*."

I'd come home from yoga Saturday afternoon, still distracted and stressed, to find every television in the house blaring what was known of the shooting that had happened hours before, replaying clips of interviews and the beginnings of protests. My parents shook their heads and worried over the state of the world and made disturbing oh-thank-God declarations similar to Joshua's about where we resided and the gates we lived behind. Later that night and all day yesterday, the black community's reaction to the shooting was the only news anyone was reporting, and the opinions were ambiguous.

"What does that have to do with Isaac?"

Joshua stuck his chin out and opened his hand as though it was obvious what protests and riots in another state had to do with my supervisor.

Responses stuck in my throat, none of them exactly right. I'd never in my life called out racism except to challenge the idiotic things Leo sometimes said. But torching Leo was easy—he was a walking, talking monument to insensitivity, not a coworker.

Isaac walked in then, cup in hand, and the entire conversation felt like something I'd enabled or even contributed to, because it consisted of words said in front of me, to me, that I hadn't yet confronted or rejected. The unspoken responses unstuck and fled, and in their place came defenses to an accusation Isaac had not made. His mere presence made it for him.

Joshua's insolent smirk and glib, "Lunch later, Erin?" showed that he felt that same accusation. But he wasn't shamed by it.

"I don't think so, no."

He frowned, then flinched when the loudspeaker above our heads crackled to life and emitted Cynthia Pike's displeased voice. "Joshua Swearingen, please report to the *weekly sales meeting* in my office. We're waiting for you."

He left, mumbling, "I'm coming. *Jesus*." The clock on the wall—which he'd been facing the whole time he'd been talking to me—indicated that he was seven minutes late.

"You okay?" Isaac said, drawing his eyes away long enough to fill his cup.

"Yes. Fine."

Somehow he knew I wasn't fine and I was lying about being so. His face went blank, and he left the room without another word.

chapter *Fifteen*

Jacqueline: A couple of weeks ago, I told Lucas I thought you were avoiding me.

Me: Why would you think that?

I'd received her text three hours earlier but waited until it was midnight in Ohio, where she lived now, to respond. Jacqueline wasn't a night owl. During the two years we'd roomed together, she was often asleep before I came in, and she'd signed up for eight a.m. classes almost every freaking semester. Whenever we'd partied together, she would start looking bleary-eyed just as the club or party got going. She'd tolerated the requisite teasing like a champ.

After sending my reply, I plugged my phone into its charger, laid it on my nightstand, and opened a novel with only twenty or so pages still unread. I expected to hear back from her tomorrow, so when my phoned chimed with her texted response, I just stared at the locked screen, which read: Message: Jacqueline. It chimed with a second text a moment later.

Jacqueline: Maybe because we haven't talked in so long that I can't remember when we last talked? Every time I call you, I get your VM. I text and you answer hours later. And you've called me when (I think) you knew I wouldn't be able to answer? I'm trying not to be paranoid. I know it's been two years since I moved away, but I thought that even if we were hundreds of miles apart, we'd stay close.

Jacqueline: I've been wrapped up in school and Lucas, and I'm sorry it took me so long to realize we had drifted apart. I have things to tell you, but I don't even care about that because I can't shake the feeling that something is wrong and you're not telling me. (In case you were wondering, the not being paranoid thing isn't going so well.)

This was not the result I'd intended. Jacqueline had always been a diligent student, and I would have never resented her putting academics first, especially at her dream school. And her perfect relationship with Lucas, her perfect boyfriend… only a coldhearted bitch would have begrudged her that. She deserved every bit of her happiness. That's why I hadn't wanted to unload my emotional wreckage on her. I hadn't wanted to tell her about my nightmares or the guilt I couldn't leave behind.

She'd been staunchly supportive when I'd called to tell her about Chaz's proposal, my rejection of it, and our subsequent breakup. "You did the right thing," she said. "If there was no possibility of your changing your mind, you had no choice." When he died six months later, she'd asked if I needed her to come home for the funeral. "I'll come if you need me, Erin," she'd said, despite her grueling senior-year schedule of compositions and performances at Oberlin. "I can be on a plane tonight."

"There's no need for you to upend your week," I'd told her, certain I would survive it, as much as I dreaded that day. "Almost everyone I know will be there. I won't be alone."

Burying my ex had been as awful as I'd feared it would be and then some. I stood surrounded by almost the entire shocked and grieving Greek community. *Everyone* was crying, including the guys, standing in their ties and blazers, dozens of likenesses of the boy we had lost. Aisles ahead of me, Chaz's family sat—his parents, his older brother, his little sister—leaning against each other, their sobs anguished.

Twenty-one-year-old boys aren't supposed to die. They're supposed to build lives for themselves, start families, grow old, look after and bury their parents. Sixty or seventy years ahead of schedule, Chaz was gone, and it made sense to no one sitting in that church.

The funeral service—standard consoling words from the pastor, reminiscences from three of his close friends, a tearful eulogy from his father—had been agonizing. But the lowering into the ground of the casket containing the remains of a boy I'd cared for, deeply—that was the worst. That was the moment it became real. There was no waking up from it. Not for Chaz. Not for any of us.

Minutes later, his grief-stricken mother confronted me and

dropped her bomb on my distraught heart, and my guilt mushroomed. I couldn't escape its explosions, still. I was beginning to think I never would. Some damage is irreversible, it seems, and all the remorse in the world won't make up for it.

Me: J, you haven't done anything at all. I'm just trying to find my feet with this job, and I screwed up in the most massive, embarrassing way recently. It's fine now, but I was preoccupied for a while.

The phone rang just as I hit Send. She was calling. And this time she knew I had my phone in my hand. I took a deep breath and answered.

"Well, that was sneaky. I taught you well, young padawan."

"I did learn from the master. Are you gonna tell me what's really up?"

I started to go with *Nothing, really, I swear*, but I couldn't do it. I waded in, hoping to stay in the shallow end.

"I've just had a rough time lately. Leo seems to believe I'm trespassing on his territory or something, and I think he purposefully fucked something up with one of my clients to make me look bad."

"That dick! Your dad couldn't have been happy about that?"

"No." My laugh was more rueful than amused. "But ultimately the fuckup was my fault. And my boss had to fix it."

"So it's okay now?"

"Getting there."

"But Erin…" In her typical Jacqueline manner, she weighed and rearranged her words before uttering them. A slight pucker would have formed between her brows, and she would be chewing her lip. Turning the dilemma this way and that. Trying to sense her way through the bullshit to the heart of the matter. "I feel like this emotional slide started before your job. Before graduation. You needed me that day, last fall. Jesus, it's been almost a year. I should have insisted on coming instead of letting you talk me out of it. You were there for me during the lowest points of my life, and I wasn't there for you."

I wanted to absolve her, if only so she'd stop prying. I knew she was doing it out of love, and that meant I had to protect her from believing she'd failed me in some way. So I told her the truth. "The only thing that might have changed if you'd been there was my hearing something I deserved to hear."

"What do you mean?"

"If you'd been with me, his mom might not have come up to me after the graveside service. She might not have told me that Chaz had never returned that solitaire. That he'd never quit planning ways to win me back. That during all those months, he hadn't given up."

"Oh, Erin." Her voice wavered. "You can't shoulder the responsibility for what *he* chose to do or believe. I'm so sorry her grief made her say those unkind things to you, but his response to your ending the relationship was not your fault, and you *do not* deserve to feel guilty for it. That's what you're doing, isn't it?"

"I hurt him, J."

She dug in her heels. "What if you had accepted that ring, knowing you didn't want to marry him? What if that accident had never happened and you were engaged or even married now—just so you wouldn't hurt his feelings? You know that doesn't make sense.

You wouldn't have done it."

"I know, but—the accident *did* happen. And he spent the last six months of his life"—I swallowed, fighting tears—"miserable and in love with someone who didn't—didn't—"

"You told him the truth. The fact that he wouldn't or couldn't accept it is regrettable and tragic, yes, but it's not your fault. Is this why I haven't heard you say a word about grad school for almost a year, though being a therapist is all you've ever wanted to do? Why you're working for your dad and living at home?"

My silence answered for me.

"We can't live our lives in fear. You showed me that, once upon a time."

It had been so much easier to be wise and encouraging when it was someone else's sadness. When I didn't really know how this sort of despair felt from inside my own skin.

"After you told me about your breakup," she said, "I had an epiphany about what Kennedy had done—breaking up with me after I'd followed him to *his* first-choice university instead of applying to my own. It hurt. It unmoored me. But he had realized we weren't on the same page anymore, even if I didn't. And he was being honest with me in ending my delusions of what we were. In setting himself free, he set me free, just like you were releasing Chaz to find someone right for him.

"I don't know how Kennedy feels now about me being with Lucas, and I don't actually care. But I know if Chaz had moved on and found someone else, you would have been happy for him. Because you're a good person, Erin."

Her audible tears brought mine to the surface. We sniffled wordlessly for a minute or so.

"Well, now I feel really dumb for not calling you sooner."

"I called *you*," she said.

"Girl, throw me a bone here."

"You answered. Finally."

I appreciated what she'd done, allowing me to unload this thing I'd shared with no one but a couple of therapists I would never see again. But I couldn't tell her about the nightmares. It would only increase her concern, and I'd worried her enough. Besides, maybe they would stop now that I'd shared the principal basis for them with my best friend.

"What was your news?" I asked, redirecting the conversation. "I want to hear it."

"Oh—I'm earning my master's in musical education from Oberlin. It's a fifteen-month program. I started in June, and I'll be certified to teach any grade from pre-K through high school when I'm done."

"I thought you didn't want to teach?" I was more grateful than she knew to discuss her life and not mine.

"I'm still going to pursue other options too—joining a jazz orchestra or a band. Doing one doesn't have to exclude me from the other. If anything, they'll be mutually reinforcing. But it turns out I like working with kids, especially middle-grade kids, which is apparently really odd." We both laughed. "But they're so musically malleable at that age! And a teaching gig will keep me from being a starving musician."

"That's great." In sharp contrast to my parents, Jacqueline's were so supportive of her academic ambitions that they'd been upset with her for sidelining them by following her high school boyfriend to college. I stomped on my senseless envy before it could crawl from its gloomy well of self-pity.

"So when are you going to get those applications in, woman?" she said then, as if she'd heard my bellyaching. "Unless construction work has become your new catnip. I'm visualizing you in a hard hat and tool belt right now. They don't make a lot of sense with your customary sky-high heels and pencil skirts, but you do look pretty hot."

I snorted. "Yeah, they *do not* allow the office suits near the tools, and hard hats are heavy and smell like *feet* for some unfathomable reason." I sighed. "J, my grades senior year were shit. I barely pulled off an adequate enough GPA to graduate. Grad schools would take one look at my transcript and laugh their asses off." *Just as my parents had assumed.*

"So you'll need superior GRE scores to compensate for the not-so-glorious GPA, and maybe take a few leveling courses to prove to them and yourself that you've got this. Sign up for a GRE prep course. The warrior redhead I know and love will crush that surmountable obstacle to her dreams."

When had my pragmatic best friend turned into the chirpy optimist in this relationship? That had been *my* MO once upon a time. She was the pensive musician—cautious and sometimes in need of a positive bump in the right direction. I was the enthusiastic cheerleader—seer of bright sides, believer in silver linings, and giver of inspirational speeches. Those had been our roles.

"I'll think about it."

"Erin, what you did for me sophomore year, and for Mindi—that wasn't just you being *nice*. That was you doing what you were meant to do—being an unfaltering advocate and an empathetic guide. You believed us both when we needed it most. I'm sure you're doing a great job there and your dad would love to keep you forever, but please think long and hard before you give up your aspirations. Your gifts are needed in the world."

"Thank you for that," I said, loving her unfaltering faith in me and keeping my *But what if I've already given up?* to myself. I made myself smile and repeat, "I'll think about it." I tried my best to sound sincere, to *be* sincere. But the thought of prep courses and admission exams, letters of recommendations and personal statements, transcripts and applications… All of it was overwhelming.

I hadn't known, until that moment, how far I had wandered from myself. I'd thought being home would help me remember how to be brave, but I was only hiding from the woman I'd fought to become and sliding back into the coddled girl I'd been. I had never felt less courageous.

"You're seeing a therapist there, right? This isn't just your best friend advising you from hundreds of miles away, with no training to actually help you—unless you need to know an obscure musical term or learn how to play a scale."

This was the reason I'd avoided conversation with J. She was not a clueless family member or caring-but-easily-diverted-by-little-white-lies friend. In college, she'd seen through my smoke screen of faux positivity when others hadn't. I'd been raised to be this way. She hadn't. This was one of the odd truths we came to—the fact that her mother, cranky and anxious as she often was, allowed for cranky and anxious in her daughter, whereas I was expected to plaster on a smile no matter my inner turmoil or unhappiness. From the time I could walk, faking happy was second nature.

I swallowed. "Of course."

"Okay. Good." Her intuition was no match for a blatant lie over the phone, even if something deep inside me wanted it to be. "My parents are coming here for Thanksgiving, and Lucas and I are going to the coast for Christmas to stay with his dad and stepmom, and with this intense program I'm doing, we may not be back in DFW for over a year. I know Cleveland isn't your first choice for vacay, Miss Skiing in Aspen or Beachcombing in the South of France, but you're welcome to come stay with me anytime for a long weekend and some BFF bonding."

"That sounds perfect." I bit my lip to stop its useless quiver. I wanted to be the Erin she remembered. Fierce and confident, ready to take on the world. Was that girl still inside me somewhere? Had she ever existed, or was she a figment of my imagination, as much illusion as my Friday-night cheer smile?

chapter *Sixteen*

Isaac stood in my doorway in his deep violet shirt and tie—my preferred combo of everything I'd seen him wear. The competition was ongoing; any day could bring a new challenger to the field. But this one had been defending its title without much effort for the past month. *Yum.*

The distraction over his wardrobe choice for the day had sidetracked me from the puzzling words he'd just spoken. I replayed them in my mind: "You might want to consider costume choices before today's meeting. Departments coordinate."

"I should do what now?"

"Halloween costumes. Mandatory."

"You have got to be joking." I hadn't been around the past several Halloweens, but I couldn't remember Daddy going out the door in a costume. "How long has this been going on?"

"Since before I started." He shifted one shoulder up, unconcerned. "But if you have a complaint, you know where to go with it."

I scowled at him from behind my monitor. "Low blow, Maat."

"If the shoe fits…" His eyes flicked beneath my desk to my crossed legs and my black patent Mary Jane kitten heels. My pleated highland plaid skirt and white blouse completed my retro private school vibe for the first Monday of fall.

I recrossed my legs, loving and hating the brisk tingles I felt *everywhere* when his eyes tracked the movement for a split second before he tore them away. My heart rate sped up, for fuck's sake. His responses shouldn't affect me as though I was some virginal adolescent. I was a woman with plenty of sexual experience, dammit.

And *whyyy* was I thinking about that in capacity or connection with my boss?

Focus, McIntyre. Halloween. "Hank goes for this? And Cynthia?"

"Are you kidding me? Sales wins almost every year. Last year they did *The Wizard of Oz.*"

"*Wins*?"

"The costume contest, held during the party. The winning department, chosen by your father, gets lunch ordered in from any local restaurant they choose. Best costume, which the whole office votes on, wins a Costco gift card for a hundred bucks."

"I had no idea adults behaved like this." Okay, so I'd seen my sorority's alumnae, the height of professionalism and accomplishment, do some silly things at convention. Like when the Governing Council performed in a lip-synched video for Revelry night at the convention I got to attend. I'd also borne mortified witness to my parents getting their dance on at the country club after a few too many drinks. "I mean at *work*," I added.

Isaac smirked, lips pressed in a straight, tight line except the very edges, which twitched like involuntary half sneers. He put up a hell of a fight to maintain that smirk without allowing it to morph into a smile, but he finally gave up, leaned forward, and laughed out loud, eyes squeezed tight, fingers pinching the bridge of his nose. Deep and potent, the reverberations pushed under my skin and soaked into my unsuspecting heart.

I was grateful for his closed eyes. The man was *laughing at me*, and I wanted to twirl in a circle, jumping up and down as though I'd just won a race. This was not good.

"Welcome to adulthood, Ms. McIntyre," he said, taking two steps into the hallway before stepping back to say, "Last year, Finance and Accounting were Minions. It thwarted my ability to fully enjoy Joshua the Cowardly Lion. I'm counting on your veto for any of that nonsense."

• • • • • • • • • • •

Department meetings about Halloween were carried out like top secret military operations. Closed doors and low voices and shredding—actual shredding, in a shredder—of notes that could fall into "the wrong hands" according to the office receptionist, Kelsey, who urged vigilance around other department members, whom she called *spies*, with no hint at levity.

Isaac and I exchanged a look, and I had to stare at the memo listing the "rules" of the contest to keep from giggling.

Hank's team was composed of Kelsey, Isaac, Connie in HR, Trey and Laurel in accounting, and Rhett—our IT guy who had the world's longest comb-over, spoke in such a near-whisper he frequently had to repeat himself, and looked less like a Rhett than anyone I'd ever met—and me.

The first suggestion, a bowling ball and pins, was right out.

"There are only eight of us," I said. "We won't be able to be a strike." I did not look toward Isaac. I would have lost it.

Trey, who was somewhere between thirty and forty, suggested

green army men, but Laurel and I vetoed painting our faces green.

"Snow White and the seven dwarves?" Connie said.

"No," everyone answered.

Half an hour later, I was beginning to understand how Minions had come about. I no longer cared what costume I was going to have to wear, and I wanted to go to my tiny office and scream into the cute fuzzy throw pillow I'd bought for my chair. It wouldn't be the first time.

And that's how, the morning of Halloween, I ended up in a metallic gold cheer outfit with shimmery gold tights, holding sparkly gold pom-poms, sporting strings of gold sequins wound through my hair, which was pulled into a high ponytail. Even my makeup was metallic. Why? Because someone suggested, "Let's all be real-life trophies!" and everyone thought that was the best idea since... Minions. I had to admit it wasn't the most abhorrent suggestion ever. Also, I'd been a competitive cheer captain and a goddamned Panhellenic delegate. Representing my squad was ingrained in my bones like an eternal honor code, even if that meant showing up dressed like a freak-show disco cheerleader.

As soon as we got to work, we convened in the HR office. The more competitive among us took turns getting dressed in the cramped copy room so the other teams wouldn't see their costumes until the judging ceremony. From Connie, each of us collected a square, spray-painted box we were supposed to stand on, because yes, we had devised poses for ourselves. The boxes sported shiny plaques listing our names and the life-sized trophies we represented, courtesy of Connie and Kelsey, who were in it to win it:

TREY ROSS: 1ST PLACE NATIONAL SKEET SHOOT BATTLE
CONNIE GARCIA: 3RD PLACE COLLIN COUNTY BAKEOFF: PIES
ISAAC MAAT: 1ST PLACE SLIDE RULE COMPETITION—HUTCHESON JR HIGH

First thought: *Bahahahaha—nerd.* Second thought: *It's against the goddamn laws of nature for a nerd to be that hot.*

"Why does yours say third place?" Laurel (1ST PLACE LPGA FINALS) asked Connie.

"Because I placed third?" Connie said, as though explaining something so obvious it shouldn't need an explanation. She opened a craft-store bag and pulled out a golden Styrofoam replica of a pie, necessary to her chosen pose of a middle-aged lady holding a prizewinning dessert. I wondered if there was any gold spray paint left in Southlake in the wake of Connie and Kelsey's determination to steal the title from Sales this year.

Laurel gasped, eyes wide under her gold visor, knuckles tight on her golden putter. "Wait. They're supposed to be for *real* stuff we won?"

"I doubt Trey's ever won a national *anything*," Kelsey said. Her gold costume included a gold tiara and multi-tiered ball gown with a sash naming her Amarillo's Miss Teen Pageant Finalist. "Just go with it!"

Laurel pointed at my box. "You really won *that*, didn't you?"

My box read: ERIN MCINTYRE: 1ST PLACE DISTRICT CHEER CHAMPION. "Um, yeah." I shrugged one shoulder and she sighed.

"I really won mine too," Rhett said. "I was an athlete in college." He was wearing what he wore every day: pleated slacks and a bowling shirt, except everything was gold. His box was inscribed: MVP, INTERCOLLEGIATE SINGLES CHAMPIONSHIP, AJBC 1978.

"AJBC?" Laurel asked.

"The American Junior Bowling Congress, which became the Young American Bowling Alliance in 1982 and was incorporated into the United States Bowling Congress in 2005."

"Ah," Laurel said. "That's… cool."

"And also real," he said, staring at the box proclaiming Laurel an LPGA Finalist.

"Isaac, what's a slide rule? Some sort of dance?" Kelsey asked, my cue that my hot, nerdy, surly, inexplicably protective boss had entered the room.

My back was to the door. I didn't turn, but my posture realigned and my breath grew shallower. I could feel him looking me over in that surreptitious way of his. Or maybe I just hoped he was. None of us had disclosed our intended trophies to anyone but Connie, whose husband had engraved the plaques. Sipping my coffee, I willed myself to appear indifferent.

Indifferent. HA. Fat chance, McIntyre.

"Um, no. It's a math competition."

I stole a covert side glance as he came to stand beside me, nerdy hot in a gold lamé shirt and slacks, unridiculous even with the gold pocket protector and pens, a tie made of gold sequins, and gold-framed glasses.

"Oh." Kelsey looked disappointed. "But you look like a seventies funk vocalist. Except you'd need to let your hair grow out more." She held her hands six inches out from her head.

I choked on my coffee, but he chuckled, unfazed.

"Where did you get those *shoes?*" She pointed. "They make

actual gold Chucks?"

"Ebay," he said, giving me a rapid once-over. Our eyes met and his were warm and dark, but inscrutable, as always. I couldn't tell if he was repulsed or turned on by my golden cheering getup, but one thing was certain—he wasn't indifferent.

Trey emerged from the copy room, dressed in a camouflage cap and coveralls that had been spray-painted. The paint was scattering from him like gold dust with every bend of a knee or elbow, but the camo pattern showed through the thin layer of paint. He was holding what appeared to be an actual firearm, which had to be against company regulations even if it had been goldified like everything else in the room.

"Is that thing real?" Laurel gaped, echoing my thoughts. "Because I swear to God, Trey."

"It's not loaded!"

Uncle Hank came in then, wearing some sort of gold superhero outfit complete with faux bulging muscles. His feet were stuffed into Tony Lama boots that had been coated in gold glitter, as had the cowboy hat he shoved onto his head before picking up his box, which read: HANK GREENE, 1ST PLACE TEXAS TROPHY HUSBAND. Miranda had outdone herself.

He glanced around, taking in our costumes and chuckling until he got to Trey. "Is that a real shotgun?"

Trey repeated his defense a bit less forcefully to the CFO. "It's not loaded."

"Jesus H. Christ." Hank took the gun, opened and checked the barrel for ammo, and handed it back, shaking his head. "You didn't think to yourself, 'Maybe bringing an actual firearm to a professional office building isn't a bright idea'? A toy would have done. Soon as the contest concludes, that thing goes out in your truck—if Aaron doesn't wrap it around your neck first."

Trey dropped his defensive demeanor and swallowed. "Shit. I forgot."

I turned toward Isaac, confused. It sounded like they were talking about me.

"Aaron in marketing," he murmured. "I'll explain later."

"Ah." Every now and then, someone summoned Aaron or me over the intercom and clarified which of us they wanted with a last name or, more often, "Marketing Aaron" or "Liaison Erin"—a shortened title I did not appreciate.

• • • • • • • • • • •

After our free lunch from Truluck's—because of course we beat Sales' done-to-death *Scooby Doo* cast and Operations' even less imaginative Corona six-pack (and a slice of lime—portrayed by Ted's secretary, who won the Costco card, bless her heart)—I asked Isaac for the promised explanation about Aaron from Marketing and Trey's shotgun.

He glanced behind us on the staircase, but we were alone between floors. "Aaron's sister was a shooting victim a few years back—one of those 'disgruntled ex-employee' situations. She hadn't even worked with the guy. She was just in the hallway when he rounded a corner and started shooting. First one shot. Only one killed."

I faltered on a step and gripped the railing. Aaron was a traditional marketing type—high energy, usually smiling or joking. But I'd come into the break room one afternoon, and he'd been standing, staring out the window, his arms crossed.

"Hi there, Marketing Aaron," I'd said.

He always replied, *Hey there, Liaison Erin*, and then we'd both laugh or groan—often both.

He'd turned, mumbled, "Hey," grabbed his cup of coffee from the counter, and left the room. I wasn't having the best day—one of my clients was rebuffing every effort at conciliation and Isaac was being scowly and brusque—so Aaron's response had felt personal. I'd spent the next hour wondering if he was pissed off at me and feeling miffed at his rudeness because I had been nothing but nice.

It's easy to forget that we encounter people every day who are waging private emotional battles or enduring invisible pain—minor or all encompassing, fleeting or relentless. Some lash out constantly, their anguish so near the surface or so agonizing that it erupts from them. Some mask their pain with levity or bury it and block it off. Both need and deserve compassion. My training had taught me that fundamental truth, but I'd somehow overlooked it.

Isaac and I stopped at his office door.

"Aaron didn't seem to have a problem during the party. I guess that's good?"

He picked up the end of his sequined tie and examined it. "I called him beforehand. So he'd know. In my mind, that isn't the sort of thing to let play out."

I agreed with him, though the thought hadn't occurred to me.

"I think he appreciated the heads-up so he wouldn't be ambushed by a surprise reminder of the worst news he ever got."

"I'm sure he did."

Those yawning potholes of grief weren't always avoidable. Hearing a song Chaz had loved or seeing his fraternity letters on a college boy's T-shirt could trigger reminders of him. Passing his birthday and holidays, one by one, that he would never experience again, until I reached the anniversary of his death weeks ago. No nightmare that night. Just crying in the shower. Just overarching sadness and a stupid relief that the day had fallen on a Saturday so I could hide away from everyone. Just going over what I had done and what I could have done for the millionth time.

This was the second Halloween he'd missed. The next few weeks would bring the second Thanksgiving, the second Christmas, and another new year.

I forced my thoughts to the here and now, to the man standing in front of me who was watching whatever clues were playing across my face. *Erin mask, engaged.* I smiled up at him. "Going to any parties tonight? You've already got a winning costume."

Awareness of what I had just done lit his eyes. I had purposefully veiled my thoughts rather than sharing them, and he knew it. *Did Isaac Maat recognize my self-protective suppression because he did the same?* I wanted to ask what he was hiding, but I didn't dare reveal my hand. He wouldn't have told me anyway.

"Yeah, but I'd have to stand on my box or no one would know what I was supposed to be."

"Isaac, no one knows what you're supposed to be *with* the box."

He laughed. "You knew."

"Don't give me too much credit. I have a nerdy brother."

He angled his head. "Not Leo."

My turn to laugh. "Corona Bottle Number Six? Um, *no*."

"That's right—you said you have two brothers between you in age."

Does he remember everything I've ever said in passing?

"Foster, nerd extraordinaire, is an attorney. Pax is a minor league ballplayer."

"The Cats?"

"No, the Isotopes."

"New Mexico?"

"Do you know *everything*?"

He pulled the golden glasses from his shirt pocket and slid them on. "Yes, I do." From the pocket of his slacks, he produced a flat leather case and then removed a short, ruler-like instrument. "And the fact that I not only have this but know how it works proves it."

"The prizewinning slide rule, I assume? And oh my God, it has its own *case*." I pinned my lips, which made my eyes water. The hilarity pinging around inside was determined to escape me one way or another.

"Actually, this is a vintage Keuffel and Esser, so it deserves its own case." He cocked a brow and stared at my face, taking in my valiant but deteriorating efforts not to laugh at his geeky math toy. "But this is a pocket model. Prize winning requires the ten-inch version. Or bigger."

My lips dropped apart and my face began to grow warm, and any compulsion to laugh was long gone. *Please do not see where my it's-been-too-long mind just went*, I begged. My silent plea went unanswered. He knew exactly where my mind had gone because he'd led the way, and it had followed him like a hungry puppy stalking a clumsy kid with a hot dog.

"Either will get the job done. But the larger ones calculate more… precisely." The smirk was subtle, but I knew that smug expression too well. "When there's no room for error, precision is essential. And if I'm going to do something, I'm going to do it right."

Hellfire and damnation.

I drew myself up. "Ah," I said. "I guess me and the rest of the dummies can be grateful for calculators, ha ha." And then I scuttled to the relative safety of my office, where I decided it had definitely *been too long*. Time I did something about that.

Me: Is that invitation to join you and your friends tonight still open?

Mindi: Sure! The more the merrier. We're going to Uber over to 7th around 8.

Me: Awesome. I'll run home and grab a few things and then head your way as soon as I get off work.

Mindi: Yay! Too long since I've seen you. <3

Trophy Erin was going trick-or-treating. *Done right* was all fine and good, but sometimes a girl didn't have the time or fortitude to wait for precision, she just needed to be *done*.

chapter *Seventeen*

Mindi's squad pulled out all the stops on costumes, howling with laughter as we endeavored to pin down our shared theme for the night and ended up reclaiming the most dreaded descriptor of junior high. Ava—slutty mechanic, Claire—slutty nurse, Madison—slutty zombie, Mindi—slutty Cinderella, and Erin—slutty cheerleader.

The gold skirt worked, but I ditched the tights and the sleeveless top, which was sweetly appropriate for high school cheerleading or a work costume but utterly unsuitable for bar-scene hookup hunting. Bare legs, four-inch platform wedges with canvas sneaker uppers, and a low-cut T-backed tank later, I was ready. I kept the big gold bow and high ponytail.

Before the bar crawling began, we were meeting up with a group of guys they knew, which probably meant they were all college boys. I'd been out of school less than six months and I felt a hundred years too old for someone conceivably *my same age*. But I wasn't in the mood for a complete stranger, so friend of a friend would have to do. *One* of them had to be cute enough, for fuck's sake. *Literally*.

"This is no time to be fastidious, McIntyre," I admonished my rearview mirror reflection before getting out of the car now wedged between a TCU-window-stickered Mini Cooper and a TCU-bumper-stickered Volvo. (Thanks be to Pax for insisting on teaching sixteen-year-old me to parallel park with only inches to spare.) Grabbing my gold pom-poms from the passenger seat, I gave myself one last motivational edict. "Go get you some college-boy ass."

Mindi shared a small off-campus house with her friends. The neighborhood might have been picturesque once upon a time, but it was all student rentals now rather than manicured lawns and darling cottages like Tuli's, which was only two or three miles away. I erased the pout that thinking about Isaac's cute, artistic friend brought to my face; there would be no moping tonight.

I didn't want to think about Tuli or Isaac. Or Isaac with Tuli.

We started the night at Chimy's to load up on greasy Tex-Mex and cheap margaritas. PSA: if you haven't barhopped in a while and then do so on a costume-encouraged, Friday-landing holiday, the experience can be overwhelming. The place was packed with pre-partiers who'd all had the same idea we'd had. The weather had turned cool in the past twenty-four hours, but when a bunch of tallish guys bunched near us decided to head across the parking lot to the Reservoir, I realized I'd felt suffocated.

I needed to get out more.

Mindi and her friends watched for the guys while I kept an eye out for a clear table.

"Boone!" Claire called, waving at a group of guys across the room. They maneuvered through the crowd toward us, single file, and I took them in, one at a time, as they drew closer.

Boone—not too tall, red-haired, decent build, and wearing a football jersey, with stripes of eye black on his cheekbones. If Ed Sheeran joined the Cowboys, this is how he'd look suited up. I wasn't in the mood for looking coordinated, and a ginger cheerleader with a ginger football player was too matchy-matchy. *Next.*

"Hey, Oliver," Ava said as Boone took orders for our first round.

Oliver came into view—*hello, slutty Egyptian prince*—and distributed short hugs all around. I normally wouldn't go for someone who did his winged eyeliner as well as I did, but with his jet-black hair, smooth skin, and mouthwatering body clad only in a black-and-gold shendyt skirt, headdress, and armbands, he was hot. His quick, appreciative scan and "Well, hello" as he pulled me in for a relaxed hug told me he was a contender for Mr. Tonight.

Until I looked at Ava, who observed his response to me and visibly deflated. I'd just met her, but we were squad-for-tonight, so Oliver was out. *Dammit.*

Kurt was boy-next-door cute with a mop of hair and a goofy, engaging smile. Like a young Jesse Eisenberg—emphasis on *young*. He was wearing an over-twenty-one wristband, but he looked seventeen. He was also wearing a giant banana costume that had, by the looks of it, been through two or three previous Halloweens without being laundered well enough. If at all.

"Nice to meet you," I said.

I had one more shot to get lucky tonight. Things looked good when the last arrival was a credibly well-built Superman in a tight, non-mild-mannered costume. The muscles, unlike Uncle Hank's this morning, were not padding. *Yum.* Bonus, he looked a little older than the others—as in, he looked like a man.

"Erin, this is Rhys," Mindi said. "Rhys, Erin."

Well, damn. Because based on the fact that Rhys/Superman had to tear his eyes away from my petite friend to register my existence, I was SOL unless I fancied a banana later on, after copious amounts of alcohol and lots of sweaty dancing, perhaps. I flicked my eyes over to Kurt and he waggled his brows. *Nope.*

Mindi seemed uncomfortable all of a sudden, and my protective instincts surged.

"Is this *the* Erin?" Rhys asked, and she nodded. Smiling warmly, he extended a hand. "Great to finally meet you, Erin."

Mindi chewed her lip and pulled on her wristband, her big green eyes flicking back and forth from his face to mine. Her tiara glinted from the exposed overhead lighting as she watched us.

I took his hand and smiled my sorority recruitment chair smile—friendly, but appraising. His grip was gentleman-firm, meant to reassure, not overawe.

"Great to meet you too, Rhys," *man that I've never heard of until one minute ago*. Brows raised, I gave Mindi a favorable head tilt and a furtive wink. She smiled back and sighed, relief and joy all over her face.

Clearly, she wanted me to like Superman, and she'd confided enough of our past connection that he knew who I was and was inclined to think well of me.

"I'll get you a prickly pear margarita?" he asked her, moving slightly closer and just behind her to block some guy dressed as an octopus whose additional appendages were hitting everyone in a five-foot radius every time he moved.

"Boone's getting it," she said. She turned to me. "Boone is Rhys's little brother. Like, his actual brother, not a frat thing."

"Oh. I guess that's how you guys met?" If I wasn't going to get my freak on tonight—*I see you, banana, and the answer is no*—I would make my mission for the night ascertaining Mindi's safety and happiness with this Rhys dude. I might not have been her official Big Sis, but we'd bonded just as tightly.

"Yeah. I met Boone my first semester. We have a big, really cool circle of friends. Not even half of us are here because there's a frat thing—duh, it's Halloween so of course one of the frats is throwing a huge party—that's where the rest of them are. Rhys and Boone have an apartment near downtown, so sometimes he hangs out with us."

"The youngsters let me tag along sometimes is what she means." He chuckled, looking down at her. "I think they're afraid I'll just hole up alone otherwise, and Boone will come home some night and find me dead of boredom with no company but myself."

Mindi laid her fingers on the big *S* in the middle of his muscular chest. "You are *not* old! And you have Isaac for company when you don't want the rest of us."

Isaac?

He looked over his shoulder. "Man, he must have had to park blocks away. It's been at least ten minutes."

My heart stuttered. *There are a lot of Isaacs in the world*, I told myself. *It's not him.* I was supposed to be watching for people leaving tables so we could pounce on one, but I couldn't keep my eyes off the door.

Boone returned with drinks for the girls. Mindi sipped a bit of hers through the straw—like a lady. "Rhys is an architect. He and Isaac went to college together."

I pushed my straw aside and gulped a mouthful of salt, tequila, and lime. *Lots of other Isaacs have architectural degrees.*

"There he is." Rhys waved on hand over his head. "Isaac!"

I didn't see anyone except some ripped guy in a near cosplay-level Batman costume. He was suited head to toe except for his chin, which was chiseled, coffee brown, lightly stubbled, and all too familiar.

Batman waved back, his hand stilling when, I assume, he caught sight of *me*.

"*Table!*" Madison barked, and we all mobilized to grab the two four-tops, already pushed together, before someone else did.

Boone went back to the bar for the rest of the drinks, and Rhys said, "I see a small table clearing in the back—Kurt, come haul the chairs over here so we'll have enough room for ten."

Mindi pulled me to her side of the table and I followed, unable to think coherently or look at Isaac. We were not at work. This was outside work hours and far from everyone we worked with. I felt like I'd spotted an endangered mountain lion. I was equal parts thrilled and scared shitless.

Rhys hoisted the table over his head to get it through the crush of people, delts and biceps bulging through the stretchy blue fabric, cape wafting in the breeze from the open patio doors. Kurt dragged two chairs in his wake. A couple of on-their-way-to-hammered guys cheered, thinking Superman and Batman—Isaac, who'd just pulled out the chair at the head of the table, next to me—were about to throw down and enact a fight scene from an upcoming movie.

Isaac put up a palm and in a low, gravelly voice told them, "Not tonight, guys. I'm off duty," and they *awww, mannnn*ed but laughed and clapped. Isaac sat. I did not look his way or acknowledge him at all, but I could feel him sitting there as though we were touching.

"Oh Lord," Claire said. "The geek is strong with this one."

Boone came back with the guys' drinks. "Isaac, man, don't kick my brother's ass yet. We need some nachos and a couple more rounds first."

Mindi leaned close. "What do you think of Rhys?"

Cape swirling around his shoulders, Rhys placed the table at the other end of the two we'd seized, then made his way to the empty seat next to her. No one had taken it; everyone in this close-knit group of friends seemed to know he would sit next to Mindi.

"He's gorgeous. And he seems to like you a lot."

Her eyes sparkled, so green they almost didn't look real. "Do you really think so?"

I pinched myself so I wouldn't laugh at the earnest expression on her heart-shaped face. "Oh honey. I've never seen a guy so intoxicated." I took a sip of my very strong margarita.

"Time to get *TURNT!*" our banana hollered to amused hoots and cheers from nearby customers, which emboldened him to break into an impromptu Wobble mixed with elements of the Cotton-Eyed Joe when a new song started up—until his sweeping, stuffed tail end tripped a waitress, who was caught by a guy dressed as a pirate.

Kurt sat.

"I stand corrected," I said to Mindi and heard Isaac's soft chuckle. My arms erupted in goose bumps, and I fisted my hands on my thighs to stop myself from squirming. I had never had such uncontrollable physical reactions to nonphysical circumstances.

"Dude, save your Wobble for the dance floor," Madison said to Kurt.

"You're not my mom!" he said. They stared at each other for a full five seconds before bursting into laughter.

I was confused, but no one else seemed to be.

"They do this *all the time*," Mindi said. "It's an inside joke. None of us are in on it."

Oliver and Kurt went to get our food when "Banana man, your order is up!" was announced. When they returned to the table with heaping platters of nachos and quesadillas, Oliver looked us all over and said, "Aww man, I just realized we only got eight tickets for the haunted house."

There were ten of us. I wondered who had crashed this party besides me.

"Shit. We could get two more at the door?" Madison said. "We *have* to go. It's the one in that old meatpacking plant in Hell's Half Acre. Scary as fuuuuuck."

"I got the ones with the speed pass. I don't even know if they cash sell those at the door. Ten bucks extra but you jump the line—which will be *insane* tonight. Like, *hours* long."

"Oh—that's okay," I said, bummed. "You guys didn't know I was coming tonight. I don't have to go. I'll just…" *What the hell was I going to do in the middle of Fort Worth, by myself, on Halloween?* I'd only had one margarita. If I was going to have to drive home, I couldn't have another.

"I'll stay with Erin. I don't really like haunted houses." Mindi grabbed my hand under the table. I'd been through a haunted house once and could understand why she wouldn't want to go. At some you had to sign a waiver that made physical contact permissible. For Mindi, that could trigger a panic attack.

Rhys leaned up to speak around her. "Erin, you go. I have an optic nerve thing—strobe lights are a problem for me. I probably shouldn't risk it. I'll stay with Mindi. We'll go watch a band at Capital Bar or hang out at the apartment, and you guys can swing by and get us on the way back to 7th."

I looked at Mindi and she gave my hand a squeeze, a coy smile on her face.

"You *sure*?" I asked her, and she gave one quick nod, her cheeks flushed pink. Girlfriend wanted to be alone with Rhys. *Bad*. "Cool, thanks Rhys. Who do I owe for the ticket? Crap, I've only got my credit card."

"That would be me." Oliver finished his beer and grabbed another from an ice bucket. Elbows on the table, he leaned forward and flexed deliberately like one of those birds that puffs up during mating efforts. Next to him, Ava sighed at his display, but he didn't notice. "'Bout fifty bucks. But walk through the house with me and show me your best private cheer later on, and we'll call it even." He winked.

If Ava weren't pining over him, I might have considered his offer—except for the fact that it was a complete fucking asshole proposition to make.

Two fifties landed in front of Oliver.

"For both of us," Isaac said. "You can settle up with me when you get a chance, Erin. No unwarranted stipulations apply."

"Man, Isaac—that's cold, bro." Oliver chuckled as he stuffed the bills into his wallet.

"No, King Tut, that's being a man, *bro*."

"Schooled by the Batman, *a very special Halloween event*," Kurt said and then wedged an entire steak quesadilla triangle in his mouth. Oliver scowled, unable to respond without doubling down on being a dick.

"Thanks," I said to Isaac.

Isaac's mask concealed every trace of emotional expression but his eyes, which spoke protective volumes. "No problem."

"I didn't mean to— Uh, I'm sorry, but," Oliver murmured, hands spread, embarrassed but defensive. "I just thought—"

"Thanks," I interrupted. *I'm sorry but* was such a non-apology. "I'm sure you didn't mean to make my acceptance of the ticket conditional on anything inappropriate."

"No." His tone wasn't exactly contrite, but I hoped he had learned the difference between initiating a suggestive but no-strings negotiation and being a presumptuous fuckbag.

Boone was glaring at him and Rhys looked like he wanted to punch him. So did Madison. I was long done ignoring offhand sexism. Excusing minor asshattery too often led to more deliberate misogyny and sometimes the kind of abuse Mindi and Jacqueline had suffered.

I stood, hoping to counteract the awkwardness and salvage the night for everyone else. *Cheerleader Erin to the rescue.* "My turn to buy a round! Who wants what, and who's gonna help carry?"

To my surprise, Oliver stood. "I'll help." We gave our order at the back counter after standing in a short line. "I really am sorry. I just wanted to get to know you better, and it came out wrong, that's all."

I rolled my eyes and took a help-me-Jesus breath. "That 'it came out wrong' or 'I'm sorry but' bullshit negates an apology. Be real. Did you actually think asking me to give you a private show later in exchange for fifty bucks was romantic?"

He stared at his feet. "You're right. I'll do better." I'd expected continued petulance. This was a welcome change of pace. "I really am sorry," he added.

Kurt's voice rose above the din—no mean feat—and we looked back at the table. Our banana was doing a freestyle version of raising the roof like an out-of-control inflatable waving tube man. The bartender slid the drinks across the counter.

"Apology accepted." I picked up the bucket of beers and pointed at the four margaritas. "Now grab those and let's—in the words of that whackadoodle banana—get *turnt*!"

chapter Eighteen

"Everything good?" Isaac asked, voice low, when I returned to the table.

I handed off mixed drinks to Mindi, Claire, and Rhys before I slid into my seat and looked at my boss, weighing the fact that in a few hours, after a few more drinks, we were going to be walking through a very dark haunted house. That shouldn't have left me turned on, but I couldn't get Oliver's stupid proposition out of my head—because it didn't feel so stupid when applied to a man I wanted to take those liberties. Maybe it was my voluntary months-long dry spell. Maybe it was the cheerleader outfit. But I felt like I was sixteen, and all I wanted was his hands on my skin or his mouth on mine.

"Yes, Isaac. Everything is good."

He turned to take a beer from Oliver.

"Hey Erin, where do you go to school?" Kurt asked. "If you're a Horned Frog, Mindi needs to invite you out more. I'm like ninety percent sure we haven't met before."

I froze and so did Isaac, but we didn't look at each other. No one at this table knew we were even acquainted. I felt sure, for no reason I could identify, that he didn't want me to reveal our working relationship. I would tell Mindi at some point, but our opening to inform the rest had passed without a logical explanation of why we hadn't done so right away, and I didn't have one.

"Nope, Longhorn for life." I threw a dutiful Hook 'em Horns hand signal. "But I graduated in May."

"Didn't you used to go there?" Kurt asked Mindi.

She nodded. "That's how we met. We were sorority sisters."

He gasped, hand on his chest. "Whaaaaat? You were a sorority girl?" The seriousness of his astonishment was wrecked by the banana stem rising a foot above his head. He studied her through narrowed eyes, one finger tapping against his lip. "Okay, yeah, I can sorta see it."

She rolled her eyes and twisted her arm through mine. "Erin was the only thing I missed when I left."

I had encouraged her to try for a transfer to our sister chapter, but she'd declined and I hadn't pushed, especially after she'd asked me if we could still be friends if she didn't do it. I'd reminded her that my best friend was a GDI—goddamn independent, the term Greeks used for non-Greek friends—and swore I only wanted her to do what was best for her. All true.

"So what do you do?" Kurt asked me.

Mindful of *my boss* sitting next to me, I shot for a stock description of my duties. "I'm a client liaison. I placate disgruntled customers and work with them to get their problems resolved so they'll refer us to others instead of bashing us all over the internet."

He grimaced. "That sounds… really terrible."

I laughed. "Wow, thanks."

"I mean, it sounds hard. Working with people who are already pissed off about shit. Man. Not like an insurance company or a cable company?"

"No. Custom home builder."

"Which one?"

Well, shit on a shoelace. The fancy gauntlets covered Isaac's forearms, but his nearest hand was a fist on the table. I wasn't sure which of us he wanted to punch—Kurt or me.

"Um. J. McIntyre."

Rhys sat forward, peered at Isaac, at me, and back to Isaac. He was a local architect and friends with Isaac. Of course he would recognize the name of a high-end local builder. The questions tumbling through his head were clear, though he was perceptive enough not to voice them, so far.

Mindi angled her head, perplexed-puppy style. "That's your last name."

I couldn't blame her—I hadn't told her, *Hey, by the way, I work for my father's company, and also don't mention it to anyone.*

"Yep. It's my father's company. I work for my daddy and live at home. I have failed to launch in every way." I wanted to thump my forehead on the table repeatedly until blessed unconsciousness or Jesus took me, whichever came first. Instead, I finished half of my second margarita in one go.

"Working for the family business is an institution, historically speaking. Nothing to be ashamed of," Madison said, bless her zombie heart. "He's probably grooming you to take over some day. Right?"

They'd have to pry the reins to JMCH from my father's cold, dead hands, and I'd be close to *sixty* by the time that occurred. My life flashed before my eyes—the next three or four decades spent working for my father—a clear-cut, alternative future unlike anything I had ever imagined for myself. My pulse kicked up, and I had to remind myself to breathe. "Oh, I don't think he, or I—"

"Unless you report directly to your old man, I bet the tension between you and your supervisor is *too raw*," Kurt said. "I don't know who I'd feel more sorry for. I guess the supervisor unless he's a jackhole." He shrugged. "But then you could probs just get him canned."

I didn't dare look at Isaac, but one glance at Rhys told me his gears were clicking into place, which would only mean one thing: Isaac had discussed me with him.

I was saved from replying when a girl in a banana suit strolled by our table and Kurt popped up and gave, I assume, a banana mating call—which she returned.

"Excuse me, my dudes. An *a-peeling* prospect appears to be *ripe* with promise."

That earned facepalms and groans all around, but he ignored us and scrambled after her. Grateful for the reprieve from his cross-examination, I hoped no one else would take it up.

I side-eyed Isaac, who stood and said, "Gonna get another platter of quesadillas. Chicken this time? The tickets are for ten o'clock, but we have to get a couple of Ubers and then get there. So last round? Their website says no drunks allowed. I'll add a round of waters."

I had never heard Isaac say so many words at one time.

Rhys began to rise. From his eyes, wide with disbelief, I guessed he was thinking the same thing. "I'll help you get that."

Isaac nodded and the two of them strode off, capes flowing, crowds of people waiting for tables parting for the superhero nemeses and gazing after them. Heads together, they were talking—after Isaac glanced back to ascertain that no one had followed—and I had no doubt what they were discussing. *Me*.

• • • • • • • • • • •

Just before we left the restaurant, Isaac offered to drive Mindi and Rhys to Rhys and Boone's apartment.

"I'll tag along so everyone else can pile into an XL," I said. "No sense paying for two cars. If that's okay with you." I assessed Isaac's reaction to my proposal, or tried to. The man was almost unreadable. Almost. His mind was spinning—*abort! Abort!*

"That way you guys won't have to wait for Isaac," Mindi said to the others. "He can go through with Erin when they get there and we'll all rendezvous at the apartment later. This is perfect." She clasped her hands and smiled.

"Sure. Great idea." Isaac's tight smile fooled everyone but Rhys—who angled a brow but said nothing—and me.

"Our ride will be here in five minutes," Ava said. She scanned all of us as we began moving away from the table and another big group swooped in to claim it. "Where's Kurt?"

We all turned, looking for our missing banana.

"There he is. I'll get him and we'll meet you guys out front." Oliver strode off toward the patio.

We squeezed through the crowd and finalized plan details outside, and then the four of us broke off from the others. "I parked on Norwood," Isaac said.

My bare arms and legs were covered with goose bumps before we were halfway there, and I felt dizzier than two drinks would normally leave me, especially with food. Next to me, Mindi had just commented about the hilarity that was Kurt taking off after a female banana, and I chuckled politely but was too busy concentrating on putting one foot in front of the other without tripping to reply.

Hugging my arms across my chest and shivering, I jolted and stumbled when satiny fabric landed on my shoulders.

Isaac's warm hands steadied my shoulders through his cape, which he'd just draped over me. "Didn't mean to startle you. Sorry. It's thin and won't help much, but better than the bit of nothing you're wearing."

I bristled at the insinuation that I was dressed like a prostitute, but his gaze was open and considerate, not disparaging. I pulled the cape, which fell to my ankles, around me like a silk sheet. It wasn't warm, but it cut the breeze a bit. "Thank you."

I glanced back at Rhys and Mindi, who were walking behind us.

"Are you okay, Erin?" she asked. She was dressed as scantily as I was but didn't seem bothered by the cold. In fact, no one around us looked cold. I felt like I was standing in a meat locker.

"I'm fine! No worries."

"You sure you want to go to the thing?" Isaac asked. "We could skip it."

"Yeah, sure thing. I'm fine," I insisted.

Twenty minutes later, we'd dropped Mindi and Rhys at his place, making small talk on the way. Rhys' curiosity about our nondisclosure of the fact that we worked together was palpable, but he only asked a couple of architect-relevant questions about JMCH—if we built outside of planned communities and whether our architectural and design support was exclusively in-house or delegated to subcontractors.

Once alone, Isaac and I listened to music without conversing until I couldn't stand it.

"Rhys already knew where you work, I guess."

Isaac nodded. "And you hadn't told Mindi that you work for

your father."

I shrugged, staring out the window. "It's not something I public-cize."

"Because you aren't doing what you were trained to do, or because of what you said about failing to launch?"

"Ouch. And both."

A song began and ended before he spoke again. "You acted like we'd never met."

"So did you."

We paid ten dollars to park in a field blocks from the haunted house. Isaac left his Batman cowl and cape in the trunk and handed me a dark gray hoodie.

"Th-thank you," I said, pulling it on. "I d-don't know why I'm so cold. It's like sixty-five degrees." The sleeves fell past my hands, but I didn't care because that just kept me warmer.

He frowned but didn't reply. *Great. Even my being cold irritates him.*

The speed passes were a godsend, though a collective murmur of animosity rose from the long line of patrons when we bypassed all of them. "We shouldn't let any of those people waiting in line catch up to us inside or we might become gory displays of our own. It could take days for them to figure out that we aren't part of the show."

The acrid, sweat-drenched odor permeating the air overwhelmed all my other senses. Glued to Isaac's solid arm, face pressed against his right shoulder blade, I barely noticed the pulsating, deafening music or shrill screams of other patrons and the chainsaw-wielding maniacs. The skeletons lunging out of the dark and psychotic clowns grabbing our ankles as we squeezed through confined spaces didn't scare me much. I was too busy trying not to inhale too deeply.

I vaguely registered the butchered corpses on meat hooks swinging by on a mechanized conveyor belt, like the goriest dry cleaner ever, and tried to convince myself that the floor was damp with water—which was dripping down walls and misting out from nowhere—and not other liquids. The smell said other liquids were a distinct probability; I would be tossing these shoes in the garbage without a conclusive answer to that question, however.

We reached what looked like an unlit maze and were handed glow sticks to navigate the pitch-black and given instructions I couldn't hear. The walls were too close to walk side by side. Isaac led, glow stick aloft, and took my hand behind his back.

After what felt like hours, we entered a room full of bubbles, higher than our heads, and my ability to deal passed peak containable level. I gasped and swallowed soapy foam, panic mounting. Unable to see, I whimpered and gagged, and even with the hoodie, the chills came back full force and evolved into violent tremors. Isaac turned, picked me up—front to front, my face against his shoulder like I was five—and walked straight outside.

Air had never tasted so sweet. I gulped mouthfuls. Before setting me down, Isaac had moved to the side so we wouldn't block the exit where other patrons streamed out—some laughing, some crying, some screaming and flailing.

"That's probably how Kurt looked," he said.

I tried to laugh, hands on my thighs, and choked instead, realizing belatedly that I was going to puke. More horrified than I'd been at anything inside the haunted house, I ran to a large metal trash can and added the contents of my stomach to that of others, which made a second wave rise and gush forth.

The sleeve of his hoodie was the only thing available to wipe my mouth. I did not want to turn and face him. I wasn't sure if the fact that he was my boss and not a date made the situation of vomiting in front of him—*and being forced to wipe the final dribbles of it on his hoodie*—better or worse. Possibly this rock bottom was so low that it no longer mattered.

"All done, or more coming?" he asked, just behind me.

I moved away from the noxious can, shivering again, and realized I was soaked to the skin from the misters inside the haunted house and the bubble room at the end. "Done, I think. My stomach actually feels better."

He gestured toward the can. "Was that from the bubbles or the margaritas?"

"I felt a little nauseous before the bubbles, though they definitely didn't help. Two margaritas have never laid me that low. Jesus, how embarrassing."

He led us toward the food truck at the edge of the lot and asked for two bottles of water. The smell of barbeque wasn't tempting, but it didn't bother me either.

He handed me a bottle. "It's no big deal."

I gargled and spit into yet another huge trash can. "I, uh, ruined your hoodie." My face prickled as it warmed. Hopefully it was too dark for him to see the hateful blotches. "I'll have it cleaned and bring it to you Monday."

He smirked. "No rush. I have others."

At his car, he retrieved my bag from the trunk, stowed the stained hoodie, and grabbed a beach towel and a heather-gray blanket so our now-wet costumes wouldn't wreck his leather seats. I wrapped myself up like a fuzzy mummy, belted in, and pulled out my phone to check my messages. I felt instantly better and worse.

"The good news is it wasn't the margaritas. The bad news it was some questionable chicken salad only Mindi, Ava, and I had when I got to their place earlier. Madison and Claire and all the guys are fine. Mindi and Ava have both been throwing up."

He started the car and switched on my seat heater, and I swore to myself that I would absolutely *not* fall asleep in his car again, no matter how cozy I was beginning to feel.

"How are you now?"

If he was worried about the risk of my puking in his car, I couldn't blame him, but the combination of upchucking the offending chicken salad, rehydrating, and removing all the assaults on my senses—cold, flashing lights, vile smells, and noise—had done the trick.

"I think I'm okay." Even so, I cringed at the idea of rejoining the partying crowds. Mindi and I could crash at her place as planned, just a lot earlier than intended. "But I don't feel like going back out."

Isaac was reading his texts. "Sounds like they got it even worse than you did. Rhys says it was like a live-action version of *The Exorcist* for the past hour. She's asleep now. At his place."

Great. I couldn't stay at her place if she wasn't there.

"Poor thing. She's the size of a Barbie doll, and Ava ate twice as much because she'd missed lunch. I guess scarfing two of Ted's frosted zombie cupcakes this afternoon saved me. I wasn't hungry enough to eat much chicken salad, thank Christ." I sighed. "My car's parked in front of their house. If you could drop me there, I'll just head home."

He drove for a minute or two, passing under the freeway and navigating without his GPS. "We could hang at my place for a bit. If you want. You shouldn't drive home right now. You're still a little shaky."

I was beat as hell and the thought of driving home was unappealing, but it was his *hang at my place* suggestion that had me shaking in my unidentified-liquid-dampened, landfill-bound wedges. "Don't you want to meet up with the others? You're not sick, and I've ruined enough of your night."

We sat at a stoplight. In the dim light afforded by the streetlamps arcing far above the intersection, his gaze was steady. "You haven't ruined anything."

I wanted to see where he lived. What things he believed to be useful, beautiful, worthy of possessing. What style of art he preferred, what types of books he read, what sort of housekeeper he was. We would be alone, I assumed, but didn't know. Would he offer me a drink? A candid conversation? A pillow for the sofa? A kiss?

"Okay," I said.

chapter *Nineteen*

He took a left, and after a few more turns, I recognized the area where we'd eaten lunch after the visit to Tuli's studio.

Sheila Anderson had been overjoyed with her artistic fix to my brother's debacle, and she'd acknowledged both the gifted rising artist and her "marvelous home builder" in a lavish multipage spread of the house that began on the cover of a local luxury magazine. Daddy had been triumphant. Leo had not. It had been a monumental effort not to *HA! HA!* straight to his insufferable face.

Isaac pulled into a parking lot and circled around to enter an underground garage where he had an assigned spot. A key fob accessed an elevator bank. When we entered a posh, gently lit hallway on the upper floor, he said, "I'll need to take the dog out, but it shouldn't take long."

The dog?

My mother couldn't leave Jack alone in the house all day, or he'd gnaw through a table leg, ingest the corner of a bedroom door, or chew half a loveseat into downy confetti. He had a variety of monogrammed dog beds throughout the house, a mechanized food bowl, a water bowl *fountain*, and as many toys as I had as a child, but if left alone for more than an hour he became an anguished cyclone of distress, bent on total destruction.

I steeled myself for a dejected, crated dog—Jack's fate after the loveseat's untimely slaughter—and the inevitable jumping, barking, and licking following its release from captivity. Luckily for Jack, my mother was seldom away from the house for very long. Isaac's poor dog would be home alone for multiple hours per week.

The apartment extended, long and narrow, to wall-to-wall windows at the opposite end, through which the luminous skyline of downtown was visible. The ceiling was high and industrial, with imprinted concrete and exposed pipes curving just below, painted to maintain a cohesive look. Music played softly from somewhere inside, mixed with faint echoes of cars and patrons of restaurants and bars on the street below. I heard a joyful whine just before a canine face appeared from one of the doorways along the right.

"Hey, boy," Isaac said, tapping his thigh. Nails clicked across the wood floors toward us, and he leaned to intercept his dog, which had a retriever's build and chocolate-brown fur, light with age around the brows and muzzle.

"Pete, sit," Isaac said, reaching to grab a leash from the coatrack mounted on the wall.

Spotting me, Pete sat. Head angled, he sized me up, maintaining eye contact as I stood there, wrapped head to toe in the now-dampish blanket, but he didn't move from his appointed spot.

"Can I pet him?" I asked.

"Sure." Isaac discarded his costume's cowl and cape on a small table, clicked the leash into place, and said, "Up."

Pete stood.

I smiled and offered a hand to be smelled. "Hi, Pete. You're such a handsome boy." He took a polite sniff, long tail wagging slowly, and looked to Isaac for reassurance or permission, I wasn't sure which.

"This is Erin," Isaac said, as though Pete might reply, *"How do you do, Erin?"*

Pete nuzzled his soft head into my hand and stared into my eyes as though soul-searching.

"How old is he? You've had him a while, I guess."

Isaac cleared his throat. "The vet says he's between ten and eleven. I adopted him about a year ago. His owner had passed on, and he was dropped at the shelter."

As I scratched behind his fluffy ears, I looked at Pete's sweet face, incapable of reflecting on his fate if Isaac hadn't come along. "That's terrible." I was positive Mom would haunt the unholy hell out of us if she died and we abandoned Jack at a shelter.

"Make yourself at home. There's bottled water in the fridge. I'll make some coffee when we get back from the dog run." Pete's ears perked at the final two words and he faced the door, tail wagging eagerly.

When the door snicked closed behind them, I was alone in Isaac Maat's home.

I removed my grimy shoes and dropped them into the lidded garbage can in his utility room. The pale taupe ballerina flats in my car often rescued my feet from my more hostile stilettos at the end of a day. I would wear those to drive home after Isaac dropped me at my car.

At the doorway where Pete had emerged, tall, solid pocket doors were pushed wide to reveal a bedroom, softly lit by sconces on either side of the bed. I had eschewed the use of the haunted house's porta potties, so I had a perfectly reasonable excuse to walk through Isaac's bedroom to the bathroom. While there, I scrubbed the melted, smeared cosmetics from my face and used the folding toothbrush in my bag with a bit of Isaac's cinnamon toothpaste.

I left the room more slowly than I'd entered it, fingers trailing across surfaces. A velvety plaid duvet, haphazardly tossed over the bed, matched the colors of Pete's fur—by design, I'd guess. The smooth chestnut dresser displayed neatly arranged stacks of architecture and urban-planning books across its top, beneath a wall-mounted flat-screen.

There was one framed photo on the night table of a young boy and his parents, dressed for church or some semiformal event. Isaac, who couldn't have been out of grade school with his say-cheese grin, full cheeks, and a bow tie only a parent could have chosen, was nevertheless recognizable. His father's lean build and facial structure was so like present-day Isaac that I could have mistaken them for each other if not for the medium Afro and clean-shaven face. His mother, hair swept into a twisted updo and makeup on point, shared only her son's arched brows. Her face was less angled—rounder, softer. Against her sleeveless pink blouse and a classic A-line skirt, high-waisted and powder blue, her skin was darker than husband and son. Her hand rested on Isaac's shoulder; her husband's arm encircled them both.

I moved to the kitchen and took a bottle of water from the fridge. The walls of the open living/dining area—three times my height—were bare but for another television. The music I'd heard was playing through a sound bar beneath it. His sectional leather sofa was Pete-toned; I sensed a theme. Still huddled inside my borrowed blanket, I walked to the window and stared at the skyline in the distance. A bark echoed from below, and I looked down to see a man and dog approaching the building from the dog run on the other side of the lot.

Even without Pete alongside him, I'd have recognized Isaac's walk—posture balanced and straight but not inflexible, bearing confident without the sort of conceited strut Joshua Swearingen displayed. Just before he and Pete vanished under the entry overhang, Isaac turned his face up and looked at the window where I stood watching him. I didn't know if he could see me from eight floors below.

I perched on a barstool instead of the sofa to wait for him because my clothes were still damp. By the expression he wore when he came around the corner—brows lifted, eyes widened, mouth tensed—I could have sworn he believed I might not be there.

"Hi," I said, wondering if I saw relief or resignation in his eyes just before he passed behind me.

He dropped a small stack of mail atop the closed laptop on his built-in desk. "Hi." At the island's sink, he filled the coffeepot.

"Are you still wet?" he asked, lifting his gaze to the startled face I fought to bring under control, lips pursed tight to stifle a juvenile *That's what he said.*

He turned quickly to make the coffee, or to hide his discomposure from having read my mind. "In the breeze outside, I noticed that my clothes aren't dry yet and thought maybe yours weren't either," he explained.

"Mine are still damp too." I was chastised but still struggling to subdue a giggle.

"I can lend you a T-shirt. Most of my sweats are too big—but something with a drawstring might work." He clicked the coffeemaker on. "C'mon. Let's see what I've got."

I followed him to his bedroom, marveling at how odd this was on the face of it, and how much odder it was that it didn't *feel* odd.

He opened a dresser drawer and pulled out a dark red tee with blue lettering: PENN QUAKERS.

"*Quakers?*" Taking the shirt, I bit my lip.

"Don't throw shade on my school now. Your mascot is a *cow*."

I gasped and laughed. "Heresy! It's a big scary cow with long pointy horns."

"Aiight, girl—if you say so." He searched through neatly rolled sweatpants. "Here we go. Matching drawstring drawers."

The sweats were blue with a red Penn crest on the front. Both were soft and would feel like heaven after spending the past several hours spent soggy and chilled.

"Thank you." Our eyes connected. We were standing in his bedroom, alone, and he'd just spoken to me in the playful tone he'd used with Tuli. A tone that meant I was worming my way behind his wall of Erin-aversion.

My one-track brain screamed, *KISS. HIM.*

I screamed back, *He's my BOSS. I can't just KISS him.*

He looked down at my bare feet. "I don't recall your being this short, comparably. I guess I've never stood next to you without your everyday high-rise footwear on."

"You're still wearing superhero boots. So we don't really know our relative heights."

He sat on the bed, crossed one foot onto the opposite knee, and began picking at the black laces. "Why don't you get out of those wet clothes—I mean, get into the dry ones." He nodded toward the bathroom, lips in that fixed line I recognized. He was determined to keep from flirting, even when it was inadvertently done. "Once you're out, I'm going to shower off, if you don't mind. I know I promised you coffee."

"I'm sure I can find a mug. Also, you're home. You should be able to relax and do whatever feels good." I had no anti-seduction qualms. If he wanted to take what I said as legitimate flirting, I was prepared to encourage him.

Attention on the tightly laced boot, he didn't respond.

I shut the door to the bathroom and stared into the mirror as I dropped the blanket to the floor and peeled every piece of damp clothing from my body, which had altered since my actual cheerleading years. Eating disorders had been common among the squads, freshmen to varsity, a fact that my adult self looked back on in horror. I had been rail-thin; my genes decreed it. No cheer coach or team captain or cheer mom had ever mentioned, oh-so-casually, that I might want to lay off the potato chips, *sweetie*, though I'd heard it done.

Gaining curves and becoming women is biologically natural; cisgender girls should be able to celebrate those changes. Instead, we went hungry all day, only to binge eat whatever was handy once our bodies—certain we were starving to death—demanded food. Meanwhile, articles in print and online warned against the deadly sins of stress eating or developing bulimia while cleverly placed ads featured photoshopped models no one could ever be, not even the models themselves.

At almost twenty-three, I was finally rocking curves of my own. I would not be my mother, submitting to anesthesia and knives and needles in an effort to preserve my adolescent body. This was the first moment I knew it, and the acknowledgment of that resolution made me feel powerful—and reckless. A precarious combination for a woman standing naked in her hot boss's bathroom.

I pulled on the sweatpants, which were so loose and long on me that I laughed out loud. I yanked the strings tight and tied them so the waistband would sit above my hips and stay there. I rolled the bottom of each leg until my feet extended enough to walk without sliding. The cottony-soft T-shirt slid over my head and fell to my thighs. I chuckled again at the *Quakers* inscription while removing the oversized bow from my head and allowing my hair to fall around my shoulders and down my back.

Running my fingers through the tangled waves, I tried to view myself as Isaac might. But I couldn't. I had no idea what he thought—or what he would think—of me. Not in my polished, professional form; not in this unembellished, shapeless configuration.

Sitting in the same spot at the end of the bed, boots now off, Isaac turned toward the doorway when I opened the door. Pete, who'd been receiving a head rub, rested his head on his master's knee and emitted a soft whine when the hand on his head stilled.

Isaac stared, his expression poker-face blank but his eyes reflecting the light from the brighter room behind me. He cleared his throat. "Heard you laughing in there," he said, gaze flicking to my chest and back. "Disparaging my school again, Ms. McIntyre?"

His sliding gaze was a weightless caress. A tenuous breath across my skin.

"I plead the fifth, Mr. Maat."

"Fair enough." He stood and took his own fresh T-shirt and sweatpants from the dresser top. "If you're hungry when I get out, I make a mean omelet. Or flapjacks."

My mouth watered and despite or because of the earlier barf session, my stomach emitted a yawning growl. "I guess I'm hungry."

"Preference?"

I am hungry for all the things, I thought. *And not all of them are food.* "Either."

"Cool. Be right out." He disappeared into the bathroom and the shower switched on.

I looked at Pete. He stared back.

"I want your master," I whispered.

He angled his head one way and then the other.

"Do you have any wise-old-doggy advice for how I can either get over myself or under him? Because this unreciprocated-crush thing is kinda grim." Pete whined in response. "You're right. I did bring it on myself." He burrowed his head under my palm and leaned against my leg, his tail thumping the dresser in rhythmic commiseration.

I settled into the corner of the sectional with Pete and checked my phone while waiting for Isaac to reappear. Ten minutes later, he emerged in a T-shirt and sweats combination similar to what I'd borrowed, but on him, everything fit. Perfectly. I was well acquainted with how he looked in suits and dress shirts and a full-on Batman costume. But *this* was something else. The knitted fabric hugged and accentuated muscular quads and shoulders. Sculpted biceps bulged from the short sleeves of his white T-shirt.

"Erin?"

"What? Huh?" *Oh damn.* My brain had shut down. Obviously.

"What sounds good?"

I batted several debauched responses away. "Whatever sounds good to you."

We engaged in a brief but intense staring game, and I would have paid good money to know what he was thinking.

"Omelets it is." He turned to remove ingredients from his fridge, bowls and pans and utensils from drawers and cabinets.

I got up and moved toward the kitchen. "Can I help?"

"You sit." He gestured to a barstool with a spatula, and I obeyed. "I think you've had enough excitement for one night."

He had no idea how wrong he was, though he bit his lip and concentrated on the task before him, too late to stop that phrase—*enough excitement*—from dangling like a mischievous dare between us.

"So you're an only child?" I asked. At his confused frown, I pointed toward his bedroom. "The photo on your night table."

His forehead relaxed. "Oh. Yes."

"I wouldn't wish my brothers into nonexistence, but I envy you that a little bit."

He angled a brow, dubious. "You didn't get sufficient attention as a child?"

"I got my share by being the only girl, but their attention was always divided, never focused, and it usually went to whichever of us was the biggest whiny-ass, or most successful, or fucking up the most. Believe it or not, I was rarely *the most* of any of those things."

He chopped vegetables, beat eggs, grated cheese, and didn't respond beyond the teeniest almost-smile that ever existed.

"Do your parents live nearby?"

He turned away to pour the egg mixture in a heated, buttered pan. "They died in a freak car accident not long after that photo was taken. A tire blew on a semi and the driver lost control briefly. They were one lane over. Wrong place, wrong time." That he had related this story countless times over the years was evident in his impassive recounting of it.

I considered the photo from that tragic angle and my heart squeezed. "Please forget my thoughtless *only child* bullshit. Jesus.

You were so young. I'm sorry, Isaac."

"You didn't know." He was silent for several minutes, and I rested my chin in my hand, watching him cook. "I think I get what you mean about focused attention. I'd had that kind of attention for ten years. Took it for granted. Never had to compete for it. But then I was part of a new family unit, and as much as they loved me, the focus was gone."

Comprehension dawned. "Your cousin—the one who worked her way through college—you lived with her family, after?"

"Yeah. My aunt and uncle took me in." He slid a plate in front of me; a fluffy omelet, fat with sautéed peppers and mushrooms, oozed melted cheese. "Don't eat more than you feel like eating."

"I feel fine now, I promise. And this smells delicious." I picked up my fork and ate a small bite to test my stomach. It gurgled happily, and I gave a pleased sigh. "When we run away from home, you'll do the cooking."

He slid an omelet onto his plate and then stared, brow arched, waiting for further explanation of that weird statement.

"Um. That was a game Pax and I used to play. When we were little, before he discovered girls. He would say, 'When we run away from home, you have to wash all the underwear.' And I would say, 'When we run away from home, you have to eat all the celery.' I hated celery. Like really, seriously, hated it."

"Enough to consent to washing all the underwear?"

"I was five; he was nine. I was easily manipulated."

He leaned onto the counter across from me to eat. "I take it you hate to cook?"

"No. But our assigned duties also recognized alleged strengths. Like, we had plans for making money on the streets: he would play the guitar and I would sing."

The almost-smile returned. "Now I'll have to hear you sing."

I finished a bite, shaking my head. "Oh no. I'm a *terrible* singer. The worst. Trust me, you'd be sorry. We thought way more highly of our 'talents' than deserved. Pax could only play two chords. Even Auto-Tune wouldn't have saved us."

This confession was rewarded with the laugh that made my heart stutter. "I guess it's a good thing you two never had to survive on the mean streets."

"We would have been arrested for disturbing the peace, or starved to death."

By the time I finished eating, I was so tired I could barely help dry the dishes. After reading a text from Rhys aloud, letting us know Mindi was still asleep and he wasn't going to wake her, Isaac laid his phone on the counter and said, "I'm getting you a pillow and a fresh blanket. No way you're driving all the way home tonight." He wore a slight scowl, and his arms were crossed as though he expected an argument and was prepared to dispute it.

I knew that if I tried to drive home, I'd likely end up in a ditch, or worse. I was a danger to myself and others. "Yes, sir," I said, giving a smartass salute.

His shoulders lowered a fraction of an inch, and with a ghost of a smirk at the edge of his mouth, he nodded, mollified.

chapter *Twenty*

My chest hurt, like a heavy weight was pressing down, impeding breaths choked with tears.

"Erin. *Erin.*"

Hands gripped my shoulders and my legs were tangled, immobile. With what felt like superhuman effort, I broke free and sat halfway up, eyes flying wide. I wasn't in Chaz's car. I wasn't in my bed. Gasping, I recognized Isaac's alarmed face. *Isaac. I was at Isaac's apartment. On his sofa.* Cautious, as if afraid to unsettle me further, he released his hold and sat next to me, silent. I squeezed my eyes shut and fell back, relieved and yet unable to stop my frustrated tears.

Jacqueline's interventional pep talk had been weeks ago, and the horrific visions of Chaz's final moments hadn't intruded on my sleep since that conversation. Foolishly, I'd begun to hope they were gone for good. No such luck. The nightmare had returned, and what abysmal timing to stage a reappearance. One night sooner or later and I would have been at home, alone.

"I'm okay." The words rasped from my raw throat. "It was just a stupid bad dream. Neurons firing. Something I ate. I'm sorry I woke you." Pete appeared at my prone eye level. He rested his muzzle on my arm, his eyes on mine. "I'm sorry to you, too," I told him.

"He tore in here faster than I did, ready to rip someone limb from limb." Isaac rubbed the dog's head. "You said a name. Chaz?" Moonlight streamed in from the wall of windows and lit his face clearly—the concern in his eyes and the pucker between his brows. "Do you want to talk about it?"

I closed my eyes, unable to refuse his gentle question or the empathy with which he'd asked it, unable to voice the *no* in my mouth. "He was my boyfriend."

The silence stretched, and I thought that would be the end of it.

"Was?"

I took a shuddering breath and looked at him. "We broke up junior year. When he proposed. I cared about him, a lot, but I didn't love him. Not like that. I broke his heart. And five months later—" My throat ached, straining to suppress the words. "He had a wreck a few blocks from campus."

I would never forget my friend Maggie showing up at my dorm room with my usual Starbucks order and bad news written all over her face. In a rare blessing, Christina had spent the night elsewhere, so she wasn't there.

"Kennedy called me," Maggie said. *"He thought I should tell you in private, before word gets out to everyone…"*

"He didn't survive," Isaac said.

I shook my head.

"I'm sorry."

"At his funeral, his mother told me he'd kept the ring. He was alone that night, but in my dream I'm there with him, in the car. And he tells me to lie to him. To say I would have changed my mind. So I do—and I tell him I love him. And then I wake up and it didn't happen. It can't ever happen." *Actual vomit earlier in the evening, word vomit now.*

"This nightmare. You've had it before tonight."

"It's been happening for the past year. It's been a few weeks since last time, and I thought it was gone, but it will never be gone." My tight fists and clenched teeth couldn't banish the pointless tears. "I'm just going to have to live with it. Because I get to, you know? I get to live with it. Jesus, what am I even saying? You lost your *parents*."

"Grief is grief. It's not a contest, and there's no sense comparing them." He stared out the window, thinking. "What do your parents say about this?"

I swallowed. "They don't know. No one knows."

"Therapist?"

"I tried. Campus counselors were somewhat helpful, but I didn't get to see the same person every time, so I got mixed results and I got tired of rehashing it over and over, like running in place. I saw a private therapist—once—but he blamed the universal root cause for everything when you're female—stress."

"As though having your sleep interrupted night after night wasn't causing the stress."

"You sound like you know what I'm talking about. Did you— You must have had difficulties after losing your parents. You were just a little boy."

"I did. But I was with family. My cousins were older, but welcoming enough for a couple of teenagers." He smiled. "My grandfather lived with us too."

"What was that like? Mom's parents retired to Colorado when I was young, and Daddy's parents were hundreds of miles east."

"Pop's in a memory care center now, so I got to spend time with him before Alzheimer's started stealing his stories, and his ability to know who I am. The dementia didn't really set in until after I left for Penn. I'd visit when I was home, and he thought I was my father."

I smiled, unsurprised after seeing the photograph of his parents. "What'd you say?"

He shrugged. "I made like I was him. He would say he liked my hair short, then tell me I needed a shave. He always asked about my 'wife,' his 'baby girl'—my mom—and I'd tell him, 'She'll be along tomorrow.' It was all lies, but it made him happy."

"And now?"

He shook his head. "He doesn't know any of us anymore. I can sit with him for an hour and he'll tell me the same story two, three times, as though I don't know him and haven't heard it before. Something that happened when he was a young man, or when he was a boy."

Grandma McIntyre had Alzheimer's before she died. I hadn't really known her. Daddy's parents had always lived in South Carolina, where he'd grown up, and where his sister, her husband, and two cousins I barely remembered from childhood were now. There had been some sort of falling out. I wasn't privy to the details, but our visits to see them—already infrequent—stopped when I was eight or nine.

Daddy's father had passed away from a massive heart attack when I was in high school. My parents flew out for the funeral and came back in a snit—something about my aunt not appreciating the money they'd offered to help with Grandma's care.

"No one ordered your sister to quit her job and be a full-time caregiver," Mom had told Daddy in her best righteously incensed, middle-aged-lady voice. "That's probably what killed your father—trying to do a job that should be left to professionals. Your mother doesn't know up from down. She would be well taken care of in a home, and we would have paid our share."

"Amanda doesn't want to put her in a home—"

"Exactly. She's making that choice. Let her deal with the consequences of it."

Thus ended the conversation I overheard. Grandma McIntyre died two years later. I was away at school. Mom texted to let me know: Daddy's mother has passed away. We'll be flying to Greenville on Friday, staying at the Westin. Back Sunday. It was like she was just some lady they knew and not my grandparent.

"What's the home like, where he lives?" I asked Isaac.

"It's nice. All the residents have some type of dementia. The staff is trained to keep them safe and comfortable. They have active-ties and encourage social interaction. We're lucky. Other places are like elephant graveyards for olds." He watched me for a moment. "Don't think I didn't notice that expert deflection. Well done, Ms. McIntyre. Ain't falling for it though."

His perception unnerved me. I couldn't hide behind my habitual barricades and fortifications. I didn't like it. My lips twisted and I groaned and rolled my eyes up to stare at his ceiling. "It's kind of how I deal."

"Or how you *don't* deal. Diversion and artificial cheerfulness."

My lips parted and my eyes burned, and damn him if I didn't try to smile. "Well done, Mr. Maat. That was a direct hit."

"Masking your pain is why it's coming out in your sleep. You're professionally trained. You must know it."

"I tried, Isaac. It didn't work, okay? It didn't work because I did something I can't take back. Maybe you don't know what that kind of guilt feels like." I struggled to sit up again, hurt and furious and wanting nothing more than to disappear, but he was sitting on the blanket and I was under it. I got no farther than propped on my elbows.

He stilled me with one hand under my jaw. "Try again." His words were soft. His touch was cool on my heated skin.

My breath issued in shallow pants. I stared into his eyes, watched as his gaze moved to my mouth. Desire flared hot in my belly, a longing beyond anything I'd ever felt, and when he lifted his eyes back to mine, I knew he could see it. I leaned my face into his palm, desperate to stoke the banked passion buried just beneath the surface of his heart before he extinguished it.

"Don't step to me, Erin McIntyre." His fingers betrayed him, stroking lightly behind my ear before his mind was aware that the actions of his body contradicted his words.

I'd never heard the phrase before, but what it meant was plain—and spoken far too late.

"I'm already here," I said, a whispered surrender and a plea. He was near enough that I could taste his breath. Inches separated his mouth from mine, but I was trapped beneath the blanket and could get no nearer. Despite his words, he would be the one to close the space between us—or not.

He leaned closer and his lips touched mine. I had never been kissed so carefully. Our eyes were open, gauging every fragile trace of emotion, savoring every measured point of contact. His tongue traced along the surface of my bottom lip, pressing for entrance. I fought to remain still under his hand, calm under his mouth, responding only, afraid to wake him to what we were doing. Afraid he would stop. Lips slid together, tasting, assessing. I wanted to thrash free of the constricting blanket and climb him. I wanted to wrap my arms and legs around him and pull him in and never let go.

All at once, he deepened the kiss and shoved the blanket to my waist, freeing me. I rose like a sliver of iron to a magnet, hands twisting into his T-shirt to pull him closer, eyes falling closed, trusting him, mouth opening in unrestrained submission as his tongue swept forward, intoxicating and sweet. I was terrified and recklessly alive, certain those disparate states of being weren't meant to be so strongly intertwined.

His hands slid to my shoulders, down my arms to cup my elbows, leaving trails of fire on my skin. Until he used that leverage to disconnect his lips from mine by self-inflicted force. "We can't do this. I'm sorry, I shouldn't have—"

"Why?" My arms were still folded between us, still clinging to him by his shirt, which was suddenly a too-insubstantial hold.

He stared, unmoving, still holding us apart. The room was lit with the picturesque light pollution of downtown and a glowing half-moon in a clear pre-daybreak sky. "You report to me. I'm your supervisor. This is highly unethical, not something I've ever done or intended to do."

"My father owns the company—"

He stood and backed away as I came onto my knees, my hands reaching out but no longer able to touch him. His eyes bored into mine. "Is that a threat?" He passed a hand over his face and breathed a quick, juddering sigh. "You were emotionally vulnerable, and it's my responsibility as the person with the supervisory power not to cross that line. There is no excuse and you have every right… But I wasn't alone in that kiss—"

"*No*." I sat back on my heels, confused and shaking my head. "There's no threat. I didn't mean it that way. I meant we're not the same as others in our positions. The power structure between us isn't like other management hierarchies. I report to you, yes, but my father is your boss's boss. It could be argued that I'm…" I swallowed. "…taking advantage of *you*."

He sighed, eyes closed, but before I could be relieved by it, he said, "Either way then. It can't happen." He crossed his arms, the physical manifestation of an emotional retreat. "You're a McIntyre. It can't happen."

"You say that like… like I'm a Capulet and you're a Montague."

Okay, so Romeo and Juliet weren't the best #couplegoals comparison in the history of lovers, fictional or real, since—spoiler alert—they both *died violently* at the end, but the fact that he said my surname like it was a disease made it an apt one.

He disregarded the comment as if I'd not said it. "Will you be able to sleep?"

Internal Erin laughed bitterly and said, *NO*. "I don't know." I turned to examine the eastern sky, still a deep indigo. There was no hint of dawn on the horizon. "What time is it?"

"Around four, I think."

I did not want to lie on his sofa for hours, restless and wide awake, mortified at vomiting in the presence of and then sexually molesting my disinclined-to-be-touched boss—*after* rousing both of us (and his dog) from a dead sleep with my nightmare. At the bottom of that glorious mental list of Erin's Fuckups, I was still horny as hell.

I lay back, studying him as his eyes shifted from the window to connect with mine.

"It would be best if you could get a few hours' rest." His arms remained loosely crossed. He'd moved no closer, and I knew he wouldn't.

"I'll try. I'm sorry I woke you."

Isaac had no obligation to my attraction to him. Zero. It was my cross to bear. All mine. But damn, that kiss. I'd been kissing boys since I was eleven, and no kiss had ever compared. The man had skills, a thought that led my sex-starved imagination to what other skills he might have. Probably had. I was thankful my face was in shadow so he wouldn't read my mind again.

"No worries, Ms. McIntyre." He clicked his tongue twice and said, "Come," to Pete, and my body caught fire as they padded away, silent but for the faint, retreating taps of Pete's toenails on the floor.

I closed my eyes and pulled the blanket to my chin, stretched taut as the elastic on a slingshot just before it discharges. *Christ almighty, Isaac, why? Why that word? Come.*

Come, Ms. McIntyre.

Aaaughhhh.

My hand slipped past the slack waistband of the sweats. I bit my lip and turned my face into the pillow to muffle the sounds I knew I would make. Fingers stroked and pressed as my imagination rioted and filled with visions of my boss shutting the door of my office behind him, rounding my desk and pulling me up from my chair, pushing my skirt to my waist and fucking me against the desk. *Come for me*, fantasy Isaac said, and I obeyed, hard, my entire body heaving on his sofa.

Face still buried in the pillow, I panted and shook with strong orgasmic aftershocks. Drifting in the delicious vibrations, I returned to earth gradually, reluctant to examine what I'd just done. My sex life had been wholly fictitious for months now. Anonymous, imaginary men. Quick and dirty fucks, to completion and no farther.

Enough to bring relief and, often, just the blessed oblivion that followed.

Was it exploitation to intentionally create personalized pornographic hallucinations about a very real someone who'd just issued the sternest and most resolute of rejections? He'd all but vowed *Not now, not ever*. My breath slowed, deep and even, as my body grew languorous, eager to sink deep into the satisfied sleep I'd just prepared it to have.

You're a McIntyre. That unalterable trait seemed to outstrip all else—our relation to each other within my father's company and whatever sentiments or cravings had just erupted between us. In the end he hadn't said, *You're my subordinate*. He hadn't said, *Your father owns the company I work for*. He'd said, *You're a McIntyre*. As if my family name was the boundary he couldn't, or wouldn't, cross.

I didn't understand, and my mind was too lethargic and full of my favorite new fantasy to try.

He sat down in my desk chair and unbuttoned my blouse as I stood before him. "Come, Ms. McIntyre."

"Again, Mr. Maat?"

He pushed the lacy cups of my bra aside and pulled me, legs spread wide, over his lap. "Yes. Now," he commanded. His hands gripped my hips, mouth sucking a nipple deep, tongue swirling around the peak as he rocked into me.

I came again.

chapter *Twenty-one*

I woke to a sunrise coloring the ecru walls a peachy pink, a low light over the kitchen stove, the drone of cars on 7th Street, and the smell of coffee. I stretched, listening for Isaac, or Pete, and heard nothing. My phone screen revealed battery life of thirteen percent, a text from a high school friend who would be in town for Thanksgiving and wanted to meet up, and the fact that I'd slept a solid four hours since my wicked, filthy, Isaac-centered fantasies.

My body tingled at the roused memory, all sensation pooling between my legs in one formidable surge. *Oh. My. God.* I had never been this strung out, every shred of erotic awareness on one person. One person who was having none of it. I groaned like a petulant child. If I weren't worried that Isaac might walk around the corner any second, I could replay one of last night's sexy-time visions or dream up a new one.

I promised my dirty little mind that it could have its treat tonight when I was safe in my own bed, and stood. *Brr.* The apartment had grown cooler overnight. With the blanket wrapped around me, I crept toward the coffeepot and found a clean mug and a note.

Erin,

Pete and I went for a run. Coffee's brewed – help yourself. I'll make breakfast when I get back. I assume your phone's dead or dying, so there's a cord on the counter.

Back soon.

Isaac

I plugged in my phone, set myself up on the opposite end of the sectional, and curled under the blanket, facing the engrossing sunrise view that stretched across the width and height of the apartment like Sheila Anderson's mural, but lovelier for its ephemeral existence. Gauzy clouds hung over the horizon, under-lit by the rising sun and backed with bright blue. In half an hour, this sunrise would vanish forever. Like last night's kiss, which hardly seemed real.

The only exposed parts of me were my head and the hand holding the steaming mug. I breathed in coffee vapors with a contented sigh and listened for the sound of the door latch turning. I didn't have to wait long. Pete came straight to me when they entered, as though I belonged there. He snuggled his head into my lap and wagged with his whole body.

"Hello, Pete. Did you get your exercise whether you wanted it or not?" I extended my warm hand outside the blanket to scratch behind his ears, which felt like thin, flappy shavings of ice.

I heard Isaac pouring a cup of coffee in the kitchen behind me.

"His ears are freezing!" I said, turning.

He was shrugging off a hoodie. Not the one I'd puked on, obviously–he had claimed to have others. This one was a vibrant royal blue and matched the tank underneath. The combo was almost as yummy on him as his purple shirt and tie. Folding the hoodie over a barstool, he rolled his shoulders and picked up his coffee.

"They'll warm up. It's cool out this morning." He sipped from the mug, staring absently out the window.

I blinked, ogling him like a sex maniac, which after last night I had to concede might be the case. The oversized armhole of his sweat-soaked tank was cut low enough to display the curve of his ribs and the rippled edges of abs when he moved. The rising sun made his perspiration-slicked skin glow golden brown, darker where individual muscles were demarcated.

I'd learned the names of fundamental muscle groups in freshman biology, but I was salivating with lust and my recall was momentarily shot. His arms were solid, defined. *Biceps*, my brain said, stupidly proud of itself. *Biceps*. Black mesh shorts exposed equally impressive, rock-hard legs. *Calves*.

He toed off his sneakers under the barstool and turned toward me.

My fuck-me eyes were activated, and I couldn't flip the switch fast enough to hide them. Flustered, I rotated back toward the window like a guilt-ridden addict whose self-reproach did not extend to a resolute cessation of unauthorized fantasies. I rubbed Pete's icy ears, pretending wholesomeness, and wished Isaac would offer himself up for breakfast.

The refrigerator door opened. "Blueberry waffles?"

I wondered if whipped cream was involved. *What is wrong with me?* "Yes, please."

"I'm going to shower real quick first."

The heavy doors to his room slid closed. The shower switched on. I fought to keep from imagining his big, soapy hands sliding over my skin and wanted to cry over the injustice of it being make-believe.

I scrambled up and out from under the warm, tempting blanket, embracing the chill like a cold-air shower. From his sunspot on the oblong rug, Pete lifted his head. "More coffee, that's what I need," I explained.

He lowered his muzzle back to his outstretched paws and huffed a little sigh. Even the dog knew I was full of shit.

By the time Isaac emerged, I'd rummaged through his cupboard and fridge to assemble the ingredients and utensils on the counter. The waffle mix was whole grain, the blueberries frozen, the milk skim, and everything was organic. I hadn't encountered a single bit of junk food in the whole place—except for a half-eaten pint of ice cream. Butter pecan, my favorite.

"You make a good sous chef," he said, pouring and stirring. He'd dressed in worn jeans, hems frayed on his bare feet, and a blood-red, long-sleeved henley. The sleeves were pushed to his elbows. For months I'd seen him in nothing but slacks, dress shirts, and ties. Now, in a short span of hours, I'd encountered Batman Isaac, sweats-and-T-shirt Isaac, sweaty-tank-and-shorts Isaac, and now this. I was being tortured.

"I'm good at all sorts of things." I was not in the mood to be subtle.

In typical Isaac Maat fashion, he took an eternity to respond. I waited him out, because I was learning. He heated and buttered the waffle iron, folded the blueberries into the batter, and poured the first batch before speaking.

"What do you want from me?" His eyes, dark and unwavering, gave nothing away.

"I think you know," I said, hedging.

His brows hitched, but he kept silent, taunting me to answer his question.

My heart leaped. In a futile attempt to appear composed, I took a slow, shallow breath and exhaled it in jittery stops and starts that signaled the final ineffective warning against the words about to leave my mouth. Words I couldn't make unsaid once they were uttered.

"I want you."

His eyes glowed like polished obsidian. "You want me to fuck you."

Freshman-year cheer practice, I'd been dropped during a basic basket toss, landing on my back so hard that I couldn't breathe for several seconds. That vividly graphic sentence from Isaac Maat had the same affect.

"Yes." My face went hot. My fingers tingled because all the blood had left them to pool elsewhere.

"As we established last night—"

"I know you want me." If he denied it, he was a liar. His kiss had lit me up like pyrotechnics gone rogue, every nerve plugging in and igniting, and he was the power source.

"Whether I *want* you or not is irrelevant." He made our carnal power struggle sound like a debate over eating junk food or sleeping in.

"But you don't deny it."

"Regardless, any association between us beyond our working

relationship is out of the question. I'm sorry if anything I've said or done made you think otherwise." His eyes slid away. He was fortifying his resolve no matter his desires. "You're just horny. It's not me you want."

The volatile temper for which gingers are known burst into flames in the center of my chest and snarled out. "So you think I just want to get laid?" He flinched, which was gratifying, but I wasn't done. "I just want a dick and anyone's dick will do?"

My conscience *ahem*-ed and recapped the fact that I had gone out last night with that very objective, evaluating each of Mindi's male friends with the intention of getting laid. Clearly I was horny as hell. But if any old dick would've done, Boone was plenty cute, Oliver was hot enough to stuff a sock in his mouth and ride him like a living dildo, or I could have picked door number three and made that banana's whole year.

Isaac glowered at the blameless waffle maker, which sizzled happily and was beginning to emit appetizing aromas.

I didn't wait him out this time. "I will take your suggestion under advisement, Mr. Maat. I'm sure someone's dick will accommodate me." I felt like a total bitch, but that didn't put the brakes on my mouth. "Maybe Joshua? He's not my boss, and I don't think he'd be afraid of my father. Or my name."

In trying to goad Isaac into arguing back, I said the first name that popped into my head. Never mind that Joshua's unpantsed penis would never find itself anywhere near me unless it had a masochistic hunger to discover The Lawnmower, a self-defense move I'd been waiting three years to use since it wasn't one we could test out on the RAD coaches. Joshua would be a worthy candidate.

I wanted Isaac to vow that his was the only dick for me. Instead, he handed me the first waffle, a miniature pitcher of warmed syrup, and a can of Reddi-wip. When his waffle was done, he took his plate to his desk, sat on his ergonomic rolling stool, opened his laptop, and began tapping at it.

I finished my meal in silence, rinsed the dishes, and went to brush my teeth and wrangle my unruly hair into a knotted bun.

Not a word passed his lips until he handed me a Target bag containing my clothes from the previous night. "I looked for your shoes and found them in the trash?"

"They were covered in dirty water and I think bodily fluids."

"Ah." He was holding his keys. "If you're ready then."

I wanted to flounce back down on his sofa, cross my arms, and pout like an oversized toddler.

I wanted to put my arms around him and beg forgiveness for being the selfish, horny person he thought I was.

I did not want to leave. He stood there, waiting for me to get out of his home if I couldn't have the decency to get out of his life.

I squatted and hugged Pete's neck. He sat patiently and let me, like a movie dog. My parents' dog, Jack, would have scratched up my arms, poked me in the eye with his nose, and wriggled to get loose until he peed. "Goodbye, Pete." I rubbed his ears, which had warmed up, as Isaac had alleged they would.

I had a wayward thought as we approached the door. Without questioning the impulse, I slid my phone into my pocket and set my other things on the entry table. "I, um, need to use the bathroom first. Long drive home." I hurried, hoping he would stay where he was by the door to the hallway, because there was no sound explanation for what I was about to do.

When I left the bathroom, I detour-tiptoed over to the framed photograph, lined it up in my phone's display, and took the illicit shot. I would run it through filters later, adjusting the color and lighting. I dropped my phone back in my pocket and returned to gather my small purse and bag of clothes.

I felt like Indiana Jones with a stolen treasure in my pocket, anticipating flying darts and body-flattening boulders and displeased Nazis. My heart hammered at a guilty pace all the way to the parking garage, but I wasn't sorry. I was captivated by that image of Isaac as a cheerful, innocent child with his jaunty, checkered bow tie and his attractive, ill-fated parents, and I couldn't stand the thought of never seeing it again.

"Be careful. There could be glass or broken concrete somewhere," he said, more mindful of my bare feet than I was.

As we emerged from the parking garage, my phone rang; Mindi's face appeared on my screen.

"Hi, girl! How're you feeling?" I asked, my artificially chirpy Erin voice now super apparent to my own ears. *Thank you, Isaac Maat.*

"Much better. I'm so sorry I abandoned you last night—"

"I'm great. Never better." *Liar, liar, everything on fire.*

"Isaac took care of you, then?"

"Yes." *No.* I side-eyed him. He pretended not to notice.

"He's one of Rhys's best friends—he's always been really sweet."

Sweet? Isaac? Um. "He was great."

The hours since leaving dinner last night scrolled by: Isaac covering me with things because I looked cold. Carrying me through a panic-inducing underworld of bubbles several feet over our heads—which sounded fun but *wasn't.* Feeding me and lending me clothes. Admitting that he had adopted an old dog, on purpose, because it needed a home. Keeping a photo of his deceased parents near his bed. Encouraging me to talk about my biggest failure as a human being.

Sonofabitch, he is sweet. I sighed.

"Erin," Mindi said, "I have to tell you this before Rhys gets back with breakfast. We're going out tonight. *Alone*." The elation in her voice was palpable. She was squeaking with it.

"I take it that's not happened before?"

"Never. I've been hanging out with Boone and them for over two years, and Rhys almost as long. But Boone says Rhys never really hung out with them until I showed up. I've tried literally everything. For a while he kept telling me I should date guys my age, until I told him what happened."

"You told him?" That was huge.

Mindi's parents had been perfect, supporting her through pressing charges, urging her to get counseling. With baby steps, she'd progressed past the devastating PTSD she had suffered after the assault. She'd left home again to finish college and established a new group of friends on a new campus, in a new city.

But she hadn't dated or hung out alone with anyone, and she hadn't disclosed her past to any of her new friends but Madison. The fact that she had confided in Rhys was remarkable. Tears blurred my vision, and I made a fervent wish that he would prove deserving of her faith in him, no matter what transpired with their potential romance.

"He was so angry and upset for me. But it backfired a little." She sighed. "He stopped telling me to date other people, but he started treating me like I was made of glass, which is just bullshit! And then last night happened, and at one point my guard was so far down from all the throwing up that I told him to please goddammit stop treating me like I was broken."

"Wow."

"Hi honey, I'm home!" I heard in the background, followed by a whispered, "Oh crap, you're on the phone."

"It's Erin," she told him. "I'm just letting her know I'm alive and that I'm very, very sorry for the rancid chicken salad."

My stomach churned resentfully. "Ugh. Please do not say rancid. Or chicken, for that matter."

"*Deal.* Claire and Madison had to take poor Ava to the ER. They gave her meds to stop the vomiting and hooked her up to an IV to rehydrate her. Madison texted around six to let me know they were back home. I'm glad you and I didn't eat much of that you-know-what."

"Jesus, no kidding."

She thanked Rhys for her latte and then, with the verbal equivalence of an exaggerated wink, said, "Well, Erin, I'll, uh, talk to you *tomorrow*." Subtlety had never been Mindi's strong suit.

I wanted to laugh and say *Get it, girl!* but Isaac was sitting next to me.

"Yes. I'll want all the deets."

Isaac pulled up behind my Prius, parked where I'd left it a mere thirteen hours before. I grabbed my small handbag and the plastic bag that held my costume. He'd added my gold pom-poms, which we'd left in his trunk outside the haunted house.

"Got everything?" he asked.

"Yep. I'll bring your clothes back Monday. Thanks for letting me crash on your couch, and the food, and… everything."

His hand tightened on the gearshift, but he needn't have agonized that I was going to have another go at persuading him to reconsider his Erin moratorium. After his coup de grâce assertion regarding my horniness and the myriad choices available to fix it (namely, anyone's dick but his), my wiles were demoralized and going on hiatus.

I popped the rear of my hatchback, stowed the bag, and removed my flats, mindful of Isaac's car idling behind me, Isaac watching me, Isaac thinking who knew what. Once I started my car, he reversed and drove away.

I clunked my forehead against the steering wheel a few times for good measure, inhaled a deep breath, retrieved my dark-lensed sunglasses from the hinged compartment over my head, and drove home.

chapter *Twenty-two*

Isaac's office door didn't stand open anymore. That was the first change I noted.

On occasion it was shut when I passed, but more often it was cracked open a few inches. Enough to say *I'm here* and also *Keep out*. The latter was more than likely *I'm busy*, but I was taking everything he did or didn't do personally, from his now-commonly-shut door to his seeming avoidance of eye contact during meetings and even when I was in his office, reporting on client progress. He listened and replied in conventional ways, but his eyes were on his monitor or a printout in his hand. Instead of looking at me, he straightened his desk or filed something while I was speaking.

When forced to look at me by Western conventions of conversation, he stared at my ear, or my nose, or the pulse beating at the base of my throat. Anywhere but my eyes—or my mouth. As before, my questions were answered, my opinions validated or negated in a professional manner, and that was the end of the interaction. No crackling current remained between us. It was like it had never been there.

I did my job autonomously for the most part, and when that should have been and maybe was a sort of praise, a gratifying endorsement of my proficiency, it wasn't. I didn't know why.

I contemplated pushing his door open and asking, "Why are you avoiding me?"

He would raise one derisive brow and affect a perplexed, confused frown. "What do you mean? I'm right here," he would say, or something similar. Not so long ago I would have believed it was all in my mind. *Silly Erin. Isaac Maat never looked at you any differently.*

A kiss had changed everything.

I was in the break room, inspecting a salad I'd brought for lunch—salads and leftovers were no longer indiscriminately trusted to not contain murderous spores—when Isaac entered, coffee mug in hand.

I saw him from the corner of my eye as he pulled up before entering and came to a full stop in the doorway. He took a step back, planning to steer clear of the room until I'd left it, no doubt. Whipping around, I said, "Hi."

He froze and stared at my ear, forcing his face into a pleasantish façade. "Hi." Walking straight to the sink, he rinsed his mug and made it clear he had no intention of making conversation.

I rolled my eyes behind his back, poked at my perfectly fresh salad a few more times, and took a sniff. *Is that odor from the goat cheese or a lethal microorganism?* I wasn't sure.

"Hey, Erin." Joshua did not hesitate at the door or stop with a greeting. He left his unrinsed coffee cup in the sink for the janitorial staff to deal with. He ignored Isaac. "Keep that salad for tomorrow. I'm in the mood for Zushi—we haven't been there in forever."

The visual juxtaposing of these two men didn't happen often. In a larger organization, they would have had little to no contact. But JMCH was a small firm—*a family place*, Daddy said—so it was like a small town. Everyone knew everyone. Even so, Sales was front end. Finance was back end. If not for the client liaison responsibility he'd assumed, Isaac would have been chest-deep in numbers all day with little to no direct interaction with the people we built homes for. By the time he saw them, the sales department's job was done.

Isaac stiffened at Joshua's invitation. There was an enmity between them that had nothing to do with me. The earliest things Joshua had said regarding Isaac exposed entrenched animosity, not jealousy that had begun with my arrival. That said, I felt like one of those miniscule neutral territories between two warring factions. I was no one's property and never would be, but I couldn't shake the feeling that they both saw me that way in relation to each other. I didn't like it.

"Sure. Lunch sounds great. I'm not trusting this salad anyway." I stepped on the floor lever of the trash can and dropped the boxed salad in. "I'll run up and grab my bag. Meet you at the front."

I glanced at Isaac as I moved between them. He was toweling his mug dry, but his eyes were on me. For the first time in almost three weeks, his eyes met mine, and he was not happy. His eyes were black, whether from fluorescent lighting or dilated pupils, and they would have scorched me to the wall if they'd had their way. I would have been a sooty cutout. A full-sized Erin silhouette.

My step faltered and I tore my gaze from his. This was what the phrase *playing with fire* meant. I left the room and sprinted up the stairs instead of walking for no reason except the absurd feeling that I was being pursued. I owed him nothing. He'd kissed me and pushed me away. *Literally*. Beyond that, I had never allowed anyone to dictate my friendships and wasn't about to start now.

My imagination, which hadn't ceased its almost nightly Isaac fantasies, now pictured Joshua and Isaac standing in the break room below. Well. Isaac was standing. Joshua was on the floor, holding his rapidly bruising jaw. *Don't speak to her again. No lunches, no coffee dates, no conversation whatsoever. Do I make myself clear, Swearingen?*

My breath caught as I entered my office and stood there for a moment, hand to chest, breathing erratically, aroused as hell, and trying to remember why I was there.

"Holy shit." I steadied myself, one hand on my desk, the other assessing the wild beat of my heart. My fantasies hadn't intruded on my workday before, for chrissake, nor had any of them ever included another person. Okay, there was one time I included another girl, but I dismissed her a minute later. *I don't share*, I'd said as she vanished, taking her voluptuous body (because if I was going to imagine a girl in my bed, I was going all in) with her. *Neither do I*, he'd answered.

In a flash, I knew why there had been no invasive daydreams, even in the place many of my nighttime fantasies transpired. Isaac had rendered me invisible to him here, and my mind knew it, even if my heart—*I mean my body*—didn't. Here, we were colleagues, nothing more. Here, we weren't friends. I hadn't told him my deep dark secret. He hadn't recounted the worst, most heartbreaking memory of his childhood. We hadn't kissed. I hadn't met his dog.

He and Joshua could decide on pistols at dawn for all I cared. Their bad blood had nothing to do with me.

I closed my eyes and took a slow breath. When my brain rebooted, I asked myself why I was standing in my office, remembered, and grabbed my purse from the hook on the back of the door. I passed Isaac's office as his door was snapping closed.

By the time Joshua and I reached his car, I regretted my decision to join him for lunch. Whatever retaliation I had heaped on Isaac in the moment had ricocheted and clobbered me in the head. Joshua spent the entire mercifully short drive boasting about his sales for the current month in comparison to his female counterparts. He didn't come right out and attribute his success to his superior gender, but he skirted close.

Overall sales hadn't been good, per usual in November because few people approach the holidays and say, "Let's begin a custom home project!" I knew for a fact there were only three new contracts, and one of them was already having complications—one of Joshua's two deals. If it fell through, Megan would move ahead because her one sale was the highest of the month.

I didn't bother mentioning it. His momentum was so strong he was having a one-way conversation.

We were eating before he interrupted his monologue with a series of progressively personal questions. "So, what're your plans over Thanksgiving? I'm heading to Jackson Hole with a couple of buddies to do some snowboarding. They've already had like seventy inches."

I'd erected a little barrier of glasses and condiments between us to thwart any food stealing. "My family goes to my grandparents' cabin in Colorado every year."

"Ah—the venerable Leonard P. Welch." He chewed a slice of tuna sashimi and continued talking around it. "Is it true he's a billionaire?"

He knew my maternal grandfather's name? What kind of stalker shit was that?

"I… don't…"

"I know McIntyre Welch Inc. operates under the name Jeffrey McIntyre Custom Homes, but it's common knowledge—well maybe not *common* knowledge, but it's no secret—that your grandfather bankrolled the company in the beginning, along with Ted's grandfather and a secret stakeholder they eventually bought out. He's not on the *Forbes* list yet, but he's probably really fucking close, right?"

I knew Ted Sager's father had held the VP of Operations position before he did, but I hadn't known his family was involved in founding JMCH. I had no idea of my grandparents' net worth either, not that I would chat about it over lunch with some guy I barely knew, for fuck's sake. Also, Joshua had searched the *Forbes* Billionaire List, looking for my grandfather?

"Um, I don't feel comfortable discussing my family's financial assets."

My maternal grandparents were loaded; that was plain. Their "cabin" in Colorado was as impressive as my parents' place, but with mountain views, thirty acres of land, a wine cellar, a private stocked pond, and a horse barn. They had live-in help, and the horses had their own caretaker. Mom had been raised like that from birth; Daddy hadn't. He'd embodied his up-by-his-bootstraps story and never let my brothers forget it. Never mind his early aggrandizement by way of Grandpa Welch.

"All right, all right—it was just for bragging rights, you know? 'I work for a billionaire' would be a cool claim."

I assumed lots of people worked for billionaires, technically speaking, but I wanted to escape the awkward topic. "So Jackson Hole—that's in Wyoming, or Utah?"

• • • • • • • • • •

Isaac pulled his office door open as I passed it. "Please get me those updated numbers before you leave tomorrow. End of month is Friday." He either had incredible timing or he'd seen me return from his window.

The wispy hairs at my nape bristled at the thought of him tracking my return from lunch with Joshua. "You aren't working over Thanksgiving, are you?"

He'd begun to shut the door but stopped at my question. "I'm not leaving town. Just picking my cousin up from the airport Thursday morning and driving us to my aunt's place in Arlington. I can get a lot done Wednesday and Friday and hold on to the vacation days."

"I guess it will be kinda dead up here those days. Less interruptions." His shirt today was a deep orange, a shade that would look hideous on ninety-five percent of men. On him, it was gorgeous. "You look like a tribute to the return of pumpkin spice."

He glanced down and touched fingers to his tie—angled stripes in silver, forest green and shades of orange. One brow hitched up and his mouth quirked to the side as he looked down at me.

"That's not an insult, I swear! I really like pumpkin spice."

"So it's no celery, I guess."

His comment, an allusion to the night at his apartment, snuck beneath my breastbone and pinched my heart. I couldn't reply. I just shook my head slowly.

"All right, then—"

"I'm not seeing him."

He straightened but didn't look convinced or appeased. If anything, his body seemed to shrink from mine even though he hadn't stepped away. I was losing my mind.

"Or any part of him."

"Not really my business, is it, Ms. McIntyre?"

"No, I suppose it isn't." I dug my nails from one hand into the palm of the other, an always handy method I had discovered in childhood to keep the pain focused somewhere other than my trampled pride or my unguarded heart. By some miracle, I even managed a smile. "I'll have your numbers to you tomorrow, Mr. Maat."

• • • • • • • • • • •

My seat was next to Leo on the flight to Boulder, with our parents in front of us. Our middle brothers had always staged a best-of-five rock-paper-scissors match to decide which of them had to sit next to Leo inflight, but Foster the workaholic was flying in Thursday morning and back out on Friday, and Pax and his fiancée, whom we'd never met, were en route from Albuquerque and would meet us at the cabin.

My eldest brother wasn't a conversationalist, and our first-class seats were roomy enough that he couldn't manspread into my space without making a malicious effort. His laziness won out. He spent the flight dozing, drinking, and playing games on his phone. I popped in my earbuds, started an audiobook, and stared out the window at the field of white clouds below, bare landscape peeking through here and there.

It was Wednesday morning, the day before Thanksgiving, and Isaac would be at the office along with one or two other people. I wondered if he'd wear his usual shirt and tie or if he would dress down. Knowing Isaac, he would cut the difference. Jeans and maybe a soft sweater—dark jewel toned, fine merino wool, worn over a T-shirt.

I had to rewind my book a number of times; I kept losing the thread of the story. After the fourth or fifth time, I gave up and switched to music, accepting the fact that I wanted to daydream about Isaac. I wanted to dress him up or down like a Ken doll in my mind. I cycled through the outfits I'd seen him wear and invented others.

Lumberjack Isaac, an ax balanced on his shoulder and a gallant *I just chopped down a tree to keep you warm this winter* look on his face. Swim trunks Isaac, walking out of the ocean like a glistening aquatic god. Tuxedo Isaac, hand outstretched to request a dance… or my future.

I breathed a sigh that became a soft chuckle. *Jesus take the wheel, because I am about to drive off the mountain.*

Once upon a time, my boyfriend of two years had proposed to me. As I'd stared down at that solitaire, there had been no vacillation in my mind, only shock followed by self-contempt that I'd been so cavalier with someone else's heart. I hadn't premeditated the end of us. I hadn't planned my exit. I had let myself be a carefree girl enjoying her life. I had allowed the finale of Chaz and me to play out, with devastating results.

And here I was, fiercely aware of the different answer I would give a man I'd known a matter of months. A man I hardly knew at all. A man who would not cross trip-wired battle lines for me. A man who viewed me as something he might desire but would never allow inside his heart. Despite all of that, I sensed the jigsaw fit of us to my bones.

I pulled up the appropriated photograph on my phone, the screen angled away from my brother. I knew that smile, as rare as it was in the man that little boy had become. This was my penance for being careless with Chaz, then. To find I was capable of falling in love after all—with a man who would never love me.

chapter *Twenty-three*

Virginia Foster Welch ruled the family like the matriarch she was. At eighteen, she'd married my grandfather, a wealthy, ambitious man ten years her senior. A judicious and respectable ten months later, she'd given birth to my mother, a cherished only child she had trained up in her image. They'd always behaved more like sisters than mother and daughter, and where I resembled my mother physically, they were similar all the way through.

Neither of them circumvented the will of their husbands; their power was influence, not mandates, but that influence was considerable. Mom told me once, after one too many glasses of wine, that if not for Nana, my brothers and I would not exist.

This is the sort of statement that gets your attention when you're a tween who thinks you've just about got everything figured out. At that age, your philosophy of existence is simple and Cartesian: *I think, therefore I am*. I was the daughter my mother wanted so much she'd kept "trying for a girl" after three sons. I had never considered the ways in which I might *not* have existed. Her startling disclosure knocked the ladder right out from under me.

"When I brought your father home to meet my folks, Daddy didn't believe he was quite up to snuff," she'd said. "Your father's people believed in hard work, climbing the mountain to success, yada yada. Mine believed in *owning the mountain*. I saw Jeff's potential, but Daddy forbade me to marry him—until Mama persuaded him that all he needed was a little boost."

That little boost had resulted in the company my parents owned and a new generation of McIntyres—my brothers and me.

Mom squinted at my face then, realizing belatedly that advising a twelve-year-old how close she'd come to nonexistence might be insensitive. "And here you are!" she said, as though exclaiming *Ta-da!* And then she offered me a sip of her wine.

Controlling an assortment of children was a whole other animal, especially once they became adults. A certain amount of leash was allowed before the collar tightened. I just didn't know that yet.

I found myself sharing a bedroom in my grandparents' house for the first time—with Bailey, Pax's fiancée, with whom he shared an apartment. No reason was given. We were simply shown to the same room and expected to share it despite the fact that we'd just met.

"Nana, Bailey and I live together," Pax said.

"You don't live in my house, Paxton," Nana answered, no give in her words.

Bailey ran her hand along his back, calming him and forestalling further argument. When it was time for bed, they kissed and whispered in the hall like teenagers on a front porch. My hands tightened on the book in my hands until I closed my eyes and reminded myself that was my brother heavy petting just outside the bedroom door. " *Eww,*" my brain said.

After ten minutes or so, Bailey strolled into the room. "It would really shock the shit out of them if we were bi, eh?"

I laughed, my estimation of her rising. "How do you know I'm not?"

Her brows rose and she smirked, nodding. "Pax said you were

the cool one." She sat on her twin bed and examined me. Her chin-length bob was darker than it was in Pax's profile pic and lacked the fuchsia ombré at the ends, and her makeup was less dramatic. She had toned down to meet his family. I would bet a lung Pax hadn't liked that. "He also said that magnificent red hair was natural. I was predisposed to hate you a little for it."

"Good thing I'm cool and maybe bi then."

She laughed. "Yeah, good thing." She looked around the room after removing a small bag from her suitcase. "This place is insane. When Pax said *cabin*, I expected rustic. I asked if we should bring our sleeping bags, and he laughed at me." She pointed at the dual-sided fireplace, visible from both the bedroom and the bathroom. "This is not rustic."

"Don't tell Nana that. She believes the stone and timber architecture plus acreage absolutely equals rustic. That is literally one of the principal words she uses to describe the place."

"Yeah, no. I have no intention of crossing her. Or your parents." She arched one dark brow. "Leo, on the other hand..."

Bailey was bright. She and Pax had arrived just after dinner, and she'd already figured us all out. While brushing her teeth, she appeared in the bathroom doorway wearing pink-and-black-plaid flannel pajamas and a tiny black tee. Her navel was pierced. "So, Pax's room is the second doorway to the left?"

"Yep."

• • • • • • • • • • •

The indication that everything was about to go south occurred not long after the traditional long-winded blessing of the meal from our grandfather, during which Pax made a face at me from across the table as he'd been doing for nearly twenty years in an effort to make me laugh, after which—when it worked—he'd close his eyes and feign utter piety. This year Bailey poked him in the ribs, eliciting an "Oww!" and earning him a dirty look from Mom.

Business as usual, Grandpa carving the turkey while side dishes made the rounds and Nana's culinary skills were praised. To pass the time while waiting for the main course to circulate, we each voiced a thing we were thankful for—another tradition that often degenerated into humble-brags of achievements that thanked one's own hard work or coincidence more than anything else. Pax surprised me by being thankful for Bailey's *yes* two months ago, and she made us laugh by being thankful that her hair had accepted a found-in-nature shade to meet his family after years of being all sorts of unnatural hues.

The turkey platter had gone full circle when Grandpa, forking a pile of white meat onto his plate, said, "Well, I'm thankful none of that protesting bullshit is taking place around here. It's like people don't know how to be grateful for what they've got."

Pax put his fork down. Bailey's hand tightened on her own as she stared at her plate. "Like the Rice family, you mean?" Pax said. "They should be grateful that the twelve-year-old who should be making off with the turkey leg won't be at their table ever again? That what you mean, Gramps?"

"*PAX*," Mom said. "This is not the place—"

"Oh, I'm sorry Mom, what *is* the place? Am I not allowed a dissenting opinion? I've been listening to this shit for twenty-six years—"

"Not at this table," she said at the same time Daddy barked, "No cursing!"

"They've got a president in the damn White House," my grandfather began, his bushy white eyebrows lowered over his eyes like heavy swag curtains. No one barked a *no cursing* edict at him. "That shooting was a damn shame all right. Damn shame that kid's parents let him have a toy that looked like a real firearm and let him out of the house with it."

I gasped and heard Foster's murmured, "*Shit*," next to me. My face flushed hot. I wanted to get up and leave the table but my legs and arms felt numb.

Pax was undeterred. "I've got teammates who are routinely stopped for DWBs. Know what that is? Driving While Black. It happens so often they don't even fucking mention it."

"*PAX!*" Mom tried again. "That is *enough*."

"I was with a teammate a week ago when it happened. This dude is two hundred pounds of lean muscle. Prime shape. He's law-abiding, tax-paying. No reason to be scared of *anybody*. We got pulled over, and he was *terrified*. 'Hands where they can see 'em, man,' he told me. He put both windows down and gripped the steering wheel, ten and two, like he might get sucked out of the car if he didn't hold on tight enough. I asked him, 'Should I get your insurance card out of the glove compartment?' and he nearly came unglued. '*NO*, man, just keep your hands on your legs!'"

No one said a word. My ears were buzzing, and in that silent beat of time all I could think of was Isaac. Was that true for him? It had to be.

"I told him okay and did what he asked. Officers came up to both windows with their fucking hands on their fucking halfway-drawn guns. They shined flashlights into the car, all over the console, our laps, the floor. One asked for license and registration, and I've never seen anyone move so deliberately, commentating the whole time. 'I'm getting my wallet,' he told them. 'I'm getting the insurance card.' His hand was right in front of me, shaking."

Bailey put her silverware down, leaned into Pax's shoulder, and took his hand under the table. She knew this story. He swallowed. "They ran his license and registration, conferred behind the car, then let us go with a 'Watch yourselves out there.' Like what does that even fucking mean? He punched the window buttons and I said, 'They didn't say why they stopped you' because I'd just realized it. 'Doesn't matter,' he said. 'They'd just say the car fit the description of one they were looking for.'

"'But they're supposed to say why they stopped you, right?' I was getting all pissed off. 'Yeah, man. Sure,' he said. We went on to another teammate's place for poker night. Neither of us mentioned it to the others. We both lost every game. We couldn't concentrate. Couldn't think of anything but how powerless we had been. How powerless we *were*. I was a shit-for-brains teenager with a lead foot and a low respect for authority. Everyone at this table knows it. I've probably been stopped a dozen times, for good reason. I was a semi-polite smartass every time. I never once worried that I might get *shot* for going fifty in a thirty-five or doing donuts in the church parking lot or having a taillight out." He stared at our mother, laser-focused. "And neither did you."

• • • • • • • • • • •

Minutes later, Nana and Mom began chatting blithely about the food and the weather, and one of them tried to blame the tension on the fact that the Cowboys had been thrashed 33-10 just before we sat down to eat. Everyone—with the exception of Foster, who didn't care about football enough to get emotional about it—came to the table like growly bears, but no one believed the loss was the cause of anything that came after. The general reticence lasted throughout the meal. My easygoing youngest brother, never so heated about anything in his life, had made his point, and no one had a rebuttal, though I could see one trying to form on at least three faces.

When people began to push away from the table, Mom eyeballed my brothers and began clearing plates. "All you boys go get changed to hang lights outside! We'll have cider, cocoa, and dessert after we've all worked off some of that delicious turkey and stuffing." Her wide eyes took aim at me, flicking to Pax and back as she piled serving bowls in a haphazard stack. "Erin, you and Bailey can help Nana and me decorate the tree!" Her voice was all holiday cheer. Her face was do-not-defy-me maternal directive.

The fragrant thirteen-foot white fir had been procured from a Longmont Christmas tree farm that morning and hauled home, placed in a stand, and now claimed its prime spot in a windowed corner of the two-story great room. Boxes of decorations, assembled into organized piles, lined the room in anticipation of the after-meal ritual: the men hung the lights outside while the ladies decorated inside.

I had looked forward to trimming the tree at my grandparents' house every year of my life. Stringing multicolored lights all across the room before twirling them around the branches. Removing passed-down ornaments from their felt-lined wooden boxes and dispersing them among newer baubles. Arranging the antique porcelain nativity scene so that every person and animal gazed at the cherubic infant in the manger and no one could see that the donkey was missing his tail and one sheep had lost half a leg.

Obedient Erin stood and began clearing dishes, but I couldn't incite joyful Erin to appear.

Pax leaned to Bailey. "You don't have to. We can say you aren't feeling well. Erin will cover for you." He looked at me.

"Absolutely." I didn't want to be left alone with Mom and Nana and their identical masks of merriment, but I wouldn't beg Pax's fiancée to participate in the farce to save me.

She shook her head. "I can fake it as well as they can. I pretended to be Goth the entirety of seventh grade just to piss off my mother. I knew it wasn't for me about a week in, but I'd made a stand and I wasn't gonna back down no matter how much I missed pink."

He chuckled and kissed her, then whispered, "I love you. I'm going to go change to help put up the fucking lights, but I'm moving our flights to tomorrow morning. We'll go home and decorate our place. Real tree and all, like you wanted."

When I got out of the shower Friday morning, Bailey had just finished packing her bag. She and Pax planned to head to the airport with Foster. Foster knew; no one else did yet. None of us believed our parents and grandparents would continue the strained silence they'd managed to maintain through dessert last night.

"Nana and Grandpa will be slighted that they're leaving early," Foster told me.

I had no problem imagining the whole scenario. "And Mom will take that offense up like a torch. Daddy too."

For once in our lives, Foster and I wanted to be wrong.

I slumped onto the end of my bed and towel-dried my hair. "I wish I was going with y'all." Bailey had no idea how strong that desire was.

"I'm sorry it had to come to a head right after I met all of you, in the middle of a holiday meal." She sighed and leaned down to zip her bag.

"Grandpa's been saying shit like that his whole life, or at least all of mine. I don't know if anyone's ever called him on it. I've never been prouder of Pax. Whatever you do, don't tell him I said that. His fat head is big enough."

She shouldered her bag and smiled. "I think I'm going to like having a little sister."

Once they were gone, I would be left alone with Leo, my parents, and my grandparents for two days. I didn't relish the daunting thought of saying my piece with no one there to back me up. Then I remembered the things I hadn't said to Joshua months ago, how they had backed up in my throat, suffocating and shameful, when Isaac walked into the room.

I couldn't stay silent anymore, even if I didn't say the exact right thing in the exact right way. Maybe there was no right thing, no way of fostering empathy in a heart determined not to feel it. Maybe there was only the rebuke of the wrong thing, even if no one accepted it.

Me: May I ask you something? It's personal.

Isaac: You can ask.

Me: DWB – is that something you've experienced?

There was an intermission of two or three minutes, with no blinking ellipsis to indicate that he was answering. No furious response—*yay*. But no reply at all would mean I had colossally overstepped. The dots appeared and I stared at the screen, waiting.

Isaac: Why are you asking this? Why are you asking ME this?

Me: I trust you. You'll tell me the truth.

Isaac: And/or you don't know anyone else to ask.

Well, fuck.

Me: Ok. Yes. No one I know well enough.

Isaac: And you think you know me well enough?

Me: I'm sorry. This was rude of me. Please forget I asked.

The ellipsis appeared immediately, blinking happily. Or furiously. My palms sweated, watching it. And then it disappeared, not replaced by text, or more dots, or even a poop emoji. I couldn't put the phone down. It might as well have been glued to my hand. I walked into the bathroom, squeezed toothpaste on my toothbrush, and brushed my teeth, still holding the phone. Finally he answered.

Isaac: I have experienced it. It's real.

Me: I didn't doubt it was real. I just didn't know how widespread it was. How common.

Isaac: Widespread enough. Common enough.

Me: And you're sure it was that, not a legitimate stop?

Isaac: I have no way to be sure, do I? But I have a question for you.

Isaac: How often have you been stopped for nothing? Asked to step out of your vehicle? To put your hands on the car and keep them there while they run your license, your plates, your description? How often have you been patted down for weapons for no reason you're ever told? And then let go with little to no explanation?

Angry tears blurred my vision. He was telling me how it felt to be purposefully reminded again and again how little power you had over your life. Some would be inspired to keep fighting to obtain that promised freedom from discrimination. But for how long, if those toxic reminders never stopped? If no means of dissent was ever acceptable to the other side because of course it wasn't. At what point in a lifetime of resisting do you lose hope?

Me: Once I got a ticket for running a stop sign when I was sure I'd stopped. The jurisdiction was one of the tiny towns between Austin and the coast. The ticket was $200 and I was really angry about it. That's the sum total of my grievance over unjust treatment by law enforcement.

Isaac: What prompted this line of questioning? TV show? Tweet? Outraged NYT article? Outraged network pundit?

Me: Something that happened to a friend of my brother. Not Leo. Pax.

Isaac: The Isotope

Me: Yes. Thank you for answering. Sorry for bothering you.

Isaac: You aren't a bother, Erin. I'll see you Monday.

chapter Twenty-four

When my conversation with Isaac finished, I perceived raised voices coming from the main room. Everyone had figured out that Pax and Bailey were leaving early.

"The tickets have already been changed. We're leaving this morning." Pax and Bailey stood near the front door, holding hands, their backpacks propped against Foster's wheeled carry-on behind them. They faced Mom and Grandpa, whose backs were ramrod straight with indignation, like father like daughter. Nana appeared at the doorway to the kitchen, arms crossed. Her expression—shifting from piqued scowl to wide, blinking eyes to a trembling lip—couldn't decide between anger, confusion, and hurt.

Daddy came up behind me, holding his razor, his face lathered with shaving cream. "*Goddammit*," he said under his breath.

Foster stood a few feet away, typing on his phone. "Our Uber will be here in ten minutes," he murmured, sliding his phone into his front pocket. He shrugged on his coat. Pax and Bailey were already zipped into theirs.

"So you're just going to run off two days early because of a difference in politics?" I had rarely heard my grandfather sound incredulous, and it struck me that there was an obvious reason for that: things usually went his way. *You're used to getting your way, aren't you?* Isaac Maat had once asked me. He'd found a sore spot and pressed it. I had squirmed away from the truth before realizing that I didn't want to be a woman acting like a spoiled child.

My grandfather was in his mid-eighties, and was a man with a lifetime of experience in getting his way. That was the reason for his disbelief that someone, anyone, would openly defy something he thought or said. For decades now, challenges had almost never transpired—not within his family or among his subordinates—and he'd grown so used to his status as a man never naysaid that he was floored by it.

In old photos, Daddy and Grandpa stood shoulder to shoulder. He was no longer quite as big as my father. Age had shrunk him. I thought of Joshua's comments. *The venerable Leonard P. Welch*, he'd said before asking me how much money he had. Grandpa's wealth and reputation were the only things important about him now, aside from his value to those who loved him and those who were financially dependent on him.

Grandpa Welch had doted on his only daughter. He had been a kind, benevolent grandparent to my brothers and me. For those reasons, we had respected and humored him. We had loved him despite his flaws. The unfortunate consequence was his present belief that he had none. No one in this room was perfect, and if we refused to hear that from the mouths of people who loved us apart from our imperfections, we would never hear it.

Pax's jaw flexed. "This isn't *politics*."

"What the hell is it then? Moral judgment?"

"Your words."

I couldn't see my grandfather's face from my position, but his ears and the back of his neck went red. "Well then, I guess you don't need your trust fund if you're gonna judge the hand providing it to you."

"Leonard—" Nana began.

Pax chuckled and shook his head. "Really? Okay, sure. Cancel it. I don't need it."

"*Pax*," Foster said. "Give everyone time—"

"I'm not going to have my ethics dictated by a bigoted old man with money."

Everyone but Bailey gasped. Over my shoulder, Daddy cursed under his breath again.

"No one's trying to dictate anything here but you, Paxton," Nana said, stepping forward. "We've been around a lot longer than you, and we see things more clearly. You'll understand when you get a little older. Don't throw your family away over this silliness."

"I'm twenty-six, Nana. Believe me, the world has never been clearer. And there's a difference between throwing people away and calling them on their racism. I'm doing the latter." He looked at our grandfather. "I don't need your money. I wasn't ever here for that. And if you can't see that, I feel sorry for you."

"Our ride's here," Foster said. He hugged Mom, who remained stiff, and came to hug Daddy and me. He stopped before Grandpa as Nana moved to his side. "Sir, you and I see eye to eye on a lot of things. I tend to agree about the protests and riots, but I think Pax has the right to feel differently. To be worried for his friends."

"Not when his friends appear to be more important to him than family."

"I don't think that's true, Grandpa."

I walked forward to hug Pax and Bailey, wishing now more than ever that I was leaving with them.

"Come visit us anytime, little sis," Pax said into my ear.

Bailey added her agreement, and then they were gone.

"What's going on?" Leo appeared, his hair going in every direction. He'd slept through the whole row, a sort of metaphor for his life.

"Your inheritance just increased, that's what," my grandfather growled, stalking down the hallway toward his library.

Nana followed. "Leonard, give him time…" Her voice faded as she went around the corner, leaving the four of us standing alone in the great room. The decorated tree twinkled cheerily in the corner. A fire crackled in the enormous fireplace, its stone column extending to the vaulted ceiling, its mantel draped with garland and fairy lights and topped with Nana's collection of antique Christmas snow globes.

Leo was smiling. "Sweet." He lumbered toward the kitchen in search of food.

"Jesus Christ," Daddy murmured, turning to finish his shave.

I was left alone with Mom.

Her arms crossed tight, as if she were on the verge of freezing to death, she stared into the blaze. "You haven't said much, Erin."

If you didn't know her, you might think that was an impromptu observation. I knew from the pitch of her voice and the rigidity of her spine that she'd just drawn a calculated line in the sand and her remark was a demand to know on which side of it I stood.

"I agree with Pax." I forced my balled fists to relax, my lungs to take normal instead of shallow breaths. There would be no flight-or-fight. I had just watched my brother walk away, possibly disinherited, and instead of being terrified, I was realizing all at once that the only power my family had over me was what I allowed them to have.

"I see." Her mouth, lips as full as they'd been at my age,

produced a ghostly smile. She continued to stare at the fire.

We were on our way home Sunday morning before I recognized the fact that she must have taken that knowledge and used it, with Nana's help, to steer every conversation away from anything that might make me voice my opinion to my grandfather. That was a protective gesture. But she hadn't looked me in the eye even once in the past forty-eight hours, so I wasn't sure who she was protecting—me or herself.

• • • • • • • • • • •

Monday morning, my inbox contained an email. Its subject line reminded me that I had worked at JMCH for six months. I had known Isaac Maat for six months.

> From: Maat, Isaac
> To: McIntyre, Erin
> Subject: Six-month performance evaluation
>
> Erin,
> I've attached the standard employee review paperwork. There's a short self-review section you'll need to fill out and return to me by end of day tomorrow. Check your calendar for Friday. We can do your review anytime before noon. It will only take half an hour or so.
> Isaac

The first section of the self-review asked me to assess my performance over the review period, noting accomplishments and strengths. The second asked me to comment on challenges that prevented me from working effectively and how those challenges might be overcome. "Challenges" seemed like a polite way to keep from saying "failures." The final section asked me to list my future goals.

In six months, I had moved twenty folders from below-green status to green. Several of those deals had closed successfully—the Andersons and the Hoopers were the most notable. I had a dozen current, active clients in various states of uproar, but only one threatening to slide to red, and they had good reason as the subcontractors working under their foreman—Leo—had fucked up one thing after another. The rest were moving the other direction thanks to my guidance.

I felt positive about those achievements, as distant as they were from counseling students about anxiety and class load, or coming out to their parents, or sexual assault, or being bullied. I had alleviated our clients' stress in making a new house a home, and along the way I'd helped a father reconnect with his daughter, a wife stand her ground, and a gifted artist get some justified recognition from a new patron.

I left off the bit about Leo since that was something for his review, not mine, and I listed the Anderson disaster as my lesson in abiding by tried-and-true procedures and following directions from my supervisor. I came to the section about my future goals and was stumped. Having already confessed to Isaac that my future was not with JMCH, pretending now that it was would be tantamount to lying.

And then there was the real issue: Did I have future goals at all, let alone pertaining to my father's company? *Keep doing what I'm doing and keep putting Jacqueline off when she asks about grad school until she gives up* hardly seemed like a goal, but it was all I had.

In the large blank space given to list my goals, I wrote: *Continue working to resolve any impediments keeping our clients from having a satisfying home-buying experience and help JMCH give them a quality custom home they and their families will enjoy for many years.*

I dithered over the wording on all three sections until I wasn't sure and no longer cared whether any of it made sense, and then I returned it to Isaac a day early with a brief message:

From: McIntyre, Erin
To: Maat, Isaac
Subject: Re: Six-month performance evaluation

Self-review attached. I can meet with you anytime Friday morning. I don't have any appointments until the afternoon.

He beat my brevity:

From: Maat, Isaac
To: McIntyre, Erin
Subject: Re: Six-month performance evaluation

Friday 9:30

• • • • • • • • • • •

Cynthia Pike asked me to join her for lunch on Wednesday. She ordered in deli salads, set up at the turquoise acrylic bistro table in the corner of her mod office, which looked like a pop art, DayGlo set in an Austin Powers movie. (Leo owned all three; they'd come out when he was a teenager. His sense of humor had never matured past thinking a character called Fat Bastard was hilarious.)

When I arrived, she shut the door behind me. "I wanted us to get to know each other a little better. See what I can do to convince you to come work for me." She smiled, unabashed, opened a tall, chilled bottle of mineral water, and poured us both a glass. We slid into the molded seats. "My proposal is that Hank and I swap you and Ashley. Not that she could client liaison as well as you do—she's sweet and dependable but no miracle worker. But she wouldn't *need* to work miracles, because you, in Sales, could prevent problems from occurring."

I took a sip of water to stall. "Have you discussed this idea with Hank? Or Ashley? Or… Isaac?" I prayed not. I remembered his reaction when I'd told him, flippantly, that Sales wanted me. The flash of his eyes and tension in his jaw. Either he didn't want me to leave, or he wanted me all the way out the front door. At the time, I'd been certain it was the latter.

"I did broach the subject with Hank. Ashley will never be a hungry piranha like Joshua or Megan. As the client liaison, however, she could problem-solve without the pressure of making sales quotas. With your bubbly personality, shrewd people skills, and loyalty to the company—even if in your case that came with the surname—you would *shine* in Sales. You remind me of a younger me!"

With effort, I smiled as if delighted by that comparison. She saw me as someone she could mentor, and that was a huge compliment.

But sales of any kind were as far as could be, vocation-wise, from working as a high school counselor or a therapist on a college campus. Not that being a client liaison was in the vicinity either.

She lowered her voice as though someone might overhear through her door. "And don't be concerned about Isaac. If you decide to jump over to my department, I'll make sure it's a smooth transition, and Ashley will do a good job in your stead. No burned bridges, I promise." She mistook what worrying about Isaac entailed for me.

I didn't want to work in Sales, shoulder to shoulder with Joshua Swearingen on the daily, comparing quotas and suffering through his competitive crybaby denigration when I beat him month after month. Because Cynthia Pike was right about one thing: I would be a bang-up addition to the sales team.

When my sorority had hosted our requisite bake sales, I'd been renowned as the girl who could sell our priced-for-profit treats to anyone. My sisters would designate a hopeless target—a slim bookworm who veered to the other side of the sidewalk to avoid us or a cranky-looking professor who'd been teaching since the dawn of time—and I would choose their poison. A baggy of Rice Krispy squares for this one, a thick slice of pound cake for that one. Homemade salty-sweet granola. Fudge brownies with icing so thick your face and fingers would be covered in chocolate by the time you'd consumed it. Owl-shaped sugar cookies, our specialty.

More often than not, I returned to the table, cash in hand. I was legendary.

Of course Cynthia would want me.

"As for pay, you would move from a salaried employee to commission based. If you average what Joshua and Megan rake in, you'll beat your current salary by at least fifty percent. The top salesperson each month also earns a nice little bonus."

I hardly cared about the pay, which made me feel like more of an entitled brat than I already knew I was. On the other hand, cheating Joshua out of said bonus would be its own reward.

"Give me a few days to think about it?"

"Certainly. Take your time! I'd love to have you settled before the holidays though. If you could let me know by Monday, we'll have time to get Ashley and Isaac on board and get your offices swapped since you'll need to be downstairs to be available to potentials. This will make Vegas next month even more fun! I can hardly wait to have you on the team."

Take my time? Monday was only five days away. But it would get me past my performance evaluation.

• • • • • • • • • •

Friday morning, I walked next door to Isaac's office at nine thirty sharp. His door stood open, and I paused just outside of it to watch him for a moment before he saw me. He was reading over a printout, probably my evaluation, while tapping his lower lip with one long finger. That hand had cradled my face just before he kissed me and launched a hundred no-holds-barred fantasies.

Eyes flicking up to mine as if I'd spoken that wayward thought aloud, he held my gaze, and a reckless, unprecedented thought drifted through my mind. What would I surrender to win his heart?

We'd barely spoken all week, and he was looking at me as if committing me to memory, and I wondered if he knew about Cynthia's offer? Hank might have informed him on the down low to ensure that he wasn't blindsided by my departure. Or to give him cause for celebration. *Good news! You may not have to manage the owner's daughter for much longer!*

Uncle Hank wouldn't say such a thing.

Even if I left Isaac's direct supervision, we would still work in the same small building, leading to the overreaching notion I'd returned to a hundred times since lunch yesterday. If being my boss was the impasse he couldn't cross, I could eliminate it by reporting to Cynthia instead.

If I'd wanted the job she had put on the table, it would have made sense on every level to take it. Higher pay. The opportunity to rub Joshua's nose in failure. The possibility of coaxing Isaac to see me as a colleague, not a subordinate. Persuading him to meet me in the middle—to see that I was already there, wrapped in a white flag.

But I didn't want the job.

My guilt over Chaz had caused a soul-deep avalanche, and part of me would always feel shame for causing him pain. But somewhere under the rubble, I'd begun to feel the first sparks of desire to fight my way out. I didn't know how long it would take, but I would find that girl I'd once been, rip the fake-Erin mask from her face, and tell her she was enough until she believed it. I would forgive her for not being perfect. I would absolve her for losing her way.

"Erin, come in," Isaac said.

You're a McIntyre, I heard.

chapter *Twenty-five*

My parents were preparing for the Ellises's annual Ugly Christmas Sweater party, held on the first Friday of December. There was always a prize for the ugliest sweater—something like a bottle of Macallan, to foster real competition—and if Daddy didn't win this year, I did not want to see what could defeat the grinning, homicidal-snowman sweater he was wearing.

I had a web series to catch up on and every reason to escape pointless efforts to make sense of real life, so I was in the kitchen heating up an entree from the freezer. The lady who catered Mom's parties and the occasional brunch also offered personal-chef services, so my mother rarely cooked now. Once a week, she ordered from an extensive menu like a noblewoman in a period piece, and voila, Chef Laurie prepared and delivered gourmet meals, à la carte items, and desserts to our freezer once a week. Everything was tasty, but none of it topped Isaac's freshly prepared omelet.

The microwave hummed, my sesame-crusted scallops in wasabi over buckwheat noodles rotated, and I pressed two fingers to the ache in the center of my chest. I had promised myself not to summon my supervisor tonight in thought or deed, and there I was, standing in the kitchen, breaking that vow. I shoved that night and his cooking skills and his kiss from my mind, only to have those musings replaced with our interactions earlier, during my review. Trying to expel him from my thoughts was like digging in dry sand. It was wasted effort. He kept refilling my mind.

"Erin, come in," he had said. I'd taken the chair in front of his desk as he slid my evaluation across the dark surface. "This is your copy. The original"—he gestured with the one in his hand—"will go into your file in HR."

I looked over my copy, skimming the self-review and skipping ahead to the sections he had completed, rating my performance by bubbling a circle for each attribute, like a Scantron exam. *Outstanding* for Punctuality, Initiative, and Problem Solving. *Exceeds Expectations* for Productivity and Judgment. *Meets Expectations* for Communication.

"You basically gave me a C for Communication?"

He arched a brow and waited for me to recognize why.

I continued to keep client confidences to myself, a periodic cause of frustration for him, though he'd grown more tolerant of it. Sort of. "Ah."

"I expect you'll keep that C. As you implied once upon a time—it's working, isn't it? Also, you're following the procedure you'll want to follow when you're a licensed counselor."

I blinked. "You believe that will happen?"

He folded his hands on top of my review. "I believe you were meant to do it. Moreover, I attended one of the most challenging grad schools in the country, and you're capable of doing the same." He pressed his lips together and shook his head, eyes crinkling at the corners. "Quit smirking at my saying *moreover*. It's a perfectly ordinary word."

"Sure, if you're forty. And maybe a liberal arts professor." In reality, I found his old-fashioned vocabulary sexy, but teasing him about it was too easy. When he rolled his eyes, I bit my lip and decided I'd have to let him off the hook and tell him so, soon. Not now, but soon. "What about you? Urban planning?"

"Where did you—?"

"The books on your dresser."

He picked up a pen and tapped it against his opposite hand. My casual observations rattled him. He tried so hard to be unknowable. To keep his personal life entirely separate from his professional life. One night and one unexpected mutual friend had botched that objective.

"It took me a little while to realize what I want to do with my life," he said. "Believe it or not, there's a shortage of little boys aspiring to optimize land use and infrastructure. I don't think I knew what it was until I was in grad school."

"But now you know. So what are you going to do about it?"

He stared at me across the expanse of his desk. "The hardest thing to do when you realize you're off course is make the decision to get back on." He wasn't just answering my question; he was challenging me to do the same. He turned the page on my review, and I did the same with my copy.

Under *Suggestions for Improvement*, he'd written: "Work on asking for help, advice, or support when needed." Under *Commendation*: "Erin is a strong client advocate. She listens and sincerely cares that clients are satisfied. She tackles challenges head-on, isn't afraid to think outside the box, and learns from her mistakes. JMCH is fortunate to have her."

The doorbell rang in the same two-second span the microwave finished heating my dinner. Jack scampered and yipped his way down the stairs, ran to the front window, and commenced barking.

His stubby legs were just long enough for him to see out the low window. A moment later, the intercom beeped and my mother's disembodied voice said, "Erin, check on that, would you? Probably just a delivery."

I'd changed into yoga pants and a UT sweatshirt when I got home from work, but my feet were bare and chilled quickly on the marble floor. The sun had just set, and the automatic lights surrounding the house had begun to flicker on, along with thousands of white holiday lights encircling columns and tree trunks and strung artfully through branches and wound between the pointy finials of the wrought iron fence.

Every year after we got back home from Colorado, Mom had our house professionally decorated inside and out—a rare dissimilarity between Nana and Mom. The results were always stylish and magazine-spread worthy. Reindeer-themed one year, white and silver with red accents; Victorian the next, everything blue and gold. Whatever the designer recommended—whatever was *au courant*—cool and hip and impersonal.

This year's trendy holiday motif was angels. Outside, they sat and stood along the roofline and gables like joyful gargoyles. Inside, they perched on mantels, were featured on velvet stockings, and covered the tree in silvery angelic poses.

Checking the peephole and expecting to see our UPS guy dashing back to his truck after leaving a pile of boxes by the door, I was not prepared for the person standing on our front porch.

I pulled the door open. "Isaac?"

He paused before replying, like he was surprised to see me, though he knew I lived here.

Jack tore around the corner, ran up to Isaac like he intended to take his leg off for a snack, and began sniffing and jumping on him. Isaac offered a hand and Jack growled, licked it, and resumed jumping.

"Jack, get down," I said. He ignored me, per usual.

Isaac was wearing a lightweight tailored coat over what he'd worn to work, where I'd left him an hour ago, and he was holding a two-inch stack of documents. For a moment he seemed to be deciding whether to leave without saying or doing what he'd come for, and then he said, "Good evening, Ms. McIntyre. I need to speak with your father."

His formality would have hurt, but it didn't make sense. I started to ask, *Are you okay?* but Daddy, in his hideous sweater, appeared in the foyer and turned toward the door.

"Isaac. What's happened? Is there a problem?"

Mom appeared on the stairs, but she stopped halfway down, listening. Jack ran to cower behind her legs when Daddy spoke.

I felt the same draw to Isaac I'd felt for months, but he trained his gaze on my father as though I weren't there.

"I've come to bring you some information." He didn't move to hand over the documents in his hands. "I'm going to leave this with you, but first I'm going to give you a warning you don't deserve."

Daddy scowled, but the attempt to look stern in that sweater was beyond his ability. "I'm not sure what you mean by that—"

"I've found evidence of fraud and embezzling inside JMCH."

Daddy's glare was replaced by shock. He blinked, openmouthed. "What the— Jesus Christ." He stepped back and gestured. "Come on in. Let's go to my office—"

"I can say what I intend to say right here." Isaac paused. I felt my father's impatience build, mistaking caution for indecision. He'd started to interrupt when Isaac said, "I took a job at JMCH with a specific goal in mind—to find evidence of illegal activity. Because of what I knew of you, I believed you incapable of running an aboveboard company."

"That's a goddamned—"

"My uncle was Ezekiel James."

Daddy jerked at the words, and my mother's short gasp from the staircase was audible.

Isaac, filling the doorway like an avenging angel, reacted visibly to neither of their responses. "I see you remember his name. Good. Maybe you'll remember that because of your greed or your racism or some combination of the two, you cut him out of the company he helped develop. You stole his design concepts and the location he'd scouted and proposed. You betrayed his trust."

Daddy swallowed but said nothing, his jaw steeling and his eyes burning into Isaac's. I was glad for the door at my back. My God, no wonder he'd wanted nothing to do with me.

"In my mind, a dirty cheat is always a dirty cheat. All I needed was the evidence to ruin you. But it didn't go down like I thought it would. It made me a little angry at first. I'd come to wreak vengeance, not render aid. But then I saw the beauty of it. The betrayer becomes the betrayed. Fitting, really."

A chill passed through me like a ghost. A fine mist of rain began falling behind Isaac, and when the wind gusted, I smelled the clean, sharp scent of it. I felt the cool moisture settle on my face and the tops of my feet. The slate stones of the sidewalk and circular drive began to darken in the glow of the landscape lighting. My father was silent, awaiting his sentence.

"Leo has been taking kickbacks from certain contractors. They bid an amount he feeds them ahead of time, beating out other bids. JMCH includes that expense in the cost of the home. When the contractor is paid, Leo takes a bit off the top. A few hundred here, a couple thousand there. In finance, we call it a haircut. Paid for by JMCH and, ultimately, our clients. He doesn't do it often, and only with certain contractors. Like his friend, Phil."

"*Godfuckingdammit.*"

Isaac continued. "What I couldn't figure out was how Hank hadn't caught it before I came on board. Few people can pull that sort of thing off for long without it being noticed. I found it when Leo's numbers didn't mesh with Erin's. The foremen used to turn them in to me directly. Now she's in the middle, getting information directly from clients and correcting discrepancies. He should have realized he was in more danger of getting caught, but he was too stupid or greedy to stop."

I'd thought he was just too stupid to add. It had never occurred to me that my brother would steal from his father's company.

"One of the things you'll need to check is whether safety standards were met. There's a chance—given what happened with the Anderson home—that quality was compromised on some homes, going back years. I didn't find evidence of city-inspection bribery, but I didn't look very closely. It's a possibility."

My parents would be ashamed of their son's deceit, of course, but I knew them too well. They were as embarrassed that someone outside the family had caught it as they were that it had occurred. Daddy sighed heavily and held his hand out. "Thank you for bringing this to—"

"I'm not finished, Mr. McIntyre." Another pause. No interruption this time. "I mentioned that I couldn't figure out how this petty skimming hadn't been caught. Last week, I finally made the connection. What a surprise to find that the trail didn't lead to you. My first clue was evidence that a JMCH construction crew had recently performed extensive upgrades on an employee's home. A slight conflict of interest, but nothing major—until JMCH picked up the tab for it. It was overreaching, and it was the reason I started digging in places I hadn't dug before. JMCH has been paying fake contractors, vendors, and suppliers from accounts Hank Greene controls. The money is being routed to offshore accounts. Millions over the past decade. I didn't bother to go back farther than that because this is not my problem. It's yours."

He handed the heavy document stack to my father, who almost dropped it. Daddy's face was pure fury—the face of a man who wanted to tear the door off its hinges and throw punches into walls. Most people would be terrified of this enraged version of my father, terrified to relay this sort of news to him. Isaac's expression exhibited no fear.

"I suggest you call Russell Spellman and start discussing what legal avenues to take. Get Rhett up to the building to lock down the system and copy Hank's hard drive before he can cover his tracks. Tomorrow morning at the latest. If it were my decision, I'd do it tonight. Feel free to have him take me off clearance. I have copies of everything I need to prove what I've told you as well as the fact that I'm not involved. I've cleared out my office and wiped my computer. I'll cooperate to provide legal evidence, but I won't be returning to the office.

"One last point. I care about the people I work with. That's why you're getting that stack of documents and this heads-up. Most of them are good people, and I hope for their sakes you can fix this. For your own sake, I don't care one motherfucking iota."

"Is Zeke— Is he… is he okay?" My father's question was pathetic, and he knew it. He wanted some sort of absolution. Some sort of *It All Worked Out In The End.*

Isaac did not give him what he wanted. "After your betrayal, my uncle went back to construction. He eventually started his own company, but he didn't have a rich father-in-law as a financial backer, and high-interest business loans don't have any give. Mere wobbles in the housing or construction sectors put him underwater. Just after his second bankruptcy, he lost his little sister, Lila—my mother. He took out a life insurance policy not long after we buried her. A week past the two-year clause prohibiting payout after suicide, Pop and I found him."

My father's face lost all color. My eyes glassed with tears as Isaac delivered those blows, reliving the painful memories with every word. His hands, now empty, were balled into fists, and his narrowed eyes held no mercy.

"If you have something to say to him, he's buried at Oakwood. Don't bullshit me with your justifications or regrets. I'm not hearing them."

He moved his gaze to my mother, who was standing, white-knuckled, at the bottom of the staircase across the foyer. "Mrs. McIntyre, my aunt Selma wanted me to pass on a message. She's grateful to you. The two of you were friends once upon a time, she said, planning lives and babies together. Until out of the blue, there was no partnership between your husbands and no friendship you would claim. 'She dropped me like trash,' she said. 'It hurt, and I felt like a fool. But I learned who and what not to trust.' I'll let you decipher what she meant by that."

I was going to be sick. My stomach heaved, my face burned, but my hands and feet were so cold I was shivering. My family had done those things to Isaac's family. I hadn't been wide of the mark, likening us to Romeo and Juliet. But I was not his sun, and a McIntyre was a McIntyre just as a rose was a rose. He did not love me, and I was both heartbroken and thankful, for his sake, that he didn't.

He started to turn and stopped, staring at his feet, and I knew he was debating whether to look at me before he walked away forever. I was silent. If he needed to leave my parents' house without ever laying eyes on me again, I wanted him to turn and go.

He raised his eyes, and the soft light of the porch lamps reflected in their depths. "Remember what I told you this morning, Ms. McIntyre. You were meant to do it." He turned, resolute. The sidewalk was lit like a runway that would take him away from me forever.

He'd rounded his car and opened the door before I lurched from my stupor as though I'd been picked up and shaken. "Isaac!" Heedless of the wet pavement, the cold, my mother's voice calling me back, I ran.

He stood and waited, the faint crease of his brow disclosing his bewilderment.

I stopped a foot in front of him, hugging my arms around myself to keep from grabbing hold of him, and stared up into his eyes, close range. "I'm sorry. I'm so sorry my family did this to you." As if a switch was thrown, I felt the cold, rain-soaked asphalt beneath my feet and the drizzle of light rain on my face. I felt the reality of never seeing him again. A concentrated shudder began in my chest. I locked my teeth together and fought tears.

"I don't hold you responsible, Ms. McIntyre." Drops beaded in his hair like tiny crystals.

What's in a name? Sometimes everything. "Please don't call me that."

He took pity on me. "Erin. I don't hold you responsible." He stepped closer, mindful of my feet, and took my face in his warm hands. One thumb moved over my quivering lips, the other wiped wetness from my face, and I wasn't sure if I was crying or it was just rain. "You're freezing," he said. "Go back inside."

I untwisted my arms and burrowed into his chest, sure he would push me away. His heart beat just beneath my ear, strong and steady. His arms slid around me, more to warm than to embrace, I thought. His spicy aftershave, barely detectable this late in the day, blended with the smell of the rain and the subtle musky scent I recognized from the one night we had been this close.

"Will you kiss me?" I mumbled the request into his chest.

I knew he heard me, because his chest flexed beneath my cheek. He loosened his hold, and I braced for the refusal he had every right to make. His body twisted, repositioning, and his hand slipped beneath my chin to tip my face up. His back to his car—and my house—he pulled me in and leaned his face to mine. I stretched on my toes to meet him, my body arcing into his.

Our first and only kiss had been a trial run—cautious, hesitant. An exploratory assessment. This was none of those things. Our lips met, and his eyes closed as if in inescapable surrender; mine fell shut as his mouth claimed mine. Spark. Ignition. Detonation. *Fireworks.* The hand at my jaw skimmed behind my neck, forked into my hair, and cradled my head. Prying my mouth open, he swept his tongue across mine. My feet were no longer planted on the ground. I was no longer a singular entity. I was a million bits of chemical flame, illuminating the sky for one dazzling moment before vanishing.

The sweet friction of his lips sliding against mine, pressing forward, pulling back, a fraction harder and deeper with each advance, made me breathless. He led without controlling, setting the pace as I dragged him closer. Nothing mattered but the small portion of the universe we inhabited. An insignificant bubble of time and space that belonged to us. As angled as my body was, there was no danger of toppling backward. His arms were firm, one at the small of my back and the other inclining my head just so. He held me securely, but I was falling all the same.

The rain had grown heavier. No thunderstorm, but drops had begun to form. I felt them on my lashes and the strands of wet hair affixed to my face. I heard them pattering against the roof of his car. When he withdrew his mouth from mine, I felt the drops on my lips. I opened my eyes to his. They were as dark and mysterious as they'd ever been.

"Go back inside now. It's cold, and you're getting soaked."

Lower lip between my teeth, I took in every detail of his face, committing it to memory. "I want to come live in the city you plan someday. Will you let me know when you've done it? I want a little cottage like Tuli's. And a dog like Pete." *And a man like you. Strong. Kind. Honest.*

"I'll hit you up. Save you the best tiny old house I can find. Build you one and make it look old, if that's what you want. Please go inside, Erin."

I nodded, thankful for rain that hopefully blended my tears away.

He leaned his forehead to mine and sighed. "You're gonna be

okay. I believe that. I want you to believe it too."

My throat constricted. It hurt to swallow. "Will you be okay? You didn't get what you wanted." My father would likely sustain both his reputation and fortune, though perhaps Isaac was right in his prediction of what the joint treacheries of his eldest son and one of his oldest friends would do to him. That cost was immeasurable.

"I'm good. And I didn't really know what I wanted until now."

I leaned up, palms holding his face, and kissed him once more—a chaste graze of our lips, nothing more. "Go get it, Isaac."

His hands at my waist squeezed and let me go. I ran back to the house. The front door was closed, and I heard nothing when I opened it. No yelling, no conversation, no barking—nothing. When I turned back to shut the door, Isaac's car was pulling away.

chapter Twenty-six

My parents were so silent, I almost passed them without knowing they were in the great room. I heard Jack's whine and turned my head. The only light in the room came from the lightly flocked, angel-laden tree, strung with hundreds of white lights and reflective silver ornaments. Mom perched on an ornate chair near the fireplace, posture straight as a queen, Jack at her feet. My father, feet away, sat with his head in both hands, elbows on his knees.

I switched on a lamp and they all started, Mom squinting in annoyance and Jack stuffing his face between her leg and the chair.

Before I could speak, she asked, "What's going on between you and that boy? Is that the cause of what happened at your grandparents' home a week ago?"

"Isaac is a *man*, not a *boy*—"

"I didn't mean—"

"I kinda don't care what you mean right now, Mom. And Grandpa was the cause of what happened last week." My father hadn't moved beyond his flinch when the lamp came on. "Daddy, call Rhett. Ask him to meet us at the office. Tell him it's an emergency, but make sure he understands not to contact anyone else about it. I'm going to get dressed."

His face, full of grief, emerged from his hands, years older than it had looked an hour ago. "You're going with me?" He deserved everything happening to him, but I didn't intend to let my brother and Hank Greene get away with what they'd done, and there were dozens of people dependent on JMCH for their livelihoods.

"Yes," I answered. "I'll be back down in five minutes." I called Foster while I changed into jeans and pulled my boots from the back of my closet.

He went from stunned to livid in five seconds flat and agreed to look into the legal implications and liabilities immediately since the attorney Daddy kept on retainer might not be reachable until Monday. Then he said, "Fuck—Spellman may have been referred or hired by Hank when prior legal counsel retired. Tell Dad to hold off calling him until I do some digging."

I took a deep breath and closed my eyes, overwhelmed. "Jesus."

"This isn't your responsibility, Erin. The guy that brought this to Dad's attention—Isaac? He's in finance, right? He can help with this."

"I appreciate what you're trying to say, but please don't patronize me. *I* can help with this. And Isaac has resigned, so you and I are it."

"I didn't mean to— Wait, he resigned? Why? How do you know he isn't involve—"

"He isn't."

He sighed. "Okay. Talk soon."

Our in-house IT guy, Rhett, had seen too many white-collar-crime movies. When he realized his part in helping secure JMCH from further financial loss, his eyes bugged like Jack's did when someone said, "Turkey jerky." He wondered aloud whether Hank might show up, mobster style, to destroy the evidence and gun down the witnesses, or if he was more likely to flee to the Caribbean on one of multiple passports.

"Just copy the damned hard drive. This isn't *Law and Order*, for chrissake." My father stormed out of Hank's office and went next door to his.

"This is pretty painful for him," I said. "It's not meant to be directed at you."

"Sure felt like it was at me," Rhett mumbled.

"Have you had dinner? I missed mine, and I'm going to order a pizza."

He perked up and gave me his order, and I walked around the corner to Daddy's office. My father was opening the little cabinet above his credenza that served as a liquor cabinet. He grabbed a decanter of something amber-colored and splashed a liberal amount into two short glasses. He handed one to me. I wasn't generally a straight-up whiskey sort of girl, but knowing Daddy, it was high-end stuff and it had been one hell of a day.

I took the glass and sipped. My stomach burbled like it had been rudely awoken. I was about to ask my father what he wanted on his pizza when he said, "What the hell am I going to do about your brother? I've got to tell Rhett who to lock out as soon as he finishes what he's doing. Leo should be on that list. Jesus Christ. I've done everything for that boy."

"That *boy* is a thirty-two-year-old man who stole *from his father*. And maybe doing everything for him was the problem."

He was silent several minutes and then said, "Damn inconvenient time for Isaac to resign. I need someone who knows finance to keep everything working until we can get someone new in here as CFO."

"Are you fucking kidding me?"

He flinched and scowled at me, like I'd just spoken out of my forehead.

"He owes you *nothing*."

"But his coworkers—"

"Are *your* employees and *your* concern." I slapped the glass down on his desk, splashing ten or twenty dollars' worth of liquor onto it. "Your friend—Zeke?—he had two kids, Isaac's cousins. His father lived with them too. And when Isaac's parents died in a car accident, making him a ten-year-old orphan, his Uncle Zeke and Aunt Selma took him in. That's who *you* stole from."

"Jesus Christ." He slumped into his desk chair in his ridiculous sweater and stared into his glass. "I didn't want to cut him out. I fought it, but they weren't going to agree to fund it with… There wouldn't have been a company at all."

Clarity. Blinding clarity. "Grandpa Welch wanted him out because he was black. And *you agreed?*"

"If I'd said no, there wouldn't have been a company at all."

I sat in one of the chairs in front of his desk. "You don't know that. Some other funding opportunity might have come up. All that can be proved now is that you caved and betrayed a *friend* for *money*."

"I'm not like your Grandpa Welch—"

"Which part of him? The racist part? Or the part suffering from insatiable greed? What you are in deed, you are." I shook my head. "Funny, isn't it, that Nana is where I got that?" I picked up my glass and took a bigger swig. It went down my throat like molten lava, and my eyes watered. "Goddamn, this family is *fucked. Up*."

"But we're your family."

I couldn't reply to that. "I'll help you till the end of the month.

And then I'm done here."

"Princess—"

"No, Daddy, I'm not your princess. I'm not that girl anymore. I don't know where I'm going yet, but it's a big wide world, and I'm too young to give up and throw in the towel on my life."

"Is that what you've been doing here?"

"My ex-boyfriend, Chaz, proposed to me junior year, right before spring break. In front of all our friends. I cared about him, but I wasn't in love with him. And I think, even if I had been, I wouldn't have wanted to be twenty-one and engaged. So I said no, and we broke up.

"A few months later, he had a wreck a few blocks from school. He didn't survive. And ever since then, I've had recurrent nightmares about that night. I drove my roommate batshit those last few months, waking her up crying or yelling out. That's why I barely graduated. You and Mom thought I was partying or maybe that I'm just dumb, but I was in so much pain."

"We never thought you were dumb—"

"Well, you sure as hell didn't think I was *smart*." My head swam, whether from anger or alcohol on an empty stomach, I didn't know. I put the glass down.

"Why didn't you tell us this before?"

"We're not that kind of family, are we? I learned really early that I was there to be Mommy's little dress-up doll. Daddy's little princess. If I didn't like something, I was supposed to smile through it and pretend. Mom groomed me to be just like her, and neither of you thought I was capable of following *my* dreams. I wasn't going to let you make that decision for me. I was going to take care of everything, go to grad school, get a fellowship to pay for it, show both of you how capable I was. And then everything went off the rails."

I heard Isaac's voice from this morning, or a hundred years ago. *The hardest thing to do when you realize you're off course is make the decision to get back on.*

"Your mother and I just wanted to protect you—all of you—"

"Let me give you a little free amateur therapy. Leo stole from you. He's compromised the quality and maybe the safety of the houses he's built, hiring drinking bros who may not be qualified to tackle a DIY project, let alone professional construction. You're humiliated and hurt. But if you don't give him serious consequences, he'll just keep doing this shit the rest of his life. What he did is small potatoes next to Uncle Hank, and I know Leo's your kid. But what would you do if he wasn't?"

His eyes fell to his glass again and I hoped he would listen but knew he might not.

"I'm going down to my office for a few minutes and ordering some pizza because I'm starving. You and I are having pepperoni—unless you want to share Rhett's hamburger, anchovies, and pineapple."

• • • • • • • • • • •

I walked down one flight of stairs and passed Isaac's office. The door was open. His diplomas were both gone from the wall; his bookcase was empty of finance books. The room was dark but for the hallway light spilling in from the doorway. Without switching on a light, I sat down in his desk chair and imagined myself standing in that doorway, wide-eyed and smiling and holding a stack of file folders.

Excuse me, Mr. Maat?

I'd been so hacked off at his groundless animosity. His inexplicable exasperation. His conceited prejudgment. My first impression had been so inaccurate. He had so many reasons for not welcoming another McIntyre into his life, and yet he was one of the most patient, compassionate men I'd ever known.

My phone pocket buzzed. Foster was heading over. He felt almost certain that Russell Spellman was on the level, but after tonight, none of us trusted our instincts. He wanted to be here when we called him. He also wanted to confer with Daddy about our elder brother.

Foster: Dad could be liable if one of Leo's dickwad friends did substandard work, especially if they were unlicensed. JMCH may need to provide free inspections and repairs.

Me: JFC. Thank you for helping out.

Foster: Of course. We're family.

Foster: Also, I'm ready to give Leo the beatdown he's been asking for since he urinated on my signed copy of The Giving Tree.

Me: I forgot about that.

Foster: I have not.

Hank called Daddy on Saturday, panicked when he couldn't get into the system, but Foster had predicted that likelihood and fabricated a plausible explanation. I heard my father delivering it when I came downstairs for a coffee refill.

"Yeah, the whole network crashed Friday night. Rhett's working to get it back up and running by Monday or Tuesday," Daddy said. He was standing in the kitchen, staring into the backyard, phone to his ear. "The Christmas party? Weekend after next, I think. Yep. See you Monday." He put his phone on the counter, unaware of my presence. "Goddamn it, Hank," he said under his breath. "Goddamn it."

Monday came. Daddy met Hank at the door and led him into one of the conference rooms, where Russell Spellman and a security guard waited. He was required to turn in his keys and fobs and given two boxes of his personal belongings. He was not allowed to go up to his office, and was informed that he was no longer allowed on the premises from that moment on. Finally, he was advised to retain his own legal counsel.

When he walked robotically across the atrium, white as a sheet, I watched him from the second floor, where Isaac had stood to watch me arrive on my first day.

Cynthia, almost as appalled as we were for the failure to have detected Hank's deceit, was gracious when I turned down her invitation to join Sales. She relinquished Ashley to be trained for the client liaison position I would be vacating after Christmas. Ashley, as expected, was delighted to escape her inconsistent paychecks. She was also happy to escape Joshua, whom she couldn't stand.

The DA sent a certified fraud investigator to find out how much money had been siphoned and where it had gone. We were told that it could be months before there was an arrest made. Between the shock of Hank's duplicity, the upcoming holidays, and the need to replace the CFO and financial analyst immediately and the client liaison by the end of the month, my parents couldn't cope with the idea of prosecuting their son.

They did, however, wring enough confessions out of him to fire Phil and every other contractor who'd abetted his skimming operation. Daddy wanted to fire Leo, too, but they compromised by demoting him back to construction with zero management or fiduciary power. Leo being Leo, he was an ungrateful jerk about the demotion, cursing and threatening to go work for a competitor.

Daddy's face went red. "Good—it'll give me even *more* of a competitive edge if they hire your incompetent ass!"

Leo slammed the front door so hard on the way out that the angel wreath fell off the door, shattering the tiny glass globes and warping the wings of the angel in the center, though she maintained her radiant smile.

• • • • • • • • • • •

Christmas dinner, not even three weeks later, was a somber affair. Pax and Bailey visited her family in Oregon. Leo was still being a surly man-baby, complaining about having to work under someone who'd been hired well after he was, but Foster told him he was lucky he hadn't found an orange jumpsuit under the tree this year, so he should shut the fuck up. Our parents said little.

I got a text from Jacqueline—a pic of her boyfriend holding his little sister, who was eighteen months old, on his shoulders so she could hang an ornament high on the tree.

Jacqueline:	My ovaries are rioting.
Me:	Ha! Yeah, that's pretty hot. Thinking of getting yourself knocked up with a mini-Lucas are ya?
Jacqueline:	In 8 YEARS or so, yes. Biology is so unfair. *sob* He taught her to make a fist and punch his palm last night and I was SO. DEAD.
Me:	Thank God for birth control?
Jacqueline:	GAH. Merry Christmas! Love you! I'm going to go find my BF.
Me:	That's right girl – get that practice in!

She replied with a thumbs-up emoji. I no longer had to avoid her, as I had confessed everything I hadn't been telling her—the nightmares, the family upheaval, the fake-Erin mask that everyone but she and Isaac fell for. She made me swear to find a new therapist, which reminded me of Isaac's *Try again* weeks before. Jacqueline being Jacqueline, she prompted me daily until I'd done it. Dr. Richey was young and progressive, using both in-person and FaceTime sessions. She treated me like someone with attainable goals who just needed, as Isaac claimed, to find my way back to the trail.

While answering texts from Pax and a couple of college friends, I got one from Mindi.

Mindi: Merry Christmas! Rhys and I are having a New Year's Eve party at his and Boone's apartment! Please please please come?

I felt my heart speed up. If Isaac was still in town, he would be there. I didn't know if he would want to see me. He might bring someone. I didn't know if I could take that.

Mindi: BTW, I know your dirty little secret.

Me: Huh...?

Mindi: ISAAC? Y'all worked together and didn't tell us! Rhys knew where Isaac worked, so when you said the name of your dad's company, he recognized it. Are you secret lovers?!? You can tell me! I'm a vault!

Me: Neither of us expected to see each other that night. It's so weird to see a coworker in the wild. I didn't say anything because he didn't, and I think vice versa, and then we both felt awkward because we hadn't said anything.

Mindi: So you worked for him. But now you don't. I mentioned I would be inviting you in front of him. He's tough to read, but he didn't seem disappointed. ;) Please come to our party. You HAVE to be there.

Me: Shoot me the address. I'll be there.

chapter Twenty-seven

Once upon a time, Chaz and I had a huge fight over the he said/she said between Jacqueline and his best friend, Buck. Buck had assaulted her and then spread rumors about her, trying to make it look consensual. I told Chaz the truth, expecting him to believe me immediately. But believing me turned Buck into a monster, and Chaz had a hard time reconciling that image with his best friend. I'd broken up with him.

At the next party we were both attending, I'd gone *all out* to make him wretched. I wore a short, shimmery, body-hugging dress and the highest heels I could manage. I flirted with everyone but him. My spiteful plan worked. I'd made him miserably aware that he'd made a very bad choice. After a lot of groveling on his part, we'd gotten back together, and a year later, he'd proposed.

Now the memory of that night of revenge only added to my remorse over everything to do with him.

When I walked through the door of Rhys's apartment, the shoe was on the other foot. It only took me seconds to locate Isaac, tall and handsome, wearing the violet shirt I hadn't seen in a month, standing with Rhys, Kurt, and Madison. Mindi ran up to welcome me, and I focused on her. Her wavy blond hair was adorned with a headband proclaiming 2015! in green glitter, and her teal dress made her green eyes shine. Or maybe her eyes were glowing because of

Rhys.

"I'm so glad you're here!" She hung my long sweater and called, "Rhys! Erin is here!"

For half a second, I was worried that she'd tricked me into a surprise birthday party, but I was relatively sure no one knew it was today. Having a birthday six days after Christmas and *on* New Year's Eve had been a blessing and a curse all my life. I've kept it off social media.

I followed her toward Rhys—and Isaac, whose eyes had lighted on me in the same moment I'd spotted him among two dozen partiers. He hadn't looked away yet. It was a chore not to stumble, and I never stumbled. I was runway model skilled in heels.

The volume on the music decreased, and Rhys put his hands in the air and said, "Excuse me, everyone!"

Mindi moved to stand next to him, hands folded in front of her. If she'd been a painting, her title would have been *Demure Girl with Secret*.

He slid his arm around her. "You're all here now, and my little brother can't keep his lips buttoned another second, so I have an announcement and then everyone can go back to dancing and drinking."

"WOOOO!" Kurt hollered. Madison punched him in the arm. "Oww."

Rhys looked down at Mindi. "Christmas morning, in front of her family, I asked this beautiful girl to marry me."

Gasps and squeals started up all around us, and Kurt *WOOOOed* again.

I watched Mindi's face. As Rhys removed something from his front pocket and slid it onto her finger, she beamed up at him. Then she held her left hand up and so everyone could see what her answer had been. Rhys pulled her close, angled her back over his arm, and kissed her, and it was the most disgustingly romantic thing I'd ever seen in my life. When they surfaced, she was crying, his eyes were glassy, and everyone in the room looked like we were standing in an onion-cutting factory.

They were mobbed, Mindi accepting tearful, bouncing embraces and demands to see the ring, and Rhys shaking hands and hugging everyone. Boone popped champagne and started filling glasses. I congratulated them both and accepted a flute of bubbles two hours before the new year began, and when I looked for Isaac—because I couldn't help looking for him—he was making his way through the crowd to me.

"Hey," he said.

I wanted to hug him, but I didn't have an excuse, so I clinked my glass to his. "Hey, yourself."

"How are you?"

I took a sip. "Today was my last day at JMCH." I had so many things to celebrate.

His brows rose. "Oh? What are your plans from here?"

"I've signed up for an online prep course before I tackle the GRE. I'll choose graduate programs based on my scores and then write essays and gather recommendation letters. I'll figure it out. It's time I get back on track."

His mouth tipped up on the sides. "That's great."

"What you said—that I was meant to do it? I needed that. I've known for years what I wanted to be when I grew up." He answered my wry smile with one of his own. "But the reminder, the encouragement, reinforced that awareness. Thank you for that."

He nodded once. "You're welcome."

We sipped champagne, the party swirling happily around us.

"Isaac. I don't work for you anymore. And you don't work for my father."

"That's true."

I wanted to grab his shoulders and shake him. Instead, I tried to telepathically remind him of the words he'd thrown down two months ago, right before telling me it was impossible for reasons that no longer existed. *You want me to fuck you.*

He blinked. "Are you saying you want to come home with me, Erin?"

I had never wanted anyone like this. I ached with it. *Remain calm.* "Yes."

He took another sip of his champagne, and I watched his throat swallow it down. "We should probably be good guests and wait until after midnight."

I nodded, cheering internally.

Two agonizing hours of invisible public foreplay later—a firm hand at the small of my back here, the slow brush of a fingertip at my wrist there—we were in his car. I was of a mind to start there, but Isaac, as usual, was in control of his desires. He had kissed me at midnight, quick but deep, and the familiar heaviness settled between my legs and refused to budge until satiated.

The short drive felt like hours. We parked, and he took my hand as we walked to the elevator. I wanted to make out all the way to the eighth floor, but an older couple, covered in glittery confetti, called, "Hold the door!" She smiled at our grasped hands as he pressed the seven. In their eyes, we were just another couple returning home from a party. I smiled back, wanting to dismiss the thick, dull ache in my chest. I loved Isaac so much, but I would always be the Capulet to his Montague.

Once inside the apartment, he locked the bolt and turned to drag the sweater from my shoulders. The whisper-touch of his fingertips lit a path of goose bumps in their wake and my stomach fluttered.

I was nervous. *Maybe because it's been almost a year since you've gotten some?* my brain suggested. I stuffed a sock in the internal dialogue. "You're moving, I guess." That wasn't a difficult observation; boxes were stacked everywhere.

"My lease is up, so I thought I'd move in with my aunt until I know where I'm going. Most of this is going into storage though." He hung my sweater, shrugged out of his jacket, and placed it on the hook where Pete's leash had once hung.

"Where's Pete?"

"I took him over earlier today. Moving on Friday."

"Oh." I hadn't known how much I wanted to see his dog.

He stared down at me, weighing his words. I'd missed his pensiveness. His restraint. The care he took before every word, every step.

"I've applied to a few urban studies programs, but they all start next fall. I haven't heard back from any of them yet. I figure I'll be in limbo for a few months at least. Thought maybe I'd travel a bit in the interim."

"Oh?"

"Nothing fancy. Pack up the car and go hike some national parks. Visit a few cities I've always wanted to explore. Camp out on beaches I've never seen."

"That sounds perfect."

"Does it?"

"Yes."

Another excruciating pause. "Wanna come with?"

I lost my breath, looking at him. I was dreaming. I had to be dreaming. Isaac never said what he didn't mean. "You're asking me to come with you on your adventure?" Dammit, I was tearing up again. I wanted to laugh with this man, not blubber like a child every time he said or did something that moved my heart.

We'd drawn closer, magnets shivering with the need to touch and snap together. He slid his arms around me, hands smoothing over my hips to cup my bottom and drag me up his hard body to his lovely mouth.

"Say yes," he said against my lips.

"Yes." I wrapped my legs around his waist and my arms around his neck as he kissed me. Shadows shifted across my closed lids as he walked us from the bright entryway to his darkened bedroom.

He sat me on the edge of his bed and knelt at my feet, sliding the zipper of my heeled boot down slowly, grasping my calf in his warm hand to pull it off, and then repeating the process with the other boot. He stood and toed his shoes off, loosened his tie enough to pull it over his head, and began sliding buttons through buttonholes at a maddeningly slow pace. Cuff links clinked into a small dish on his dresser, and he shrugged the shirt off his broad shoulders and down his arms.

Taking my hands, he drew me up. There was fire in his eyes now, and a promise to make me feel it before we were done. He placed my hands on his bare chest, where they looked small and pale. My freckles, my personal all-over constellations, matched the deep sepia tone of his skin. I felt the drum of his heart beneath my right palm. His fingers grazed from my wrists to my shoulders, over and behind.

"Happy birthday, by the way. Although I guess technically I missed it."

"How did you know?"

"I'm your boss." His smirk was downright devilish. "I know everything about you."

His words cued my favorite fantasy to power up. I switched it off. I wouldn't need it tonight. "You *were* my boss."

He pinched the tiny hook at the top of my dress's zipper before drawing it down. His eyes didn't leave mine until the fabric began to part and slip down to pool at my feet. Every tiny hair on my body rose and strained toward him as his eyes took a leisurely perusal from my collarbones to my ankles and back. The strapless bra and panties I'd chosen were lacy and red beneath my understated charcoal-gray dress.

"Mmm." His voice was a resonant hum, echoing through my body. "Red is my favorite color."

"Is it?" I twisted my arms behind my back and unhooked the bra. Let it fall.

He reached to pull his fingers through my hair and brought a long copper strand to loop over my chest and curve around my breast. "It's been my favorite color since the day you walked into the lobby of JMCH, hair like flame, body like a besetting sin, there to wreck my plans and turn my life upside down."

The ends of my hair tickled my nipple, and it quivered and hardened. He brushed a fingertip over the other, and it responded in kind.

I gasped, hands kneading his chest like a kitten. "I didn't know."

One side of his mouth turned up. "That's what slayed me."

I bit my lip. "I wanted you immediately."

He angled a brow. "I was a total asshole to you. On purpose."

"Which made me kinda pissed with myself for wanting you anyway."

He unbuckled his belt, unfastened his slacks, and pushed them down. My hands began to slide down his solid, muscled torso. His skin was smooth but for the soft trail of hair leading into his dark boxer briefs. I stroked my fingers over him and he groaned, picked me up, and laid me down in the center of his bed after sweeping the covers to the floor. Bracing himself over me, one leg between mine, he said, "You sure about this?"

I nodded but said, "I have a confession."

His brows rose, one a little higher than the other. "Hmm?"

"I've been inventing fantasies about us. Dirty, *dirty* fantasies. In my office, over my desk. In your office chair. In this bed. In mine."

His brows lowered and his eyes went black, pupils dilating. "Jesus Christ, woman."

"You were wrong. I only wanted you. No one else." I licked my lip and he stared at it. "But you were right that I was horny."

"Are you still?"

"*Worse.*"

He pressed his thigh between my legs. "Let's take care of that."

I should have known, or maybe I did, that Isaac would be unhurried, even here. Taking his time was his defining characteristic, and I knew there was nothing I could do or say to convince him to do any blessed thing until he was ready to do it. He sat back, hooked his fingers in the lace at my hips, and drew my panties down. When he stood, his rapt gaze swept over my body, careful and deliberate. My hands grabbed handfuls of his sheets on either side of my hips, legs moving restlessly.

He shoved his underwear to the ground, removed a condom from the drawer of his night table, and rolled it on. He was big and strong and, for tonight, all mine. No man had ever moved so slowly over me or kissed me so thoroughly, tongue making languid promises, fingers teasing and checking my readiness as his thumb circled my clit with gentle skill.

"Yes, yes, please," I begged, not that it hastened him along.

I dug my fingers into his biceps and whispered into his ear. "I had my first fantasy about you before going to sleep on your couch after you kissed me. I imagined you stalking into my office and shutting the door behind you. I turned my face into the pillow so you wouldn't hear me when I made myself come."

He choked back a strangled, un-Isaac-like roar, rocked forward, and filled me. I came before the third stroke, but *oh my God,* he slid a hand beneath my thigh, tilting me at the precise angle to make the aftershocks go on forever.

Somewhere during all that, I was aware of the rigid muscles of his arms tightening, expanding, shaking with effort. I was aware of him surging harder and deeper, aware of his low moan of release. I was glad for all of it, because I'd been too blissed out to have consciously helped it along. For several minutes, we lay side by side, facing the ceiling and panting, waiting for our heart rates to return to normal.

His weight left the bed and came back a moment later. He pulled the comforter over us and tugged me into the circle of his arms. I still felt like a bowl full of wobbly noodles. I couldn't imagine how he'd managed to walk.

"That was quicker than I intended," he said, almost to himself.

I snorted into his shoulder. "I think if you'd have gone any slower, I'd have expired from anticipation." I turned my head up. I couldn't see his face, but I could tell from the position of his chin that he was smirking.

"That's not a thing."

"How do you know? I swear I almost died back there." I snuggled against him. "Please do it again after I rest for a few minutes." I yawned, eyes closed, warm and drowsy.

I'd almost drifted to sleep when he asked, "Did you really do that? On my sofa?"

I leaned to kiss the spot at the edge of his jaw, exactly where that little muscle tic showed up when he was cross with me. "*Twice*."

His whole body constricted and he covered his face with his other hand. "You. Are. Gonna. Kill. Me." His cock sprang up a little against my thigh and I giggled.

"Oh, look. Someone's *horny*, and it's not me this time." I reached between us and wrapped my hand around him, gratified by his answering moan and how he went from partially erect to raring to go. To hell with sleep. I was a kid in a toy store with a wagon full of allowance money. I leaned up on my elbow, my hair tumbling over my shoulders to pool on his chest.

I crept lower as he breathed deeply, letting me lead, probably doing math in his head to help prolong the moment and see where I was going with it. The thought of math brought another memory. "Mr. Maat, I *love* your slide rule."

"Oh God." He laughed quietly, abs tightening beneath my mouth.

"Will you teach me how you do those *precise calculations* now?"

He swept a firm, gentle hand from my waist to my breast, stroking, circling, pinching gently. All my Isaac fantasies scurried in malfunctioning circles, crashing into each other and going up in smoke. "As to not being horny. You were saying?"

I moaned and mumbled something incoherent.

"C'mere." He took hold of my upper arms and towed me back up. "I wanna tell you something." He tucked my hair behind my ear, and I waited for the question or comment he was mulling over before voicing it.

"That sounds serious." I chewed my lip. I wasn't an expert at waiting yet.

"I'm in love with you, you know."

I had not known, or even suspected. "You love me? How? When?"

He exhaled a deep breath, as though he'd been holding it in for a very long time. "You dismantled me piece by piece, I think. When you asked me why I said your name like you were a Capulet and I was a Montague, that was when I knew. I fell asleep brooding over the aptness of *My only love sprung from my only hate*. I was furious with myself. How the hell could I fall in love with the daughter of a man I saw as my enemy? I said horrible things to you the next day. I apologize."

"I said worse, completely untrue, things to you."

His fingers caressed my face, inches from his. Our bodies were pressed together, two complementary puzzle pieces who'd found each other in this big wide world.

"I love you too. And I'm sorry for saying those mean things."

"None of that matters now. There will be no poison draughts or daggers in our futures. Our stars are aligned, not crossed. And in case you're ever unsure, I can't hate the name McIntyre anymore. You've ruined that for me, or maybe helped fix it. That means you can't hate it either."

"It may take me a little while."

"Maybe someday you'll change it out for something else."

"Maybe. But only if I don't have to change my initials."

He chuckled, dark lashes sweeping down and back up. "That your line in the sand?"

"I'm afraid so. I have a truly shocking amount of monogrammed things and as a practical grad student, I can't afford to be wasteful."

"I think I can work with that, Ms. McIntyre."

"I'm sure you can, Mr. Maat."

Epilogue

January 2015

I unfolded the map and it creaked with age. The advent of GPS systems and cell phone maps had made it a relic. Isaac stared at it, then at me.

"What's this?"

"It's a map."

His smile was bemused. Indulgent. "Okay, smartass, I can see that. But…"

"I know—it's probably ten years old."

"I would say twenty?"

"Okay, yeah. I'm sure some of it has changed in the past few years, and we can use your GPS or our phones for actual navigation. But I'm pretty sure the cities and states haven't moved and major highways are the same." I smoothed it out on my lap and laid it between us. "Close your eyes."

His brow swooped up.

I waited. He closed his eyes.

"Give me your hand."

He did so, and I balanced it above the map.

"Use your finger, and without peeking, pick our destination."

His eyes opened, hand still hovering between us. "What? I

thought we were going to get breakfast, discuss our options. I made lists of possibilities and notes concerning cost of living and weather patterns and crime rates."

"Close your eyes! Now I'm going to have to rotate the map around so you don't cheat."

"I could peek and you wouldn't know."

"But you wouldn't."

"You said I might cheat."

"I meant accidentally. Because you are one of those people who probably not only know exactly where every state is in relation to the others, you know the capitals and the other major cities, too."

"Possibly..." He laughed softly, and my heart melted as I stared at his face—smiling, relaxed, the planes and angles smoothed by the curve of full lips and the tiniest little lines at the corners of his eyes, which were closed.

"All right. It's set. Choose."

He rotated his finger around in an exaggerated show, finally stabbing down—in the Gulf of Mexico. He opened his eyes. "Unless you got a yacht or a rowboat or something, we're in big trouble."

I sighed. "Try again."

This time, he took my hand in his, extended my index finger, and stared into my eyes as he rotated the map in awkward circles. "One. Two. Three," he said, and down our hands went.

We stared at the city under my finger and then at each other.

"Ever been there?"

"Nope."

"Me neither." He was still holding my hand, our arms entwined. "You sure about this?"

"I'm sure."

He tugged my hand up to his mouth and laid a soft kiss against my wrist, and then his opposite hand slid across my lower jaw to cup my face, the pad of his thumb skimming the surface of my lower lip, pressing gently. Breathless, I watched the contemplations of everything and everyone we were leaving cross his furrowed brow and the dark eyes that stared at my mouth. When his eyes rose to mine, there was no indecision there. My own burned with tears that were all relief.

"I'm sure too." Isaac did not make careless promises. He was offering his heart and soul in exchange for mine. "C'mere," he said, and I obeyed. He swept a tear away and kissed me. "I love you."

My heart ached from joy. Sliding my hand behind his neck, I kept him close. "I love you too."

A cold, wet nose snuffled between us and we separated enough to assure Pete that he, too, was loved. His tail thwacked the seat in a joyful cadence and he woofed his love back at us.

"Pete, sit on your blankie." That was the first time I'd ever given him an order. He angled his head left, then right, licked my chin, and hopped back on his blanket, tail still thump-thumping like a heartbeat. "Scamp," I said. He took it as praise, judging by his answering yap.

I dug a red pen from my bag and drew a crimson heart around the city we'd chosen. Isaac chuckled—at the profound girliness of the gesture, I was certain. As I folded the map against the creases to display our destination and the surrounding areas only, it protested by creaking and throwing off dust that all paper eventually became. But it would survive to be framed and hung in our new place. And the one after that. And the one after that, where we would settle and make a home of our own.

For now, Isaac wedged the ancient map between the dash and the center console, the heart-encased spot in the center, facing us, and then he fired up the GPS and got more current routes and directions.

"We'll take shifts and stop for the night when we get tired, but we can be there by tomorrow afternoon." He kissed me again, and we were off.

I chose "Heads Carolina, Tails California" from my phone's playlist, dancing and singing in my seat and proving beyond any doubt my months-ago claim to tone deafness. Pete howled along in delight—or agony—and Isaac laughed at the both of us until he had to wipe tears from his eyes.

Reconciliations would be made here and there with some, but not all, of my family members. Some immediate, some years in coming. Some surprising, some not.

Isaac and I would calm each other's nightmares and support each other's dreams. We would shape our futures into what they were meant to be. We would take risks and stand our ground and learn and grow and be brave, because love is a tenacious, powerful, infinite force, and it can change the world, one heart at a time.

Acknowledgments

Since 2012, Erin has been the secondary character most requested for a spinoff romance. Readers connected with her fierce, protective heart in *Easy* and wanted more of her, but I didn't see the right partner for her until Isaac arrived, as heroes do, with baggage of his own. If there is one thread running through my novels, it is that love heals at the deepest connection point between people, and these two had a doozie. It has taken me three years to bring this book to fruition. Thank you for your patience, dear long-time readers. *Brave* exists because of you.

Special appreciation is due to those who helped make this book better and/or held me accountable (in encouraging, supportive ways!) for putting my butt in the seat and doing the work: Tracey Garvis Graves, Catherine-Rose Thollet, Aimee Salter, Liza Weimer, Elizabeth Reyes, Jamie Wesley, Carmen Pacheco, Robin Deeslie, Kay Miles, Lori Norris, and Anne Victory. Thanks, too, for careful, regular nudges from my wonderful agents, Jane Dystel and Lauren Abramo, and the whole team at Dystel, Goderich and Bourret.

To my husband, Paul, my real-life hero—I could not have

survived the past two years without you. When you promised "for better or worse," you meant it. Zachary, Hannah, and Keith, I adore each of you to the moon and back and am so proud to be your mom. To my parents, in-laws, and birthmom, I love and appreciate each of you and what you've meant to my life. I wouldn't be who I am without you.

A few years ago, a brilliant oncologist-hematologist, Dr. Gregory Friess, told me that the more he knew about the human body, the more he realized what he—and medical science—didn't know. "Thinking we know everything is when we fail," he said. That sums up my experience as a published author and as a writer trying to get Isaac Maat down faithfully. The more I studied race relations and the more I thought I understood, the more aware I became of my infinite shortcomings. I was running toward a goal that was moving into the distance. I would never be able to portray him flawlessly.

Then I remembered a favorite writing quote from Margaret Atwood: "If I waited for perfection, I would never write a word," and a wise tidbit from my undergrad creative writing professor, Patrick Murphy: "You can't edit a blank page." So I wrote, and I kept reading, and I revised, and I passed the manuscript to others, and I listened, and I revised some more. The novelist John McGahern said that the reader, not the writer, completes the novel. Thank you for being part of that process as my reader. I apologize for what I got wrong or miscommunicated, and I intend to keep listening and learning with the full comprehension that this will be a lifelong process.

In previous Acknowledgments, I've asked you to realize that violations inflicted on you or someone you cared about were not your fault. I've asked you to not let that thing—whatever it was—define you. I've asked you to let go of love that was less than you deserved. I'm not asking you to face something I haven't, though the circumstances are different for each of us. I have made myself small and taken blame that was not mine. I have been silent and allowed others to define me. I have accepted love that was less than I was worthy of because I was afraid to be alone or lose someone I had outgrown but still carried in my heart.

What I've learned: You can love people and let them go. You can love people and leave. You can love people and refuse to accept (or pretend to accept) their ideologies just so they will continue to care about you. Dear reader, do not make yourself into someone you are not for someone else. It's okay to be flawed, to be unhappy, to need help. It's also okay to know exactly who you are, what you want, and what you will no longer endure. Telling your truth can mean therapy or the world. Defining yourself can be out loud or in your heart. Leaving a person, a past, or a set of values can be a confrontation or walking silently out the door when you are able. If you need to be loud, be loud. If you need to act in silence, for safety or mental health, be silent. But act. This is your life. Be brave, and live it on your terms.

Further Reading

The following are my favorite Black contemporary romance novelists. If you aren't already familiar with these ladies, please check out their work—you won't be disappointed: Nia Forrester, Christina C. Jones, Brittainy Cherry, Delaney Diamond, Jacinta Howard, and Jamie Wesley.

Baldwin, James. *The Fire Next Time*. Random House, 1963.

Coates, Ta-Nehisi. *Between the World and Me*. Penguin Random House, 2015.

Golden, Marita, and Threve, Susan Richards, eds. *Skin Deep*. Doubleday, 1995.

Rae, Issa. *The Misadventures of Awkward Black Girl*. Simon & Schuster, 2015.

Shawl, Nisi, and Ward, Cynthia. *Writing the Other*. Aqueduct Press, 2005.

Writing With Color, http://www.writingwithcolor.tumblr.com

About the Author

I'm a hopeful romantic who adores novels with happy endings, because there are enough sad endings in real life. Before writing full time, I was an undergraduate academic advisor, economics tutor, planetarium office manager, radiology call center rep, and the palest person to ever work at a tanning salon. I married my high school sweetheart, and I'm Mom to three adult kids and four very immature cats.

TammaraWebber.com
Facebook.com/TammaraWebberAuthor
Twitter.com/TammaraWebber
Instagram.com/TammaraWebber

Printed in Great Britain
by Amazon

85615199R00181